THESE

a novel

VIOLENT

Victoria Namkung

DELIGHTS

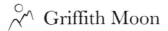 Griffith Moon

Cover Design by Sara Martinez
Book Design by Marvin Lloyd Larson
Cover Painting: "Crown of Thorns", Oil on linen, by Kimberly Brooks
Printed in the United States of America
First Printing, 2017

ISBN: 978-0-9993153-1-6
Library of Congress Control Number: 2017955876

Published by Griffith Moon
Santa Monica, California
www.GriffithMoon.com

For Natasha

In a single-sex school, a girl can comprehend her value and her capabilities in ways that have nothing to do with how she looks or whom she dates. She can be free to experiment and explore, trying out new things and trying on new roles. She can follow her ambitions without wasting a second thought or a backward glance on how her male counterparts might perceive her.

—National Coalition of Girls' Schools

Chapter One

Jane

April 2016

"What is the point of a high school reunion when you can already see who got fat and bald on Facebook?" asks Caryn, the intern working with me this semester, and I can't help but laugh because she's right.

Caryn works one desk over from me, but she often steps into my cubicle to chat—and she's quite chatty—anytime she's on her way to or from the bathroom down the hall, which feels like ten times a day on average. I sense her hovering while I glance at the digital save-the-date invitation to my twentieth high school reunion, being held next year at a forgettable budget hotel in my quiet northern California hometown.

"Do you really want to have to talk to *those* people?" Her eyes are wide and full of judgment.

"I think those are stock photos."

Nothing, including the aforementioned reunion, makes me feel older than being around Caryn. A perky-titted, size two, eyelash-extension-wearing USC journalism student who peppers her sentences with internet slang that people, and, oh fine, I, simply don't understand.

"I am never going to a reunion." She announces the decision with the conviction of a twenty-two-year-old who simultaneously knows everything and nothing about life. "What could possibly be the point?"

I decide against a minilecture about nevers and instead ask her if she's come up with any pitches for next week. Interns don't typically write stories for the *Daily*, but she's a talented reporter with a gift for putting subjects at ease, and I'm determined to get her a few more bylines before her internship is up. Since Caryn's working here for a small pittance and school credit, at a time when "newspaper reporter" has been named the worst job in America for the third year in a row by financial magazines, I figure it's the least I can do.

"Actually, there's a piece I've been working on for a while." She rolls her office chair over to sit opposite me, her heavy chain-style bracelets clanging along the way. "But I'm not sure it's *something* yet."

I didn't sleep well last night and spent fifty-three minutes in traffic driving from the Westside to our downtown office, so I'm not feeling like much of a cheerleader at the moment. Especially for someone being vague. "Do you want to at least give me the lede?"

She looks sheepish; something seems off, but I don't have time to find out what since I have to file one of my own stories within the next half hour.

"Can I just email it to you later after I work on it some more?"

"Of course."

I'm always amazed by the amount of exhaustion I am capable of feeling from sitting in a chair all day. After an epic battle on Olympic Boulevard to get home, I plop onto the couch, tired and hungry, open my laptop, and go to my work email since I'm waiting for an edit on my latest piece about the effects of California's ongoing drought. My contact lenses feel dry, but I'm too lazy to take them out and go grab my glasses from the bedside table. I see an email from Caryn in between messages from our deputy editor and PR people who are furious about the way I covered their client.

From: Caryn Rodgers
To: Jane March
Date: April 21, 2016 at 6:25 p.m.
Subject: Personal essay . . .

Hey, so I've wanted to write this for a long time. You know I went to Windemere, right? Something happened there with a teacher and it's always bothered me that he was never punished for it. I know the Daily *doesn't do first-person stuff outside of the Opinion pages, but I think this will work better as an essay—see if you agree. I've attached it here and hope you'll help me make it into something great.*

—Caryn

My eyes scan the first few lines and before I've even finished the first paragraph, I grab my phone, silently scolding myself for not getting its cracked screen fixed weeks ago, and text her.

"Do you have time to chat tonight?" Within a few seconds I see the three little dots that denote her typing.

"I wish." She adds three pissed-off-looking emoji faces. "My dad is making me have dinner with the freaking Korean Consul General. Pretty sure it's going late, especially since they are all drunk."

I sometimes forget that Caryn is part Korean, even though she has long, pin-straight black hair, high cheekbones, and dark almond-shaped eyes. But I never forget that her family is ultrawealthy. We don't typically get interns at the *Daily* who sport a two-thousand-dollar carryall as their work bag and make reference to more than one private Pilates instructor.

Since finishing her first draft, my appetite has magically disappeared, and I know I won't be sleeping well tonight, either. I guess even money can't protect you from certain things.

After hitting the Snooze button on my iPhone for the second time, I wonder if Caryn's already getting cold feet, but I change my mind when I see a message from her stating that she's coming in this morning to talk about the essay. I'm desperate to get more details before our staff meeting at two. These are big claims after all.

She's in the office before me, waiting in my cubicle.

"I can't name him." Caryn blows on her to-go coffee cup.

"Okay, but why?"

"I mean, I can tell *you*, but not the world. My parents won't be thrilled with the idea of me going public with this."

"Well, I can appreciate that they probably want to protect you, but these are serious allegations and they fully merit an audience and proper investigation. I'd like to pitch it at today's meeting. For the Sunday magazine. It could be a cover, Caryn."

"Oh my god, are you serious? Isn't that too much?" She looks scared, and maybe a little bit excited. "Windemere is going to freak out."

"I can't guarantee anything, but you did a great job with it and I think if we can just corroborate your story we'll be good to go. Of course, Eric is going to want you to name the teacher."

"I can't. In fact, maybe we shouldn't even mention Windemere. Just let people wonder which girls school it is."

"But anyone will be able to put it together with a simple online search because of your name."

"I guess." She looks distracted, like she's going through a mental Rolodex of every place she's mentioned on the internet.

"Caryn, are you sure about all of this? You know how it is now. It's not just the story in the paper. It would run online, get shared, linked to all over social media, picked up by TV. . . ."

"I have to do this. My therapist said it was okay."

"*Okay*, well, I'll talk to legal too because I'm sure they'll have some questions for you." I wonder if she's in therapy because

4

of this or because she's an anxious twenty-two-year-old young woman living in Los Angeles.

"I kept all of his emails."

"That was smart of you." She is far savvier than I thought.

"They're in my Gmail." She twirls a section of shiny hair around her manicured finger, which is appliqued with sequin-like art on the tips. "Windemere has them, too."

"You've got to be kidding me."

"I wish I was." My stomach tightens. "I'll be around if you need me, but I just want to work with you on this," she continues. "I don't want to talk to Eric or Chris or any of the other guys about it too much."

"I understand." I want to offer some kind of reassurance as she heads to the bathroom for her first of many visits today. "Oh, and Caryn?"

"Yeah?"

"I'm really sorry this happened to you. You know, it's one thousand percent not your fault."

"I know."

I recognize the terror in her eyes. It's the first time I've seen her look unsure of herself and it makes me wonder if her overconfident demeanor is simply an act.

"This is really brave of you."

"Thanks, Jane, but brave would have been writing this six years ago."

After corroborating some of the basic facts via Windemere's extensive website and combing through the emails, which made every hair on the back of my neck stand at attention, I read Caryn's story aloud at the two o'clock meeting:

My Tenth-Grade Teacher Claims He Fell in Love With Me
By Caryn Rodgers, Special to the Los Angeles Daily

Six years ago, I felt like an awkward teenager, and didn't have much experience with boys since I went to a well-known, all-girls school starting at age twelve. I was the editor of our school paper, eager to line up a new Teacher of the Month profile, when someone recommended our school's beloved English chairperson. I wouldn't have him as a teacher until the following semester, which was a few weeks later, but I knew him, of course. I knew everyone on campus in our little corner of Los Angeles.

I emailed him to set up the interview and he replied that he'd love to participate and added a few happy faces, which I found odd coming from a fortysomething man. Our meeting, held off campus at a Starbucks that was walking distance from school, made me feel extra grown-up, even though I was still in my school uniform: a standard white polo shirt embroidered with our school's logo and pleated gray skirt, cut exactly three inches above the knee as our dress code required. I'm sure people thought he was my dad, in retrospect. His answers were quick, charming, and funny. At certain points, I felt like he was flirting with me and I have to admit that I enjoyed the attention. I was flattered, which sounds delusional now, but I was fifteen. A fifteen-year-old who thought she was in total control.

Before we parted ways, he mentioned that I would be in his class next semester and I said I was looking forward to it. He paid me numerous compliments. "I know how talented you are," he remarked. "You run the entire school paper and have time to kick butt on the soccer field." I smiled, looking down at my iced tea. "I can't wait to get to see you every day," he said. We were seated on the back patio and no one was paying us any attention. He noticed this as well, because he put his hand on top of my thigh, rubbing the top of his thumb on the skin, which raised my skirt an extra inch. It took me a few seconds to fathom what was happening. I felt like I was frozen. After I moved my leg, I could still feel his hand there. I thanked him for his time, told him when the piece would run, and said I had to go. "Thank you for the great date," he said.

With my heart racing and entire body sweating, I speed walked back to campus to catch a ride home with a friend since I didn't yet have my driver's license. She asked me why I looked like I had seen a ghost. I replied that I was stressed out about deadlines and finals next week. That night, my dad asked me how my day was and I just made something up. I told no one. When the article ran a few weeks later, the teacher sent me an email, thanking me for "a most generous and completely undeserving profile of an old dude." I replied that I didn't think he was that old. He wrote back, "Really? I'm so happy to hear it because I can't stop thinking about you." I was shocked he was so bold, and that he would put this in writing, over our school's email system. I figured he was really into me if he would take such a risk.

Two weeks later, I was sitting in his class as a student. I often caught him staring at me, which was embarrassing and thrilling, and I hoped no one else noticed. He was generous in his praise of my writing, particularly an essay I wrote on E.E. Cummings. "You are the most talented English student I've had in years," he said. "And that smile could probably get me to give you an A even if you didn't already deserve one." He made me feel beautiful, which was an unfamiliar feeling. I could see him blush in my presence at times and I felt powerful and proud to have this control over a grown man. I told myself that I was doing nothing wrong and it was all pretty harmless. After all, he was the one breaking the rules, and it's not like I was enticing him in any way. I now know that for someone like him, my behavior of no behavior, really, was a bright green light in his mind. He was testing the waters.

One afternoon, when class was over and there was a free period for students to visit with teachers to talk about assignments or other issues, I found myself alone with him after two other students left the classroom. He was still sitting at his desk and I walked over to have him sign off on a form I needed so that I could miss class for an out-of-town soccer game. He did so, joking that I was torturing him by my upcoming absence, and as he stood to hand me the paperwork, he kissed me, briefly, on the lips. Stunned, I said nothing. He then asked me if I would meet him after school sometime. I felt like my stomach was in my chest, my heart in my shoes. I stammered something about having to babysit my little brother and walked out as fast as I could.

That night I hardly slept. I could see my hands shaking anytime I went to grab my phone. I was racked with guilt. I had brought this upon myself because I never told him to stop paying attention to me. I didn't want to have to tell my parents, because they would make a big fuss, and I knew if I told a friend they would go straight to our Head of School. But I knew I had to do something before facing him again the next day. So I typed a short email. "I'm sorry if I gave you the wrong impression," I wrote. "This isn't right and I just want to be treated like a normal student." He didn't reply, but after class the next day he scolded me for being "just a tease" who knew what she was doing. He thought I chose to profile him because I liked him, even though I interviewed different teachers each month as part of my job as editor. He looked hurt as though he were a fifteen-year-old boy I had denied a date to the prom.

Within two weeks, I had lost eight pounds. My friends knew something was wrong and I was having a hard time keeping up with school because I wasn't sleeping well. I had regular nightmares and anxiety every time I had to go on campus. I was basically a mess. And even though my school's mission is to empower girls, I felt helpless, confused, and ashamed—like the worst person on earth. In addition to being married, he had children, one of whom I had met casually through a friend of a friend a few years ago. My teacher sensed something was wrong, or perhaps he feared I was going to say something to someone, anyone, because he wrote me a final note, telling me he was sorry for the things he said and that he couldn't help that he had fallen in love with me.

"From that first meeting at the coffee shop, you've been on my mind pretty much every hour of the day. I truly feel like I can't control my feelings," he wrote. "Don't get me started on your exquisite beauty. The fact that you are so unaware of it makes you even more enticing." He asked if I would please just meet him one time after class and he would explain more. There were mentions of my long, shiny black hair and perfect white teeth. He said I was the most mature student he had ever met and that I was "as special as a rare rose" because there was no one else like me.

That was the final straw. I printed out the emails and put them in a folder with a card he had given me with a book of E.E. Cummings poetry and presented them to my parents. Surprisingly, they didn't blame me, but they did fight about whether it was a mistake to have sent me to an all-girls school, and how furious they were that they had given the school so much money over the years, in addition to the $18,500 tuition payments each semester. The three of us met with the Head of School the next morning. They listened, but offered very little in the way of a reaction. Because I had the email proof, it wasn't possible to get into a debate. I assumed he would be quietly let go, maybe at the end of the school year to avoid any public drama, and I would be thanked for coming forward. All I wanted was to finish the semester and my academic career without having to transfer to a brand-new school.

Instead, nothing happened. He was asked to participate in counseling and is still teaching on that campus this very minute. He is still everyone's favorite teacher. He currently has a 4.6-star average on RateMyTeachers.com.

I place the printed-out essay on our large conference table, exhaling loudly while trying to push the image of Gregory Copeland, Caryn's former teacher who I found online, easily, out of my mind.

"Jesus." Eric runs his fingers through his thick gray hair.

"How do we know this is even true?" asks Chris, the *Daily*'s assistant managing editor.

Celia, our chief metro reporter, retorts, "Who would make this up?"

"But why now? It feels out of the blue to suddenly be covering something that *supposedly* happened years ago."

"Are we really going to treat Caryn as suspect and not the pervy teacher?" Celia asks.

"I'm just saying, I think it's weird to come out with this years later. People do make these things up for attention or whatever. Maybe she saw some of these types of essays going viral and thought she'd make a name for herself off this."

"Well, by all means, let's make sure to not support her because the timing isn't convenient for Chris." Celia shakes her head. "She was just a kid. She's still practically a kid. And please know that no one wants to make their name as a writer because of something like this."

I cut them off. "She has their email correspondence. I've seen a few of them already. They're time-stamped. Everything is checking out. We have an obligation to run it."

"Why didn't she go to the police or the media back then?" asks our new copy editor, Ken. I refuse to answer him and look at Eric, hoping he'll say something so I know he's on my side, but he doesn't. I feel my body temperature rise.

"An accusation like this can ruin someone's life. That's all we're saying, Jane," Chris adds.

"Don't you find it interesting that these types of crimes against women—whether it's violence, sexual assault, rape—are the only kinds where we force the victim to make a case about their own innocence before even investigating?" The room goes quiet. I feel my face and neck redden with increased blood pressure, but I can't stop now. "If someone told you their car or iPhone was stolen would you believe them and try to help, or make them prove it to you? I'm serious. If someone walked in the office right now and said they were hurt and needed help, would you need an investigation and a prosecutor to bring charges and a judge or jury to convict them before you attempted to assist them? Why do you think this is?" More silence. "I mean, really, why do you think this is? Do I have to spell it out?"

The new copy guy averts his eyes and mumbles something incoherent under his breath while fumbling with a paper clip. Celia gives me a knowing smile.

Eric stands, ready to hit his next meeting. "Jane, let's discuss this at four. I want it for Sunday. Can you ask Anjali from legal to join us? See if Caryn is willing to stick around a bit late, as I'll want to talk to her as well. And let's talk about the photography. We need to make sure she's ready for this."

I hope I'm ready too.

Chapter Two

Caryn

I've dreamed of writing a cover story for a major newspaper for as long as I can remember, but I never thought it would go down like this. I mean, this isn't even journalism; it's a full-blown personal essay about something so private and embarrassing *and* it's going to cause a complete shit storm. Jane keeps checking on me, but never says exactly what she expects to happen. Will the police get involved? Will Dr. Copeland finally be fired? Will Windemere downplay what they already know? Will I get slut-shamed by random internet commenters who hate women and themselves so much that they have to take it out on me? Probably all of the above and then some.

My parents are conveniently out of town, as they often are, but this news will reach them in an instant. I wouldn't be surprised to learn that my father has a Google Alert on me since I know he has one for himself. Oftentimes he sees my *Daily Trojan* stories before I do, which I find incredibly creepy. His long-suffering assistant prints them out in large type and then he takes a red pen and marks up the parts he likes and the parts that he deems problematic, even though he has no background in journalism and can barely compose a letter without help. His assistant then scans the document and emails it to me. If I don't respond to the email in a timely fashion, he then calls me, which is worse. The entire process is exhausting. The freedom of writing under a pseudonym is becoming more attractive by the day.

It's Tuesday and the article will come out on Sunday, but it will be online by Friday afternoon. I realize I better comb through all of my social media accounts because once my name is out there, every public image of me is going to be dissected like a frog in my housemate Grace's biology lab. I just hope they use a good picture and not one from Windemere. I had not yet discovered the wonders of brow shaping.

"Caryn?" Jane calls and I appear in her cubicle, which is home to mounting stacks of paper and her cracked NYU coffee mug that's permanently stained by the coffees of days past. She could really use Marie Kondo. I'm positive the mug is not creating a sense of joy in her life.

"What's up?" I have butterflies in my stomach and my mouth feels oddly dry, but I'm doing all I can to appear calm.

"Have you talked to your parents about all of this?"

"I told them I may write something about what happened, but I haven't shown them the piece. I don't think it's in our best interest to show them."

"And why is that?"

"I'm pretty sure my father would have it killed."

"That would be impossible." Jane is so smart and yet so naïve sometimes.

"He pretty much gets whatever he wants. And my mom does not believe in talking about things like this in public. She will not be pleased, which is nothing new."

"I'm sorry to hear that."

"I've been disappointing her since forever. From being born on her birthday to my chosen occupation, she doesn't miss a chance to pick me apart." Jane clearly doesn't approve. "I guess you haven't known a lot of Koreans."

"Not well, no. But this is Los Angeles, of course I've met and known Korean people."

"My mom's uncle molested one of her cousins for years when she was younger and he still gets invited to family functions.

When I told my mom that I thought this made her cousin upset, she shrugged her shoulders and told me that there's no point in dwelling on things that happened in the past. Once Windemere decided not to act on the Copeland situation, I think my mom was relieved that we could put it all behind us and never speak of it again. Denial is practically a virtue among Koreans."

Jane is clearly horrified by this revelation, but doesn't push further. I'm sure she's smart enough to know that immigrant mothers are a special breed of crazy. "Didn't your father want to see Copeland punished?"

"Of course." I remember how red his face became when he found out. "If I hadn't begged and pleaded with him not to, I'm sure something would have happened to Copeland after the school did nothing."

"Something? Something violent, you mean?" If having someone chop off his dick is "something violent," then yes, I think to myself.

"I don't know." I'm unsure how much I should be discussing my dad with a seasoned newspaper reporter. "Let's just say I don't think he'll appreciate me airing my dirty laundry in public and drawing attention to our family."

I hope I'm not annoying her. I feel like I annoy her a lot.

"Well, you may want to at least give them a heads-up that this is coming out soon. I'd hate for either of your parents to be blindsided."

"I have a younger brother as well." This isn't going to be easy on Phillip, a high school senior and the star of his baseball team, once it all blows up.

"Well, I'll leave it up to you to decide who needs an advance warning." I realize my professors at USC will most likely see the essay and my byline and wonder if they'll be shocked or impressed or maybe both. "I just want you to be prepared. That's my first concern."

Jane doesn't know it, but I specifically asked to work for her during my internship. I've been reading her stories since I was a senior in high school. Last year, I saw her speak at the Los Angeles Times Festival of Books, and I was a bit starstruck, which is funny to think about now that we work side by side. I doubt she'd remember meeting me that day (I had her sign a book she coauthored with another investigative reporter just so I could talk to her), but I always remember something she said on stage: "The job of the newspaper is to comfort the afflicted and afflict the comfortable." It's a famous journalism quote, but I wrote it down in my notebook that day and thought about it all the time.

When one of my journalism professors showed us the list of available internships we could apply for, I zeroed in on the *Daily*, and during the interview process I spoke several times about Jane's impressive work covering local politics and the environment. When the managing editor gave me a choice of working for several different reporters, I picked her. As far as I was concerned, working for Jane March was like an aspiring guitar player getting to go on tour with Prince.

There's nothing intimidating about Jane upon first glance. She usually wears a thick brown ponytail with an ethnic-inspired, shapeless garment that hides everything, but if you talk to her for a few minutes, like I did during my first day of the internship, you'll realize that she's operating on a higher plane than the rest of us. She has a way of getting to the heart of a story in seconds. She unnerves subjects with her photographic-like memory and ability to recall facts and figures as though she was discussing what she had for breakfast this morning. People take her seriously, and she's written more than three hundred stories at the *Daily*. If we remove things like fashion, grooming, and general taste and style, I want to be just like her.

I finally ask Jane what I've been dying to ask. "Are you going to reach out to Copeland for some kind of comment or statement?"

"No. This is *your* essay, from *your* point of view, and I feel confident that everything you wrote is true. Perhaps there's a follow-up story, reported by someone else, but I doubt he'll talk once his life blows up. And what could he possibly say to excuse his behavior, anyway?"

I imagine the things Dr. Copeland could say to refute my essay. He could say that I came on to him and was rejected and, therefore, I had a vendetta. He could claim that I made the entire thing up for attention, although why any young woman would want this type of attention is beyond me. He could say it was a misunderstanding because young women are dramatic and hormonal and prone to misconstruing things.

Jane begins rattling on about how stories like these are commonplace and how technology has made them easier to prove in some cases. My experience seems innocent compared to some of the media accounts I've read lately, so part of me is surprised that my essay would even warrant a feature in the *Daily*. But I guess fancy Windemere, which "prepares young women to follow their passions and make their mark on the world" and has a $56 million endowment, gives it that extra allure. Eventually, someone will connect the dots to my father and then we'll be off to the races.

Plus, it's a familiar trope. One we hear about in songs, books, and films. The charismatic teacher. An insecure teenage girl. He gives her the attention she so desperately craves from boys. But there are no boys to be found at an all-girls school. And even if there were, they would not understand nor appreciate this teenage girl in the way she hopes and dreams of. Instead, there's a most-average-looking man with a toothy smile and a soft belly that hangs over his khaki pants when he goes over the day's lesson plan.

Later in the afternoon, Jane arrives at my desk. "Caryn, I need you to come meet with me, Eric, and Anjali from legal." The impromptu meeting announcement jolts me out of the constant thoughts racing through my head.

"Okay, I'll be right there." I close my laptop before feeling the eyes of the newsroom gaze upon me as I follow Jane into Eric's office.

"Hi, Caryn." Eric's hand is outstretched. I've met him before, but he never said much to me until I brought the click bait.

"How are you?" I'm trying to put him at ease, as he looks concerned. I make sure to look him in the eyes to show that I'm not scared. I don't ever let them think I'm scared even though I'm fucking terrified.

After the twenty-minute meeting I go in the bathroom and do what I do best: throw up.

The only person who knows about my essay, outside of the *Daily*'s newsroom, is my housemate and best friend, Grace. I haven't even told my therapist that I wrote it for actual publication, but I will since I'm guessing I'll need to start upping my sessions to twice a week. I've lived with Grace off campus for the last two years in a three-bedroom craftsman house in Larchmont Village that my dad bought as an investment and so I would have somewhere nice to live that was near campus, but not so near campus that bars are found on the windows of the nearby houses.

Even though we're seniors in college and have plenty of responsibility, it's hard to feel like a grown-up when Daddy still pays your way. But we had a deal: I stay local and go to USC and all expenses—from tuition to shopping to beauty treatments to therapy sessions—would be paid by him. We have not yet discussed what happens after I graduate and he loses official control of me. My father cannot imagine a world in which he doesn't have control of his wife and children.

"Unnie's home," I shout when Grace walks in the door,

carrying three bags of groceries in her delicate hands. She's only one month older than me, but I always address her as my older sister in Korean since she's the closest thing I have to one.

"Here, eat something." She tosses a bag of popcorn my way.

I push the bag back toward her. "I practically ate an entire charcuterie tray at work today." I leave out the part about me getting rid of it all a few minutes later.

"You're getting too skinny." She eyes my razor-sharp clavicles.

"I thought there was no such thing for Koreans. I mean, you gotta love how Koreans value thinness above everything else, and yet they're constantly shoving food down your throat at every possible occasion."

"That is so true." Grace laughs, but then her face resumes its expression of worry.

"Seeing as you're a size zero, I don't think you can say anything," I reply. "And don't frown so much, or you'll be getting Botox by twenty-five."

"Yeah, but I'm naturally thin," she argues, "and eat whatever I want. You know that. You see what I eat."

"And I hate you for it," I tease. "It doesn't come natural for all of us. I blame my father's giant German genes."

"I just want you to be healthy. You were already skinny when we met freshman year."

"Take it up with Mrs. Rodgers."

Grace isn't smiling. "Are you feeling extra stressed right now? I mean, I know your school schedule, but maybe with the internship and your duties at the *Daily Trojan* it's all a bit much?"

"I think I'd feel worse if I had more time to sit around and think."

If you believe there is pressure for a young woman to be thin in this world, try being a young woman raised in Los Angeles where the sun shines three hundred days of the year. Then go to a school like Windemere, and have a Korean mother, a former Miss Korea who gives you money for each pound you lose while you're still in high school. Throw in the stuff with Dr. Copeland and regular life pressures and here we are.

"I just worry about you sometimes, especially now, with everything going on." Grace arranges the fruit in a showy crystal bowl that my mom forced upon us.

"I'm fine, Unnie. Everything's going to be fine. That's what Susan says to tell myself anytime my anxiety kicks in." I close my eyes and pretend to be lost in a reverie.

Grace dismisses my attempt to deflect. "What's happening with your article? Is it official?"

"It's running this weekend and I'm excited." I grab a banana from the bowl and peel it to please her.

"I'm sure you did a great job with it, since you're such a great writer."

I ignore her compliment and close the fridge door that's been partially open for at least a full minute. "Everyone seems worried about me, like how I'll handle the reaction. They had me meet with the *Daily*'s lawyer and everything. It kind of feels parental, like I'm a kid they have to help cross the street."

"Well, that's nicer than them not caring, right?"

"Jane's been great about it all. I know we have nothing in common, but I trust her. As long as she's involved, I know it will be okay."

Grace rolls her eyes. "How can you say you have nothing in common when you're both reporters? I thought she was your idol?"

"She is my idol although I'd never tell her that, and yes we're both reporters. I just mean she wears Birkenstocks, which I know are 'back,' but come on." I grab a pile of junk mail from the counter so I can shred it.

"She's working in a casual office, and it is pretty warm out right now." I adore Grace for being willing to defend a hideous shoe.

Even though I spend more time with her than anyone else, Grace's optimism and sunny disposition have not rubbed off on me. "Call me old-fashioned, but I don't think anyone needs to see your toes at the office." I realize I sound judgmental, but if you can't be judgmental about Birkenstocks, then what fun is there left on this Earth?

"You must be learning a lot from her."

"Watching her up close is better than a master's program in journalism. She always does the right thing and she's patient with me."

Grace stacks cans of wild salmon in the cupboard. "So, what went down at the big meeting?"

"We talked about the possible fallout, and how other outlets, including television news, may pick this story up and run with it. How it could become a much bigger thing than I intended."

"Well, yeah." She unpacks the last of the groceries. "I mean it's the *Daily*, and I assume it will go viral because of the subject matter. And you."

"What do you mean?"

"Have you seen yourself? You know the world we live in. Our society loves a victim who looks like you. Someone young and beautiful, I mean."

"There are beautiful women everywhere. I'm nothing special."

"Can I tell you something I've never told you before?"

I widen my eyes, waiting for this revelation.

"I think you're more beautiful than your mother is or ever was."

"I appreciate you trying to build me up, but she was Miss Korea and I have yet to have a real boyfriend."

"If you'd actually consider letting someone in, I think you'd find a line forming outside our front door."

I can't continue to talk like this anymore so I change the subject. "I've just been feeling a little weird, like, nothing *that* bad happened to me."

"Don't you think if that were the case they wouldn't publish your essay?"

"I guess."

"Caryn?"

"Every day there are horrible things that happen to young women. A kid just shot a girl from his high school because she said no to a school dance. There are gang rapes and kidnappings and murders, not to mention little girls getting their clits hacked off on the other side of the world." Grace winces. "It's true. Google 'female genital mutilation' and then tell me I have real problems."

"It's not a contest." She's always the levelheaded one. "Don't play the Oppression Olympics. It's not helpful."

"I know, but the news is so shocking these days, I guess I just feel like my essay won't even live up to the salaciousness of the headline. It's not exactly Penn State or Bill Cosby level, you know."

"Plenty of people will be shocked and outraged and on your side. The public, especially the families that give so much money to Windemere, deserve to know. To think that he is teaching girls right this second is sickening. That bastard is about to be fired and I can't wait."

"We'll see."

"You don't think he'll be fired immediately?"

"You would think so, but the parents and community worship this man. I assume that's why no one has come forward before. It's not easy to go up against that. Against him and his fucking charisma."

"But you did come forward before and Windemere did

nothing. How could they have done nothing?"

"I don't know. You'd think they would have at least investigated the situation seeing as my dad was always a big donor."

"Forget being a donor." Grace's dark brows furrow with rage. "They should have protected you as a student and fellow human being, and if they couldn't do that, they should have taken you seriously when you told them what happened. You had email proof. What more do they want?"

"They want a perfect victim and a perfect perpetrator. Someone who jumps out of the bushes in a park in the middle of the night and drags you to the ground by your hair. They want witnesses and screams and blood. Anything short of that is considered murky or he-said, she-said, even when there's proof."

"Okay, so let's say it's murky and not one hundred percent black and white. So murky means no investigation? What about murders and robberies? It's not like those cases are crystal clear. That's the whole point of an investigation—because it's murky. We can't even figure out JonBenét Ramsey and it's been twenty years."

"You tell 'em, Unnie." I sip from the sparkling water I've been nursing for the last hour.

"I don't think this is funny."

"Part of me wants to burn Windemere to the ground and another part of me feels bad."

"Why?" Grace folds her arms across her chest. "Windemere deserves everything that's coming to them. They're going to have a PR nightmare on their hands. Are you worried about the students? Could it affect their standing or college applications?"

"No, not about Windemere. I feel bad because I'm about to ruin his wife and kids' lives. Can you even imagine? I can't stop thinking about how they are going to find out. Will his wife open the paper and think to herself, how horrible, without realizing the essay is about the man who's still snoring a few feet away? Is some nosy neighbor or friend from school going to drop this bomb on one of his kids? How can they even go to school on Monday?"

"*He* ruined their lives—don't ever forget that."

"You know that's not how it works, Unnie."

Dr. Copeland's kids are part of why I didn't go public before. I've always known about them because that's how it is at Windemere. Any girl from my class could tell you my parents' names, how many siblings I had, or if we had any pets, and I could do the same in return. We know which teachers are married, who has kids, and which staff member is suffering from an ulcer because they're going through a tough divorce. When I was in his class, Dr. Copeland's daughter was around the same age as me, and her little brother, Jack, was twelve. He kept one of those travel-size silver frames—a gift from his wife, I'm sure, as men don't do sentimental things like that on their own—on his classroom desk and I looked at it sometimes. Leah seemed like a bit of a tomboy, with cute freckles and a bob-style haircut, while Jack had big green eyes and a wry smile like his dad.

I worried about his kids when I came forward at Windemere and I'm still worrying about them. I guess there's no good time to find out your dad is a cheater and criminal. I hate that I'm the one they will forever associate with this life-changing news. But part of me feels like if I don't do something, anything, to try and stop him, then I'm somehow complicit in Dr. Copeland's actions. I don't know why it took until now for it to finally hit me that I couldn't have been the only one. There must be other girls out there—and I'm about to make a siren call.

Chapter Three

Jane

"Y ou hanging in there?" I'm surprised to find Caryn is
in the office before me on a Monday morning.

"I feel better being here than at home." Her eyes
dart around the newsroom like an animal trying to plan an escape.
"I keep thinking people are staring at me, like, even on the street."
Her voice sounds a bit hoarse and I wonder why.

"I can imagine." I say this, but I really can't imagine. Even
my biggest stories don't draw the amount of attention Caryn is
dealing with at the moment. She agreed to sit for a black-and-
white portrait at the urging of our art department, so her image—
which they blew up to a full-size page inside the magazine—has
been disseminated widely, to say the least.

And even if I had a byline on this piece, it wouldn't be the
same because I hardly have a digital footprint outside of my work.
You'd be hard-pressed to find more than a few photos of me online,
whereas Caryn has a few thousand on Instagram alone. Plus, she's
young, beautiful, and intelligent, and her dad is a diplomat and her
mother was a beauty queen. She doesn't speak much about her
personal life, and I don't push, but it was clear to me from the first
interview that she was different from any intern we've ever had.

"I know what the online reaction has been." I'm
downplaying the fact that Caryn's story was read 1.2 million times
on our site alone and was trending on Twitter in Los Angeles at one
point. "But what about for you, personally? Did you sleep? Are
you able to concentrate?"

"Well, aside from the fact that my parents aren't speaking to me, my brother being mortified, and getting hate mail from Windemere students and parents, I guess everything is fine."

"I'm sorry to hear that, but you know, you did the right thing. It's not the easy thing; it's the right thing. It was very brave of you." I sound like a mom in a cheesy after-school special, but I mean it and want her to know.

It's clear she can't take a compliment. She just continues speaking. "There's also been more support than I expected. I told myself I wasn't going to read the comments, but I saw some and they were surprisingly kind."

"We've had a lot of emails regarding the piece. It didn't take long for alumnae to connect the dots. I'm going to forward some your way. It's up to you if you want to respond to any of them."

"Okay."

"And feel free to leave at lunch today as you're surely putting in some extra hours outside the office these days. I won't tell."

"Thanks, Jane." She twists the gold pendant of her necklace in between her thumb and forefinger. "I appreciate it."

I pull a few of the emails we received that I think will make her feel better and forward them in one document:

Class of 1992 over here. Seriously what the hell is going on? I remember a few of us hating a male biology teacher and within a week of Parents Night, he was fired. How is it that someone accused of misconduct like this doesn't even warrant a firing or removal while a proper investigation takes place? The fact that Windemere gave him counseling . . . SMDH. What is the point of an all-girls school environment, which is supposed to protect us and let us feel safe?

Literally, WTF Windemere? It is such a small community (I have a child currently in attendance) and trust is a huge part of the experience. Although my daughter assures me she has never encountered a teacher like this, I am horrified to say the least. There are so many sharks circling around young girls—in the streets, online, and in their very own "safe" schools—it truly makes me sick!

Windemere is a place where you can misplace your backpack for hours and it will be safe. I remember leaving a wallet in class overnight by mistake and it was found with not so much as a dollar missing. That feeling of complete safety and trust—that you would never feel anywhere else in Los Angeles—is gone. Teachers should NEVER fraternize with their students because of power dynamics, duh. It doesn't matter if the student is mature or special in some way. Any nonacademic contact or inappropriate relationship is totally unethical.

The hypocrisy of this institution makes me sick! Most parents choose schools like these because they give girls and young women a place to feel comfortable, be heard, and pursue their true passions without judgment or the distraction of having boys around. Most girls are around twelve when they start at Windemere, which means this teacher may have known or watched her since she was a prepubescent child. When Caryn bravely spoke up, she was shot down and essentially told that her safety and comfort were of no importance. While I had a positive experience at Windemere in the early 2000s, I will not be giving a cent to this school ever again. In fact, I look forward to their next solicitation letter so I can respond accordingly. Caryn, if you read this, please know that we are behind you.

While I was at Windemere, I never heard of sexual relations between teachers and students, but I certainly witnessed plenty of instances of crossed boundaries. The faculty tend to treat students as though they are adults. While Windemere is an excellent place to prep for college life, the students are still girls and young women. I noticed numerous inappropriate actions from teachers, such as female faculty members asking girls about their dating lives, while another messaged their student in the middle of the night to check on college applications or test deadlines. Some teachers got so invested in our success that it bordered on creepy.

I'm trying to reach the author of this piece. Caryn, if you read this, please know that he gave me a book of poetry by Emily Dickinson. I'm class of 2002 and would like to talk if you are open to it.

I don't send her some of the nastier messages, which included everything from references to schoolgirl skirts to vile rape and death threats. One guy claimed he was masturbating to her image and offered to send proof. We made the decision to close the comments on the story after twenty-four hours since there were already 2,573 of them. Contrary to our society's everyone-gets-a-ribbon mentality, not all opinions need to be amplified. I miss the days when journalists dispensed the news and people had to mail in a letter to the editor if they wanted their thoughts heard on any given subject. The comments section of our stories was once a respectful discussion, but in recent years, it's become a cesspool of misogyny, racism, and other unsavory behavior, so I'm relieved that Caryn saw some of the nice ones.

I get back to work on a story about the revitalization of the Los Angeles River, but I can't help but think of Caryn, who is tapping her suede heel on the base of her swivel chair so fast that I can feel the ground shake from ten feet away. She doesn't leave to grab lunch, which isn't out of the ordinary as I've rarely seen her eat at work, but seems focused on something.

A few hours later, a notification pops up on my desktop from our internal instant messaging system and it's a link from

Caryn. Since I'm in the zone, I debate waiting to click on it until after I finish my story, but then I realize it's a link to the mass email that just went out from Windemere, and I simply can't resist.

Dear Windemere parents, alumnae, and friends,

We are deeply concerned and troubled by the recent accusations made by a Windemere graduate. This alumna wrote in detail about a former teacher's inappropriate behavior, which occurred during her sophomore year.

After learning of the situation at the time, the School immediately investigated her concerns. However, this essay contains details not previously reported or communicated in any way to the School. We regret the suffering mentioned in the article.

Our Board has met for an emergency meeting and will conduct a thorough examination of these allegations. We would encourage all current students and alumnae to come forward if they have any information or personal experience regarding the situation.

Sincerely,
Rachel Wasserman, President, Board of Trustees
Ann Erickson, Head of School

They didn't name Copeland in the email and I feel like a pot on the verge of boiling.

"Caryn?"

"I know. They aren't going to name him, are they?"

" 'We regret the suffering mentioned in the article,' " I quote from the email blast.

"They're lying, not only about caring about my suffering, but about the supposed details that are new to them. None of this is new to them. My parents and I spoke with Ann Erickson and showed her everything."

"They must not have met with a PR team yet."

"How do you know that?"

"Because a crisis management firm would tell you that you have to at least admit something, some wrongdoing, so that you can get ahead of the story and seem like you have nothing to hide."

Caryn laughs in reply. "They just hoped it was an isolated thing they could sweep under the rug. When they realized my parents weren't going to make a public fuss, they just went back to business as usual. No one ever checked on me again or even sent me so much as an email to see how I was doing. The irony of it all is their whole M.O. is to develop and nurture strong young women. From day one, they teach us to be critical and skeptical, to not just take things at face value. Windemere, above all, values teaching their students to be vocal and independent. They created their own monster."

"Caryn, you're not a monster." I sip from my mug and realize it's gone cold. I motion with my head for her to follow me.

She lowers her voice while we cut through the newsroom to the kitchen. "I'm sure they will have their team of lawyers at the ready. Half of Windemere girls' parents are attorneys and I'm guessing some of them are already involved." Caryn's walking fast to keep up with my long stride. "A bunch of parents are going to suddenly become interested in their children's lives beyond SAT scores and college applications."

I grab a tea bag. "I figured Windemere parents were overly involved. Isn't that the stereotype? Public school parents aren't involved enough and private school parents are too involved? Helicopter types?"

"Some of them are obsessed with their kids' schooling, especially the ones who had high-powered careers but then they became stay-at-home moms and now they're bored as fuck so they meddle in every aspect of their daughter's life. Sorry." She lowers her eyes like a child who's about to be scolded.

"You can say 'fuck' around me, Caryn. You're a grown woman and the newsroom is not exactly a church." I add hot water, careful not to burn myself like last time.

"Okay, thanks." She looks embarrassed for no reason and I start walking back to my desk as she trails behind. I'm not hard on her because I remember how exhausting it was to be in my early twenties, obsessing on every detail of the day, constantly apologizing for doing nothing wrong, or doubting the most basic decisions of daily life.

"There are plenty of helicopter parents and Tiger Mom types, and they aren't even all Asian," she says. "In certain L.A. neighborhoods, there are kindergarteners who already have tutors, but some of the ultrawealthy kids—especially once in high school—are essentially on their own." I wonder if she's speaking about her own experience. "I'm talking about generational wealth, not Silicon Beach new-money bullshit. Some of these Windemere students' last names are on buildings, or their parents are high-profile people who aren't interested in discipline or being in town for their daughters' big game. I mean these are kids who grew up trick-or-treating with their maids because their moms and dads were at some charity masquerade ball where tickets are twenty-five thousand dollars a seat. The parents are there, but not actually *there*."

My eyes close for a second. "That sounds sad. What's the point of having kids if you're just going to outsource parenting?"

"They have kids because that's what you do. It helps them look normal when they are far from it. Plenty of Windemere parents are involved and loving, but some of them don't have any interest in raising their kids, or learning anything about who they really are, and so girls act out. It started getting really bad during my senior year."

I act nonchalant, but I'm eager to hear any revelations about this world that is so different from the one in which I was raised. "These three girls, let's just say you've heard of their families, would host 'pharma parties.' "

"Farm parties?"

Caryn can't help but giggle, but I don't join her.

"Pharma, like pharmaceutical. A bunch of us would get together and bring whatever pills we could find in our parents' medicine cabinets. Then you dump everything into a pile and take whatever you want."

I shake my head in judgment as if kids I knew didn't do similar stupid things while we were growing up. "That sounds like Russian roulette."

Caryn doesn't appear to get the reference. "We'd be up in Laurel Canyon and there were no adults around—not even an older brother. I only went twice before realizing it wasn't my thing. I'm all for teenage angst and pissing off your parents, but these girls were dark. I honestly think they wanted to end up in the emergency room just so their parents would pay attention."

I lean closer toward her. "Well I would hope something like your story would get any parent to pay attention."

"I hope so too." She looks at the floor as if she's focused on an interesting fiber of the carpet. "Some of the parents will overreact, convinced that their daughters had their legs rubbed, and others will defend Copeland to the death because they met him a few times and know he's a wonderful man. It's going to get messy, especially if anyone else comes forward. Plus, we haven't had a good scandal in a while, and never one involving a pervert teacher."

I blow on my tea, which is still too hot to drink. "What was the last big Windemere scandal?"

"There was a cheating ring going on during my senior year with some of the juniors. Girls are superclose at Windemere until it comes time to apply for colleges, then it just turns ruthless. They're under pressure from their parents and themselves. People become competitive and want an edge or a way to stand apart because the entire class can't attend Harvard, you know?"

"No, I guess they can't. So what happened?" I'm tempted to take notes but I want her to keep talking.

"This one girl, whose dad literally bought the four-million-dollar pool at Windemere, was the mastermind and ringleader, but she was never punished. Actually, I don't think anyone was punished."

"Because of the pool gift?"

"Exactly. It was a good teacher who brought the cheating evidence to the administration, but the board decided to keep it quiet. I think there were a few teachers who would complain about how certain parents were influencing the workings of the school with financial donations."

I finally take a sip. "It sounds like there are many stories to be written about Windemere."

"Why would Windemere take the risk of keeping Dr. Copeland after I showed them everything? Why couldn't they conduct a proper investigation? Instead of firing him they chose to make me feel like I was overreacting, like I was crazy or something." Caryn's talking at a faster clip and filled with a passion she rarely exhibits.

"Well, perhaps they'll learn a lesson from all of this, although I wouldn't hold your breath. These institutions are far more concerned with protecting themselves than their students, and that's not an easy thing to digest as a student or a parent." I notice her left hand has curled into a fist.

"The school is essentially run like a business and they want to serve their own interests. I think that teacher who discovered the cheating quit the following year because she was so devastated that those girls were never even given a slap on the wrist. I mean how can they say they are preparing students for the world if they let that kind of thing fly?"

I get distracted for a moment by a stream of AP news alerts popping up on my screen. "What was the school's official explanation for not punishing those students?"

"They didn't want those students to lose their college admissions or any related academic scholarships."

"Because that would be awful for them and their parents who had invested hundreds of thousands of dollars in their education. Plus, if a group of girls suddenly didn't go to top colleges that would also affect the school's brand and standing."

"I heard there were 'gallons of tears' over it." Caryn fiddles with an errant rubber band. "At Windemere, things that should be black and white become extremely gray."

"You've really thought about this stuff and yet you still came forward."

"It's because of this stuff that I came forward."

Chapter Four

Caryn

f all the supportive reader emails Jane sent over earlier today, there is only one person I want to write back to: Miss Emily Dickinson.

From: Caryn Rodgers
To: Eva Garcia
Date: May 1, 2016 at 2:42 p.m.
Subject: Emily Dickinson

Hi Eva,

Thank you so much for your note. I know this is awkward. Yours is the only email I decided to answer for now. I assume we are talking about the same Windemere faculty member, given the Emily Dickinson book you mentioned. Would you mind using his initials so I know for sure?

Sincerely,
Caryn

From: Eva Garcia
To: Caryn Rodgers
Date: May 1, 2016 at 4:06 p.m.
Subject: Re: My article . . .

Caryn,

Thank you so much for replying to me. I'm talking about Dr. Gregory Copeland who was my English teacher when I was a student at Windemere. I feel certain that you are describing the same person. When I read your essay, I had a visceral response to some of the details and now I can't stop thinking about it, so I'm really glad you wrote me back. Now that I know I am communicating directly with you, I feel the need to share some additional things. I'm sure you're a very busy woman, so let me know if that's okay with you.

Eva

From: Caryn Rodgers
To: Eva Garcia
Date: May 1, 2016 at 4:08 p.m.
Subject: Re: re: Emily Dickinson

Yes, it's Copeland. I don't know why I'm surprised that he'd pull the same thing with others, as I think I always suspected it deep down. I'm here for anything you feel comfortable sharing with me, and I promise to keep it between us.

Sincerely,
Caryn

From: Eva Garcia
To: Caryn Rodgers
Date: May 1, 2016 at 4:12 p.m.
Subject: Re: re: re: Emily Dickinson

You are far braver than I was. I never told anyone—not even my husband—about what happened to me at Windemere. I had planned to never talk about it. Ever. There's this stereotype that girls can't keep secrets. Nothing could be farther from the truth in my case.

Once I read your article (which I just happened to see on Facebook as I never have time to read the paper anymore), all the feelings I had kept buried for so many years came right back. All kinds of memories—good and bad—flooded my mind's eye. It's so bizarre because I haven't spent much time thinking about him in recent years, but I guess the past is always there, simmering. Here's a summary of my experience (I hope it's not too long-winded):

I had him as an English teacher during my sophomore year. I was a new student and he made me feel welcome and like I actually belonged there (which I never felt at first, or ever, really). The attention he paid me was so incremental that I barely noticed things were escalating until it was too late. I've since learned about the phenomenon of "grooming," and that's exactly how I would characterize what happened. He is a brilliant teacher, but he's an even more brilliant manipulator. I am now certain that he picked me for specific reasons.

Things changed from a typical teacher-student relationship when I had been struggling with a Shakespeare assignment and Copeland suggested we meet in private to discuss the essay. I was part of Los Angeles Unified School District prior to Windemere, so I just figured this is how teachers at an elite private school interacted with students. All the extra attention and opportunities for one-on-one interaction was why I wanted to attend. At my previous school, teachers could barely keep our names straight and we sometimes had to sit at the teacher's desk due to classroom overcrowding. So we met up, and one meeting led to another, almost as if he was my private tutor.

I thought nothing of this until he put his hand on my thigh during one of these meetings, just as he did to you. Just typing that gives me goose bumps now. I think this was his litmus test. If I had jumped up and screamed, or pulled away discreetly, then I'm sure everything would have ended right there. But I wasn't horrified at the time; I felt empowered and flattered that this popular teacher was paying me special attention even though I knew it was not necessarily the kind that would be considered appropriate. I justified it in my childlike mind.

The more time I spent with him talking after class or going over assignments, the more he made me feel smart, interesting, and beautiful. There were lots of cute girls in our class, so to think that he had selected me in some way, or would choose to pay me attention over others, did wonders for the little self-esteem I had at that age. I felt more confident after spending time with him and also enjoyed having something to look forward to at school. Looking back, I suppose I had a crush on him, although I wouldn't have articulated it that way at first.

A few months after we first met, I found myself accepting an invitation to leave campus with him one afternoon after school. It's hard for me to even believe I did that as it feels so out of character for me (in the past, I've taught Bible study classes in my spare time and am considered a bit of a prude compared to typical women my age). I was a bit nervous, but not more so than when I had to speak in front of the entire class or wait for report cards at the end of the semester. I was incredibly attracted to his heart and mind, and because of that I couldn't be scared of him. He was so patient and understanding and kind.

He reassured me that we didn't have to have sex, but that we obviously had a "special connection" that should be examined. I felt the exact same way. I had never connected with an adult in any way like this and so I bought everything he was selling. I know it must sound revolting to you, especially now, but we hooked up in his car. At one point, I remember seeing a piece of mail on the passenger-side floor mat that belonged to his wife (who I'm sure you know is a prominent attorney in Century City; I believe

*she even handled several divorces of Windemere girls' parents).
I remember feeling disgusted with myself afterward, like I had
somehow betrayed my gender and committed a horrible sin. I was
totally convinced at the time that I was going straight to hell.*

*I fully blamed myself rather than holding him responsible
for these actions, which I guess are technically crimes. Facing him
on campus after that was like torture, especially because I had told
no one. By ignoring me or shooting me a dirty look across campus,
I felt he was punishing me because I decided to stop seeing him,
but I never reported it because I knew that I would come off looking
terrible. I was on a full financial scholarship and never wanted to
draw any extra attention to myself, as it was bad enough that I
never had the right brand of shoes or nice jewelry. You can't hide
class, even in a school uniform, can you? I definitely couldn't talk
to my parents and I didn't have friends who I would trust with
such a secret. Seeing how your situation was handled makes me
realize that I was right in assuming that Windemere would not
have protected me.*

*I have to run because my girls are about to kill each other
(I have twin seven-year-olds)! If you ever want to chat more or
even meet up for a coffee, I'd really like that. Just know that I
support you and am here for you.*

Eva
P.S. He also told me I was special and unique "like a rare rose."

I shut my laptop screen and walk as quickly as I can to the bathroom
without arousing extra attention, and pray to myself that no one
will be in there. I promised Susan, my therapist, and myself,
that I wouldn't read any other comments from my article, and I
actually haven't, but I can't help but check out Copeland's page
on RateMyTeachers.com to see if there's been any repercussions
from my essay. I'm also eager to learn if there are any other Evas

out there who may choose to come forward anonymously online. I see a bunch of new entries at the top of the page, published after my weekend essay:

Mr. Copeland is so inspiring—the best teacher I've ever had! This has gone far enough! He's a great person and does not deserve this slander!

He's the best teacher I've ever had. I don't know about all this other stuff being talked about. He completely changed the way I feel about literature and the English language.

I do not believe what was written in that article. He was always a great teacher and I'm so sad to hear what he supposedly did.

Oh, please. In the seventies (yes, I am a parent of a Windemere student), girls practically begged their teachers to seduce them. Many of us went on to marry them! Most of these millennials have a victim mentality and are overly sensitive. To the author of that dreadful article: you are not special and probably overdramatized the situation. Welcome to the real world—get over it!

A truly brilliant man who is dedicated to literature. That horrible essay is nothing more than the fiction we are assigned to read in his class.

Great guy. I loved him. Don't judge him harshly, please.

I wish Mr. Copeland would rape me!!

I put my phone away and take a deep breath, in through my nose and out through my mouth like Olivia always reminds me to do in Pilates. I then do what I need to do, clean up, and pop an organic breath mint. Everyone's preoccupied as I walk back to my desk. I will take relief wherever I can get it.

"Jane?"

"Yeah?" She stops typing.

"I emailed the Emily Dickenson alumna and she replied."

"And?"

"She was credible. She had a lot of similar details and she's almost a decade older than me."

"So this has been going on for many years." Jane begins writing something in her reporter's notebook. "I can't say I'm surprised; it's not like these guys get caught the first time. God knows how many times things like this happened. It could be happening right now."

"I guess I always knew that I couldn't have been the only one, but now I know it for sure. Her story is much more, um, involved than mine."

I fill her in on the general themes and contents of Eva's emails without revealing any personal details. I notice that Jane's chest is getting flush with a pink hue as though the blood coursing through her vessels is trying desperately to get to the surface of her skin.

Jane saves whatever she's working on to show that I have her attention. "Are you going to meet with her?"

"I want to, yes." I realize I'm stammering. "But, what do I even say?"

"You're a reporter." She grabs today's edition of the paper, which has an "additional reporting by Caryn Rodgers" credit at the bottom of her story, and hands it to me. "Since when are you tongue-tied?"

"I know, but this is not exactly the same as profiling Tommy Trojan."

"You're not going to write an article, obviously, but she appears to feel comfortable telling you these personal things. I'm sure it would be useful for you both to talk to one another. Does she want to come forward publicly?"

"I have no idea. That didn't come up."

Jane begins untangling the pair of white headphones she keeps at her desk. "Well, I think you should encourage her to alert Windemere at the very least. Their email asked for people to come forward, so the gates are wide open. This is the time to do it. It will force them to take this seriously if there are multiple victims."

I take a quick peek to make sure no one in the newsroom is listening to us. "I hate the word 'victim.' It makes it sound like we're on some police procedural show."

"Caryn, she reached out to you—a complete stranger—and didn't have to."

"I know, but—"

Jane cuts me off quicker than a driver merging onto the 405. "What was your end goal with the essay you wrote for us? I assume it wasn't to add stress to your life or upset your family."

"I want him to get fired and not be able to teach girls ever again. I want the Head of School and board to be held responsible." It's the first time I've vocalized my deepest want to anyone. My voice is shaking and I feel a lump form in my throat. I will never cry at work, especially not in front of Jane, so I dig my nails into my right thigh until it hurts enough to distract me from my own emotions. I stop just short of drawing blood.

Jane offers an encouraging smile. "She can help you do that. Just because your essay came out doesn't mean this is over. This is just the beginning. We have no idea where this is going to go."

"She has kids and no one knows about what happened to her. She hasn't even told her husband yet. I don't know if she's ready for all of this." I feel a knot form in my stomach. "I've been thinking about writing this essay for years. Meetings were had to prepare me. I've talked to my therapist at length. I have a supportive best friend and you and the *Daily*. She just had this brought back up in her life in the last twenty-four hours."

"She doesn't need to write an essay or even identify herself to the public. Why would she contact you if she didn't want some form of justice herself? She wanted to talk to you. Perhaps she wanted to let you know that you're not alone."

"Her story makes mine look like a joke."

"It's not a competition, Caryn. No two stories are going to be exactly the same, even if they have similar elements. The common theme here is that Copeland was totally inappropriate with you both. If you were amenable don't you think he would have taken things farther with you?" If I had been amenable, I have no doubt he would have fucked me in the bathroom of that Starbucks had I asked. "He has no business teaching at Windemere or anywhere else. No matter what happens, don't ever forget that."

I can tell Jane is getting annoyed. She already spends more time than required helping me with pitches and articles, and now this. I know how busy she is with her regular workload. It's time to go back to my desk and figure out what I'm going to do. I feel a pain in my neck sharpen.

Chapter Five

Jane

I t's been ten days since Caryn's article first came out and Eric has just called to inform me that the numbers on her piece were three times as high as a typical viral story of ours. He's thrilled, perhaps more with the online traffic than the fact that the *Daily* may help get a dangerous teacher out of teaching.

"I want you to write a follow-up piece to run next weekend." I can hear Eric pacing around his office, determined to get his ten thousand steps in each day. "Didn't you mention that another victim came forward via Caryn's article?"

"Yes, Caryn is in touch with her."

"Does she want to talk?"

"I don't know. Caryn's meeting with her soon. I guess we'll find out."

"Start digging around. We need to know if Windemere knew anything before Caryn's piece ran."

"Well of course they knew. Her piece made that clear."

"I mean, did they know anything else? Have others come forward and been dismissed like Caryn?"

"That I don't know."

"It's clear our audience is hungry for a story like this."

"Of course they are." I roll my eyes. Although I'm sure he's not rubbing his hands together like a movie villain, he still sounds like a caricature of a newspaper editor, practically salivating at what this could mean for the paper. For him.

"Let's see where this story takes us. Perhaps it will lead to some change in the end."

"I doubt that." I can't hide my cynicism and Eric knows better than to give me some pep talk about changing the world.

"It's a conflict for Caryn to work on this piece with you, so I'll trust that she won't be involved in the reporting."

"Of course not. But if she introduces me to a source, I'm taking it."

"Fine by me."

When I get back to my desk, after stopping at the kitchen to get my third cup of coffee, I see Caryn has forwarded me another official email from Windemere:

Dear Windemere parents, alumnae, and friends,

We regret to tell you that last week, another graduate of the School came forward with serious allegations of an inappropriate physical relationship with the same teacher more than fifteen years ago. In response to this shocking news, we notified the Los Angeles Police Department as well as Child Protective Services. There is no greater priority than the safety, well-being, and happiness of our students.

We are committed to transparency and wish to have a full understanding of what occurred, so today, the Board of Trustees has authorized an independent investigation and appointed a special investigative committee. This committee will be chaired by Trustee Michael Patrick, a partner at Chatham, Gilchrist & Wendler LLP and a renowned expert in the field of internal investigations. Under his leadership, the committee will appoint a neutral investigator.

If you or your daughters have any information that could be helpful to this investigation, please contact Rachel Wasserman, President, Board of Trustees, or Ann Erickson, Head of School, as soon as possible. Windemere is committed to keeping you informed of developments and the steps the School is taking during this challenging time.

We are expecting the media to report on this matter in the coming days and thank you in advance for your support and understanding. The Windemere community will work through this difficult period with dignity and determination to never let this happen again.

Sincerely,
Rachel Wasserman, President, Board of Trustees
Ann Erickson, Head of School

Once again, Copeland has not been named. Why won't they just say his damn name? At this point, Caryn's story has gone completely viral and in those articles, he is identified. Everyone knows. Reporters have dug up photos from past Windemere yearbooks and a reporter from the *Press-Telegram* even scored an interview with one of Copeland's neighbors who assured everyone he is a "wonderful father." The British tabloids have run stories, the scandal has been on local news, and we've heard rumblings of reporters from New York digging around for a possible investigative piece.

Based on my own math and what Caryn told me about the woman she was emailing with, it occurs to me that this must be yet *another* former student who contacted Windemere, and not the one with the Emily Dickinson book.

I grab my phone and head toward the patio we share with a local tech start-up.

Caryn answers after one ring, already one step ahead of me. "We have to find her. I assume that's why you're calling."

"Let me work on that." I'm exhilarated with what has transpired in such a short time. "I think this story is just getting started, thanks to you. Eric wants me to write a reported piece for next weekend. Depending on what I can find out, it could be big."

"I'm meeting with Eva today on Larchmont. I'm nervous."

"You'll be fine. Just ask questions and listen. She wants to talk, so let her."

"I don't want to freak her out by asking her to go on the record or anything."

"You don't have to mention the story right now. Does she get the Windemere emails?"

"I'm sure she does. In this world, nothing can be said to be certain except for death, taxes, and Windemere emails hitting you up for donations. You could change your email ten times in a year and they'd find you."

"If only they used that precision for school policies that would protect their students from predatory teachers."

"If she hasn't seen the email yet, I'll show her."

"It will help her if she knows there are multiple accusers. It will give her the confidence to do the right thing. No one wants to be the first one, or even the second."

"I'll let you know how it goes."

I decide to ping Ben, a former *Daily* colleague who was let go last year in one of our many waves of layoffs. I heard he's making a living by writing college essays for kids who go to schools like Windemere.

He writes back within minutes, offering help, so I give him a call.

"Chained to the desk?" Ben asks.

"It's actually not so bad lately. The paper is so thin these days, and we've lost sixty percent of the staff—there are only so many stories that can be written. And the online stuff we do is supershort."

"What did Eric tell us about writing posts for the web? Readers' attention spans maxed out at two hundred and fifty words?"

"It's more like one hundred and fifty now."

"I read your first piece on the drought," he says of my new investigative series. "Good stuff, March."

"Thanks, Ben. We miss you around here."

"I doubt that, but I appreciate the lie. So what can I do for you? I know you and your requests. They're always big ones."

"I'm sure you heard about what's going on at Windemere."

"It's a hot topic among my students and their parents. The reactions are pretty wild."

"How so?"

"Just that some people are outraged, others shrug it off like it's a rite of passage, and of course, some parents are now convinced that we're all monsters. Men, I mean."

"Aren't you?"

"Very funny, March. I work with a few Windemere kids."

"So you know that they are doing an internal investigation then."

"Yup. I actually know someone on the board. The parent of one of my students."

"That's great." I don't want to sound too overeager, although I'm secretly delighted because this could be an in. "We know that there are multiple victims. One is Caryn, who wrote the essay, and there's another woman who came forward after reading her piece."

"Jesus. I guess I can't say I'm surprised. From her essay it sounded like he was pretty brazen. He's quite popular on campus from what I've heard."

"But then there's another victim who approached Windemere directly."

"Well then it sounds like he's done."

"We'll see about that, but right now, I'm trying to get in touch with that victim. The one we don't know."

"They're not going to release her name to you, Jane. You know better than that."

"Of course they won't. That's why I called you."

"They sure as hell aren't going to tell *me* her name."

"I thought you could do some digging around for me. Maybe talk to the parent who's on the board. If they're sympathetic, perhaps they could encourage her to reach out to me. Off the record, of course."

"That's a tall order, even for you, March."

"If anyone can deliver, it's you. I know you're one of the good guys." I realize I've been twisting the phone's black cord around my fingers so tight that I've created temporary indentations.

"You know me too well, Jane. I haven't had my ego stroked in quite some time. Working with privileged kids isn't as rewarding as exposing dirty politicians, you know?"

"Look, this guy can't get away with this. He's gotten away with it for years. He could be doing this right now with some fifteen-year-old kid. I don't need to tell you how young a fifteen-year-old student looks."

There's a pause. "You know, these girls aren't always innocents." I feel my chest rise. "I mean, I've had students develop crushes on me. Some of them are bold. And I'm not exactly Zac Efron."

"No, you're not."

"Look, there are all sorts of factors: raging hormones, the fact that there are no boys their age around, and you could even argue that it's natural."

"It's natural for a child to come on to a teacher? Is that what you're saying, Ben?"

"You never had a crush on a teacher, Jane?"

"Of course girls have crushes on their teachers. Boys do as well. That's not the issue here. Are you really going to go with the narrative of it being the student's fault? That's your gut reaction? That sometimes young women come on to their teachers and so we should just ignore the fact that actual crimes have been committed?"

"No, March. That's not what I meant." I've never heard him falter before.

"Then please, by all means, articulate what you meant." My foot is now tapping the floor at a rapid clip.

"I just meant that it's natural to develop crushes or flirt with someone, especially as you're coming of age and having all these feelings. Some of these girls who go to schools like Windemere are incredibly mature, even though they're kids, and they interact with adults and are used to being in adultlike situations. What's not natural is for a grown man, in a position of power and authority, to use that for sinister purposes."

"Are you done?"

"Look, when I see a teenage girl my first thought is a feeling of protection."

"Is that because you know what certain men think about and would want with that teenage girl?"

"No, March, you're getting a bit carried away here. Let me make it clear: I don't think about fucking them. Ever."

"Do you expect me to be impressed by that?" I immediately regret being so forceful when I'm the one asking an old friend for a favor.

"No. It's because I recognize that they're just kids. No matter how provocative they may try to be, or whatever shit they're going through at home that leads to that type of acting out, they're just kids. Their brains are not even fully formed for Christ's sake."

"I don't have time to get into the blame game right now. It's a complicated subject, but in the eyes of the law, only the teacher is guilty of a crime, so why not just focus on that for now. It doesn't seem plausible that a bunch of Windemere alums are throwing themselves at Copeland and he simply couldn't resist the onslaught. You saw his picture, right? We're not exactly in Disney Prince territory. We have no idea how these relationships, or assaults, began. We have no idea how big this story is or how many women are involved."

"C'mon, March." He knows my impression of him has been altered by his initial reaction. "I'd do anything to help you. To help Caryn and anyone else who was involved."

"Just make it known that I'm here to make an introduction to the others. I think they can help each other, not just legally, but emotionally."

"March, you know I'm on your side. I didn't mean anything by what I said earlier. Of course this piece of shit deserves whatever is coming to him."

"Why didn't you just say that then?"

"Because I'm another idiot who thinks they can go toe-to-toe with you."

I can feel his contrition, even over the phone, and so I decide to let up. "I owe you one, Ben."

"Yeah, yeah."

"I mean it. I really appreciate this."

"You were always fighting for victims. That's what I remember most about you."

"Isn't that why we became journalists? It certainly wasn't for the miserable pay and harassment from internet trolls. It's to hold people, companies, and institutions accountable."

"I always thought of the definition of a journalist is a person who distributes the news, in print, online, or for broadcast."

"Ben."

"I'm teasing you, March. You are still in the trenches doing the hard work."

"Hey, we all have to do what we have to do. I could be gone in the next layoff and be joining you."

"Working with you again wouldn't be the worst thing, March."

"No, I guess it wouldn't." I smile, feeling myself blush.

"Tell you what. Let me work on the board member and then I'll give you a call this week."

"Sounds good."

"And perhaps I can tell you the findings over a drink. I never come downtown anymore, but there's that new Filipino spot on Seventh I've been meaning to check out. Jonathan Gold hasn't written about it yet so you can still get in."

"You know where to find me."

Chapter Six

Caryn

"Caryn?"

"Hi." I stand up so abruptly that I hit my leg against the table and my napkin drops to the floor. I'm not sure if I should shake her hand or give her a hug. Eva is a petite brunette with a warm smile that sets me at ease. I immediately try picturing her as a Windemere girl in a white polo and gray skirt.

"I'm a hugger." She embraces me. "I mean we've already told each other things over email that we wouldn't share with most friends or family members."

We make some awkward chitchat about where we live and what we do for fun. She compliments me on my hair and platform sandals and I tell her I like her earrings (even though they aren't my style).

"They were a gift from my husband, Jesse. What about you? Do you have a guy in your life?"

"Um, no." I look at the stream of passersby on the street. "I'm just trying to stay focused on school and my internship."

"I'm so impressed that you wrote the essay. You write beautifully."

"It's one thing I can do pretty well." I scan the room to make sure no one is listening to us.

"I highly doubt that, Caryn. You seem lovely."

"So, um." I'm acting like I've never met a stranger for coffee before in my lifetime.

"After I read your story, and the more I thought about what

happened, I realized that I couldn't hold this in any longer." Before we've even started, Eva begins to tear up and I wonder if this was all a mistake. I hate making someone feel pain just because I had to do this for myself.

"I'm so glad you reached out." I pass her a napkin. "Of course I wish it never happened, and that we were meeting under different circumstances, but it's nice to know I'm not alone."

I debate giving her a comforting pat on the hand like you see people do in movies. It's clear she's an emotional person, but I don't want to make her start bawling and have everyone stare at us. In my family, if you start crying, you are told to leave the room. "Crying is weakness," my dad always says. "Never let them think you're weak, no matter what." My mom cries once in a while, but she tries to hide it from everyone. She still doesn't understand that kids see and hear everything. Even the things that aren't ever said.

"I told you I have twin daughters, Ella and Ava. The thought of something like this ever happening to one of them is too much to handle." She wipes her eyes. "As soon as I got pregnant, I started worrying. Then, when I found out we were having twins, I was even more scared, not just because it was a high-risk pregnancy, but because so many things could go wrong. When you become a mother, there is so much uncertainty. You wonder if your children will be healthy and who they will become in this world. You already know life can be hard and unfair, but you don't want them to know that. When they were finally born, my husband and I would watch them all the time on the monitor. I would check on them night after night, to make sure they were breathing. I actually still do that."

"I can't even imagine. I'm pretty sure there's a plant dying in my house right this minute."

Eva gives me an encouraging smile. "But after the baby phase, you worry about preschool and them getting enough vegetables, and bullying and developing peanut allergies. A simple act like driving can turn you into a terrified person because all you want to do in life is protect your kids. There is no deeper pain than seeing your children suffering or hurt. You'll see when you're a mom." She dabs the corners of her eyes with a napkin and I don't have the heart to tell her I have no desire to have kids.

In an awkward transition, I share the latest news. "I'm not sure if you already saw the Windemere email that was sent out this morning, but there's at least one other person who has come forward."

Eva's mouth hangs agape as if she's frozen in a painting. I pull out my phone to show her the school's missive and her eyes quickly scan its contents.

"I knew I couldn't have been the only one, especially after reading your story, but how many people do you think there are in total?"

"I have no idea. Some women have reached out to me, with similar stories to mine, but I have a feeling there are others. I remember other friends of mine having crushes on him or flirting with him openly in class. Those are probably not the girls we have to worry about. I think about the ones who were always quiet or kept to themselves."

Eva nods as if she's recognizing herself in my description. "There was a girl from my year who began cutting herself. I didn't even know what that was back then, but now it makes me curious about what she was going through at the time. I remember she had white scars. Why was she hurting so much and why did none of us do anything about it?" It's a valid question.

"I can think of a girl from my year who left abruptly in the middle of the school year, never to be seen or heard from again. There were rumors at the time that she was pregnant and her Catholic family forced her to give birth elsewhere and put the baby up for adoption, but I have no idea if that's true. Writing the story and hearing from people like you has made me question everything. It's horrifying to think he had access to young women for decades."

"I still have a journal that I kept from around the time I was involved with him." She looks down at her lap like a toddler who knows they did something wrong. "It's really hard to read because in parts you can tell that I craved and loved the attention he was giving me, even though deep down I knew it was wrong."

"Trust me, I get it."

"But in other parts, I'm so angry. There are things in the journal I had completely forgotten about. I think I blocked a lot of this stuff out until I read your essay. It's amazing how the brain works, how it tries to protect you so you can proceed with life."

"I could sometimes go months without thinking about it, but it was always there in the back of my mind, like when I had to read *Lolita* sophomore year. I couldn't even bring myself to watch *Spotlight*. Even though I never suffered in ways remotely close to the victims of those priests, it just feels too close. Stuff like that—stories about fairness or justice—would always bring me right back to Windemere, and that was not where I wanted to be."

"I can't believe how long I've blamed myself for what happened. I seriously thought it was all my fault. It didn't even occur to me to blame him. Whether it's one kiss or a full-on relationship, you automatically assume it's your fault because that's what the world tells you. It's always 'What was she wearing?' 'What did she say?' 'Was she drinking?' These messages get internalized over the years and you don't even know it. I was fully convinced that I deserved to suffer." She is welling up again. It's clearly a wound that never healed. The aftermath is still in progress.

"You were a minor at the time. There is nothing you did that would make this your fault. He is a master manipulator in a pair of khakis." Eva laughs. Why can't I be this gentle, kind, and understanding with myself?

As we're talking, I notice a group of five teenage girls who have entered the coffee shop to order soy lattes and other tailored drinks. It's a bit past three o'clock in the afternoon and they just left school. I look at them closely to see what girls who don't wear a uniform are wearing these days. One has a pair of nineties-era Doc Martens; another is in a complicated pair of gladiator sandals, the kind that leave cage-like marks on your skin after you take them off. Some have on makeup; others are more natural in their presentation. They giggle, carefree and light, buried in their phones and each other.

"Look at those girls." I motion to them with my head. "They couldn't be more than fourteen or fifteen, right?"

Eva turns her chair to see the group, surveying their long hair and skinny legs. "Seems about right."

"Even though they're young, they seem fairly cosmopolitan, right?"

Eva nods in agreement.

"They're city kids, like we were. They know about cool cafes and art and homelessness and diversity. I'm sure most people would call them mature. I mean, they're ordering coffee drinks on their own while other girls their age are still on glasses of juice or milk after school. They have probably seen lots of things and been exposed to a variety of people in their short lives. But does any one of those girls look like they'd know what to do if their favorite teacher came on to them?"

Eva places her elbows on the table, resting her forehead on the palms of her hands. "I feel sick."

I turn my gaze away from the group of girls, who are now engrossed in looking at a photo on one of the girl's iPhones. "I feel sick a lot too. But I think there's a way out of this sickness."

Eva composes herself and sits up straight, as if she's quickly run through the stages of guilt, shame, and fear and is now ready to do something. "So we know there are at least three of us that Copeland crossed the line with. What happens now?"

"Well, if you're comfortable with it, I would suggest you contact Windemere, since they're conducting an investigation. I will be speaking with them, as well, even though I didn't have a physical relationship with him. Normally, I wouldn't trust that they were actually doing things properly, but I think the media attention is helping in this case because they know they are under a microscope. Parents want answers. The community wants answers. And I'm sure his students—past, present, and future—want to know the truth."

"I've thought about this ever since your piece came out and I decided that I have to come forward no matter what."

I give her nod of support and a closed-mouth smile, but inside I'm practically bursting with joy. Eva's case is much stronger than mine. It doesn't hurt that she's a mother who's taught Bible study in the past. I know they'll probably find a way to tear at her, to intimidate her out of the situation, but she is as credible as it gets. Plus, she has a journal.

"I'll forward you the info. They are interviewing me as well and I imagine the other woman who came forward. A reporter at the *Daily* is working on putting us in touch with her. If she's willing."

"I don't want to go public the way you did, you know with my real name and everything, but I can't hide this anymore. I'm going to tell my husband tonight and then I'll arrange to meet with the committee as soon as possible." She leans back in her chair. "It's going to be so embarrassing to share these details with total strangers."

"I know. It's one thing to write something, or talk like this one-on-one, but telling these details to administrators and board members we don't know is mortifying."

"Do you think we're going to have to talk to LAPD too?" Her frown lines deepen with every passing second.

"I don't know. I haven't researched the statutes of limitations for cases like yours." I hate when I don't have the answer to a question, but I'm not a lawyer and don't want to make any promises. "I guess we'll find out. There's one other thing, but it's not mandatory at all."

"What?"

"The woman I work for at the *Daily*, Jane March, is working on a piece about Copeland and Windemere that's going to run next weekend." I'm surprised to see that Eva looks happy about this.

"Does she want to talk to me?"

"If you're open to it, yes, I'm sure she'd love to."

"You can give her my number."

"Seriously?"

"Seriously."

I can't wait to tell Jane.

Eva has to leave to pick up her daughters from school, so we wrap up our conversation. I walk her to her dark blue minivan, which has those stick figure stickers—a dad, a mom, and two girls holding hands—affixed to the rear windshield. She beams with pride when she talks about her family, something I don't hear much of since I'm primarily around college students and grumpy newspaper reporters. It secretly makes me happy to see, although I would never admit such a thing to anyone.

"Unnie?"

"Hey." Grace is folding laundry in her bedroom. "How was your day?"

"Fine, I guess." I leave out the fact that I met with Eva today. I'm still digesting our conversation and don't want to betray Eva's trust in me. "I'm doing all this research for Jane for her series on the drought and I have, like, ten papers to write."

"Good thing you know how to write."

"Did you go on campus today?"

"I only had one class in the morning, but I had to meet with my advisor because someone left the lab a mess and they're trying to play detective so we were all interviewed. It's so annoying."

"Well we know it wasn't you." Grace is almost full-blown OCD when it comes to cleanliness and organization. She would never leave a lab in anything other than perfect condition. It's one of my favorite things about her. That and the fact that she understands what it's like to have a Korean mother. It's refreshing to not have to explain the idiosyncrasies or the style of mothering that most Westerners would call abusive. Freshman year, my assigned roommate, Kat, was an aspiring architect from Boynton Beach, Florida. She confessed that I was the first Asian girl she had ever spoken to, let alone lived with, and wanted a primer on the various ethnic groups she would be encountering on a regular basis.

"We have tons of Latinos and Haitians and other minority groups," Kat told me, "but I have never seen so many Asian people in my entire life as in Los Angeles." Even though there are more Asian Americans in San Francisco and Hawaii, I sympathized with her culture shock. I was relieved that Kat was eager to learn about my background, but I felt strange serving as the ambassador for Asian culture and four billion people. I remember the horror on her face when I'd mention things like my mom getting mad for me becoming tan during spring break or how she'd had double eyelid surgery at age nineteen in order to look more Western.

Grace's mom, who's at least a generation older than mine, is a standard-issue Korean mom. She's the proud owner of a separate kimchi refrigerator, hoards free calendars, worships Jesus, often sits on the floor, and can dress you down from head to toe in ten seconds. When she visits from the Bay Area, Grace's *umma* spends most of her time in nearby Koreatown getting violently scrubbed and exfoliated at the Korean spas or cooking Grace's favorite childhood dishes like *galbitang* and *mandu-guk*.

"I made some *chap chae* if you want some." The glass noodles remind me of the times my mom would take Phillip and me to the same dingy Korean restaurant on Western Avenue on select Sundays. We'd inhale them, along with scallion pancakes and kimchi, enjoying ourselves until a disapproving waitress or customer glared in our direction. Koreans are obsessed with the purity of their bloodlines, so kids like Phillip and I were often treated as specimens to be inspected at best, and at worst, totally shunned like we were creatures that had appeared from an enemy planet. No wonder my dad never came with us.

I pat my stomach for effect. "I'm stuffed, but thanks."

I don't feel that hungry anymore, which thrills me, but that's not the only reason for declining food. All I can think about at the moment is my conversation with Eva and what it means for going forward. I don't have an appetite for anything but this right now. I give Grace a fake smile before I retreat into my room, feeling the glare of her disappointment on me like a spotlight until I shut the door.

I grab my laptop and flop onto my bed so I can compose an email to Jane. I think about how natural it felt to give Eva a hug goodbye this afternoon even though I don't usually enjoy hugs from people, especially strangers. Superficially, we have nothing in common, and yet we have everything in common. It doesn't matter anymore that her experience with Copeland was different or worse than mine. It doesn't matter anymore that Eva was raised in Duarte, where she was like a second mother to her three siblings, while I had a cushy existence in Hancock Park with au pairs, housekeepers, and world travel. It doesn't matter anymore that I'm still finishing college and she is a stay-at-home mom who has an online store to sell her line of handmade notecards. What matters is that we are now united. It's us against him. And we have Jane. I know Jane is going to help us.

I open up Gmail and start typing her name. Her email

address automatically populates. I go to the subject line and type eight characters: *She's in*.

Chapter Seven

Eva

"Mommy!" I hear two sets of feet scamper from the kitchen and down the hall toward me before they practically throw themselves at me.

"Hi, girls." I drown them in kisses as though I've been at sea for a year, away from them. "Did you have a good day at school?"

"Yes," they sing in unison, wearing identical outfits from their headbands to their sneakers. Jesse and I think it's time they start dressing different, so they have their own identities, but our efforts have been futile. I'm sure these days will be a blissful memory once they are tweens.

"Hey, babe." He gives me a lingering hug and kisses the top of my head, inhaling the scent of my shampoo. It's almost as if he knows I'm having a rough day and could use the extra affection. "How did your meeting go?"

"Good. I'll tell you all about it later." Even though my mind is racing, I've managed to put on my default smiling face.

"What meeting?" Ava asks. "For your cards?"

"No, my love."

"Then for what?" Ella asks. I don't want to lie to them, but they are too young to understand.

"Mamá was meeting with an old friend from school." Jesse gives me a wink before I run upstairs to change.

After making spaghetti squash pasta and helping the girls with their homework, we do the nightly routine: showers, teeth brushing, selecting outfits and snacks for school tomorrow, bedtime stories, and finally, sleep. I feel emotionally drained from the meeting with Caryn, but know that this is the perfect time to talk to Jesse, as I can't risk doing it when the kids are awake.

"Everything okay, babe?" He looks handsome with his closely trimmed beard and thick black hair. I feel bad that I'm about to ruin his night.

"Not really, but it will be."

He listens, alternately nodding and squinting his eyes in disbelief, but letting me get the whole Copeland story—from start to finish, save for some especially unsavory parts—out before he asks any questions. I conclude by explaining that I am going to participate in the investigation, the article, and whatever may come after that, but that I will do everything to protect my privacy, and our family, no matter what.

When I'm done, he wraps his big arms around me, a feeling I never tire of no matter how many years we've been together, and stays that way for a full minute.

"I'm sorry I never told you about this. I didn't want you to think differently about me, like I was somehow tainted." My bottom lip begins to quiver. "I never told anyone. Not even my parents or sisters. Not even a friend or a stranger."

After we part from the embrace, he stays on my side of the couch. "I wish you trusted me with that information earlier, because I would have loved to have been there for you."

"Well, you can be here for me now." A single tear streams down my left cheek. "Honestly, I didn't know if you'd ever be able to look at me the same way. I've never known how to bring this up, especially so many years later. It's not something you want to share on a first date, or even a fiftieth. But I knew I'd have to tell you someday, because as the girls get older, I get more paranoid about something like this happening to them."

"Well, you know what I always say: If you have a boy, you only have to worry about one prick in town, but if you have a little girl, you have to worry about every single prick in town."

"I always have my eye on every dad, older brother, coach, and Bible study teacher. I just don't want to become one of those moms who projects her own issues and concerns onto her innocent kids. It's not fair to them. We just have to be diligent."

"I actually feel a bit relieved that they're twins." Jesse gets up from the couch and grabs a beer from the fridge. "Because they'll always have each other to talk to, even if they don't want to talk to us about something. I don't think they would hide such a huge thing from one another."

I know he's going to go through a litany of emotions in the coming days, weeks, and months, as will I, but for now, he's calm. I guess if I was a horrible person who deserved what happened to me, then God wouldn't have sent me such a wonderful husband. Exhausted, I wash my face, brush my teeth, check in on the girls, who are sleeping soundly in their daybeds, and then head to our own bed where I say my prayers and ask for strength for the days ahead.

For the first time since I became a mother, I slept in today. I don't know how he did it, but Jesse managed to get the girls to be quiet while they got ready for the school day and then they were gone. No one asked me a single question this morning, about what to pack for lunch or who needed to bring what for their respective sport or after-school activity. This is what it's like to have no responsibility, I think for a moment, which makes me a bit sad. I can't imagine not having people rely on me. I honestly wouldn't know what to do with myself.

It's 9:47 a.m. so I figure I better get to it since I'm meeting with the Special Investigative Committee from Windemere later today. It feels apropos that their acronym is SIC. They are talking to everyone they can: administrators, teachers, students, parents, graduates, and, of course, any of the willing "roses."

In their email to me, they said they formed the committee to "examine the allegations surrounding Dr. Copeland, including his conduct and the School's responses to reports of his conduct." While I'm in the shower, taking longer than I should, because we are in the midst of a drought, I wonder what one wears to a meeting like this. I envision a long conference table in one of the gleaming high-rises downtown. I imagine a group of men in conservative business suits seated across from me like I'm the one who did something wrong. I pray hard that there will be at least one woman in the room.

After I dress and dry my naturally curly hair straight with the help of a small round brush, I go downstairs and see that Jesse has picked a few random flowers from the front yard and placed them in a water glass next to an envelope. Inside, the letter reads: "You got this. Just tell them what you told me and you'll be fine. *Con amor*, Jesse." I immediately feel a little rush, like the butterflies you get on a first date, and can't help but smile. I text him a quick thanks since I know he's already at work, and then send Caryn and Jane a message confirming that I'm headed to meet with the committee so they know I'm not backing out.

I pull up the directions on my phone, double check my makeup in the rearview mirror, and make the twenty-five-minute drive downtown. The building, a thirty-two-story office tower, is intimidating. I park in the visitor section of the mammoth parking structure, do one final check of my hair and makeup, and take a deep breath. I enter the lobby elevator and press number twenty-three and follow the sign to the law offices of Chatham, Gilchrist & Wendler LLP.

I look up to make sure I'm at the right suite and glass doors immediately part as though we're in some futuristic movie. "How may I help you?" asks a perky receptionist.

"I am Eva Garcia." I feel my voice shake a bit so I clear my throat and stand up straighter like I teach my girls to do. "I'm here to meet with Michael Patrick."

"Yes, Ms. Garcia, we're expecting you. Can I get you anything? A coffee or latte?" I wish I knew how much she knows about me.

"Just some water would be great."

"Please take a seat." She makes a quick call in a hushed tone. "They should be with you in just a minute or two."

I sit down on the modern black leather-and-chrome chair and can't help but overhear two people around the corner.

"Did you see the feng shui memo?"

"They're using our birth dates to reconfigure offices and the floor plan just because *she* told him to. How she got that cheap bastard to do anything is beyond me. She must be blowing him." They have a quick laugh before the receptionist rises and they disappear.

"Ms. Garcia, they're ready for you. Please let me show you the way."

I'm relieved that nobody in the offices we pass appears to notice me. As I suspected, everyone is in business attire. After standing in my closet for a solid ten minutes, I decided on a crisp white collared shirt and gray slacks, so I don't look terribly out of place, but my fraying handbag is a pretty big tell that I don't really belong here.

As she shows me into the room, the floor-to-ceiling windows and city view distract me for a moment from my spinning thoughts. I've never seen Los Angeles like this. How does anyone get any work done when they can see the entire city from their office?

"You should see it at sunset," says a gray-haired gentleman in his sixties who appears to be the leader of the committee. "Thank you so much for your time today, Ms. Garcia." He stands to shake my hand across the table, which makes for an awkward moment as I can barely reach the halfway point to meet hands. "I'm Michael Patrick."

"Pleased to meet you. You can call me Eva."

Just as I imagined, I am seated alone and across from the committee. The only thing on my side of the massive glass table is a heavy silver coaster, water glass, and tall glass bottle of water. The rest of the introductions are made and I know I'll never be able to keep their names straight after today. There's Rachel Wasserman, current Windemere Board President and parent of an alumna and current student; Rick Wells, Board Vice President and parent of two current students; and Xhana Stein, Board Secretary and parent of a current student. The rest of the committee, made up of additional Windemere parents, is not present today due to scheduling issues.

"In addition to being a trustee and Windemere parent," Mr. Patrick begins, "I am also a former United States attorney, so I have a lot of experience with investigations like these." His expertise helps to set me at ease because a former U.S. attorney must know what he's doing.

He explains that they've retained the services of a top Los Angeles lawyer and independent investigator, known for overseeing countless internal investigations, including ones involving allegations of sexual misconduct. I'm relieved that this lawyer, Kim Holder, is also present, as it seems like a huge conflict of interest to have the entire Special Investigative Committee be made up of board members and parents of Windemere students. It's like a police department that investigates itself after a crime and never manages to find any wrongdoing.

After assuring me total confidentiality, he asks me some basic questions about my background and how I came to be at Windemere.

"I never even told my parents I was applying." A panel of serious faces stares back at me. "I knew they could never afford to send me to a school like that. They probably didn't even know that schools like Windemere existed. It wasn't part of their reality."

"So what made you apply?" Mr. Patrick asks.

"I was always a good student and was at the top of my class in junior high. I was already dreaming about going to college and wondering if I would get there by staying in a LAUSD school. I was at the library one day after school and I came across a magazine article that talked about the best schools in Los Angeles, and of course, Windemere was right there at the top. There was a picture with these smiling faces and I just thought, I want to be one of those smiling faces."

A couple of the board members glance at each other with a tight-lipped smile, like they're congratulating themselves on their own marketing efforts.

"I saw the tuition fee and couldn't believe my eyes. But then I saw that the article said they had a great financial aid program so I figured I could apply and see if I could get in."

"And you did."

"It was seriously the best day of my life. I felt like I did something big for myself."

"That's wonderful to hear."

I sip from my water glass etched with the law firm's logo and notice the committee members smiling. This is the Windemere they want to hear about.

Thinking back, I remember being nervous to tell my family I was accepted. I wasn't sure how we were going to work out the logistics since I would have such a long commute, but the financial aid was so great it included transportation costs, and special fees for events and field trips, so it didn't end up being a problem. Windemere was generous and I was grateful. It was difficult at first, arriving in tenth grade, because most of the girls had already known each other since middle school and lived near one another. But everyone was friendly and welcoming—nothing like what I pictured or had been worried about. On the very first day of classes, we sat together—all one hundred of us—on the Lawn so no one would feel left out.

Things like valet parking on Parents Day were totally foreign to me. The wealth that was on display, whether it was the fancy cars at drop-off and pickup or classmates receiving three-thousand-dollar handbags for birthdays, was something I had never seen or experienced before. And even though we had our uniforms, it was easy to tell who was a paying Windemere student and who was on aid. I know my parents felt out of place being on campus even if they didn't say so.

I remember thinking Dr. Copeland was smart, funny, and passionate about literature. He loved being a teacher. I found his reading list for class challenging, but I was able to keep up. I was quite shy, so I wasn't leading the class in discussion or anything. There were definitely other girls who were more confident and well spoken at the time. He noticed that I was struggling with a few of the assignments, and seemed like he genuinely wanted to help. I thought this was what private school was all about: smaller classes, more teacher interaction. I was so thankful. It's not like I had anyone else to turn to. Other students practically had staffs at their disposal in terms of college prep.

There's a rule at Windemere that a male teacher must keep a door open if a female student is alone with him in the classroom. Sometimes Dr. Copeland asked me to stay for a few minutes to chat about an essay or upcoming assignment. The door was always open so I never thought anything other than my teacher was helping me. After a few weeks of this, he suggested that we talk about a Shakespeare assignment on the Lawn. He said studies have proven that people are happier when surrounded by nature. I'd seen other students talking with teachers on the Lawn or in hallways so I thought it was fine, especially as it was right after school when there were still a lot of people around.

Dr. Copeland seemed more relaxed and happy outside of the classroom. I can still easily picture his smile and hear his hearty laugh. That day, he asked me about my family and background and if I had a boyfriend. I told him I was raised in a strict, religious household and was not allowed to date. I had a few friends who were boys from my neighborhood, but I had never been on a real date or anything like that. He teased me, in a jovial way, and said I would be a heartbreaker once I started dating. Of course this thrilled me.

Because classes were only ten to fourteen students, it was common to get really close to your teachers and your classmates. They often treated us like adults, whether it was in the course work that was assigned or personal things they shared with us. They were invested in our success and lives, which is a good thing I suppose, but I can recall instances of female teachers telling us about their dating life or relationships. We'd get invested in these stories like they were soap operas or a reality show. The culture at Windemere made me feel grown up and trusted.

I was totally flattered that Dr. Copeland would take time out of his busy day to talk to me. In my household, a teacher is like a doctor or priest. I would have never questioned his motives because in my mind he was an authority figure and someone who wanted to help me succeed in life. I met with him five or six times to talk about assignments and writing and was a little embarrassed that I needed the extra help. I didn't want my parents to think I was in over my head, as they worried about me adjusting. My goal was to improve my writing skills to the point where I wouldn't need any special attention.

I always thought my writing was one of my strengths; after all, I did get into Windemere, so I knew I wasn't stupid, but my classmates were so incredibly smart, mature, and savvy. Some of them had already traveled to Europe and Asia by age fifteen. I had never left the L.A. area. There's not much economic diversity at Windemere and I gravitated to some of the other students who were there on financial aid. I also had a few friends from choir. Friend groups naturally formed by neighborhoods or shared backgrounds.

Mr. Patrick interrupts the Windemere highlight reel that's playing in my mind to ask more detailed questions about Dr. Copeland. He removes his glasses almost as a warning that we are about to go *there*. "So, when did things change from Dr. Copeland being your teacher to something more complicated?"

I had never talked to a grown man who wasn't my dad or an uncle. And Dr. Copeland is nothing like my dad or uncle. We could talk about epic poems or our favorite sonnets. He was friendly and I started to feel comfortable around him. While I wouldn't characterize my feelings for him as romantic at that time, I definitely felt warmth toward him and from him. I saw him as a mentor at that point. I wanted to please and impress him with my progress, and I always thanked him profusely for the help.

He seemed like a romantic, and certain passages of literature appeared to move him almost to the point of tears. As a teenage girl, I found this incredibly endearing. The men in my family rarely showed emotion, even if someone died. They are macho types, whereas Dr. Copeland seemed sensitive and had no trouble expressing his thoughts. He would make passing comments, like wanting to feel the type of love we were discussing in class. Of course I wanted to feel those things too, but I knew I would when I was older. Other times, he outright complained about his wife. He'd talk about how she was sometimes mean to him or made him feel bad for not making more money. I recall him saying she worked a lot and that she wasn't much fun to be around. He made it seem like he was in a loveless marriage. I listened to anything he told me because I believed he was wise.

I felt bad for him. I didn't know anything about love or

marriage except for whatever I had seen in the movies or on TV. But I thought, here's this wonderful man who chose such a noble profession, one that doesn't pay very well, and he's willing to go above and beyond for his students, and it's sad that his wife doesn't appreciate that. Of course I never imagined what her complaints about him might have been or that he may have been telling his students a false or exaggerated story. It was a bit of a different time. Even in liberal Los Angeles, women were still thought of as less than if they chose a busy career. I heard from other students that Dr. Copeland's wife was a powerful attorney who handled numerous divorces of Windemere students' parents, but he never told me anything else, specifically. I preferred to pretend she didn't even exist.

Things changed when he gave me a book of poems by Emily Dickinson. It wasn't a book we were reading for class—it was a gift, from Dutton's in Brentwood, and it was a beautiful special edition with a hand-carved cover. It was like a work of art, something to cherish. I had never received something like that from anyone. One day after class, I think it was right before the winter break, he handed it to me. It was in a plain brown bag, unwrapped, but he did write something inside the book. It said, 'Were I with thee.'

I recall the giddiness I felt that day and throughout the holidays. I liked having a secret, something I didn't have to share with my siblings or parents. Just thinking about him handing me the book would give me a small thrill, and each time I'd open it, I could hear his soothing voice reading Dickinson's verses. I dreamed of him on several occasions and kept the book between my bed and the wall, so I could retrieve it anytime. Anytime I'd even hold the book, I'd feel warm and aroused, almost like a pulsating sensation was traveling through my body. I didn't know what to do with that feeling, but I definitely wanted more of it.

Mr. Patrick jolts me back to reality. "And you inferred that this gift was romantic in nature?"

"I don't think I would have phrased it that way, but I knew it was out of the ordinary. To my knowledge, he wasn't giving these books out to all of his students. Gifts at Windemere were always a thing, especially during the holidays, so it's easy to recall."

"Could you explain a bit more about what you meant by gifts being 'a thing' at Windemere?"

Surely they must know what I'm talking about, especially as they are parents of students, but I guess they need to make it official for the committee record. Windemere parents were supposed to each give a certain amount each year, I believe it was twenty-five dollars, and then it would go in a pool and be split among the teachers and staff members for holiday gifts. Of course some of the celebrity kids or ultrawealthy families would ignore this and give teachers giant gift baskets or expensive perfume.

Since teachers didn't make a practice of giving students holiday gifts I knew I should keep the book a secret. Dr. Copeland never asked me to. It was an unsaid thing, which made me feel even more trusted in his eyes. I liked that feeling because at home, I was just a kid who couldn't question anything my parents said or did. At Windemere, I felt like more of a grown-up. Over the break I remember missing him, and his attention. It sounds silly now, but at Christmas I went into the backyard and watched the moon rise between the buildings in our neighborhood. I thought about Dr. Copeland looking at the same moon and I felt an inherent connection to him that I couldn't explain. It's not that he had a hold on me, per se, but I felt a pull toward him.

I no longer had him as my teacher when the second semester started and missed being around him on a daily basis. I believed he was one of the only people in my life who was truly rooting for me to succeed. I loved my parents, but there was a lot I couldn't talk to them about in terms of literature or college prep stuff. They're hardworking immigrants who didn't have time or energy to nurture my passions. Their focus was on keeping a roof over our head and food on the table.

A week or two into the new semester we talked after a campus event. He saw me in the crowd and winked at me. It was so quick that no one else would have noticed, but I happened to have been looking right at him. As the crowd began to disperse, I walked toward him and he said that he missed me. I said I did too, and his face lit up. I loved the feeling of being able to make him happy. I knew this was perhaps crossing a line, but I didn't care. I felt empowered and like a better version of myself compared to the prior semester. That this brilliant man could take an interest in me was flattering and exciting. He asked if I would want to go on a walk sometime after school and I said yes.

The next day, during lunchtime, we met and walked up the hill on the west side of campus together. I was surprised no one noticed. It felt like we had a special bond since we were doing something together that was wrong. I was an inexperienced and awkward teenager, but I knew this could get us both into serious trouble. When we got to the top of the hill, I remember he was a bit winded, and made a joke about not being at his "fighting weight," and we sat on a bench for a few minutes. That's where he kissed me for the first time.

I had a feeling he wanted to do that, but I was so clueless about that kind of stuff, I wasn't sure how it would happen. He had put his hand on my thigh, and when I didn't object, I think he felt he could kiss me. We made out right there at the top of the hill, overlooking Windemere.

After I speak this aloud, Mr. Patrick's pleasant face morphs into one of stern disapproval, and various committee members are looking at one another in disbelief, as though they weren't sure these allegations were real until this very moment.

"Was Dr. Copeland concerned that someone would see you? Perhaps a neighborhood resident, someone walking their dog, for example?"

"No. He never mentioned that." They look at one another again in judgment.

"Were you concerned about appearances, as you were in public, in your school uniform with an older man?"

"No. It felt like a private spot, and I figured Dr. Copeland knew what he was doing. Of course now I believe that was not his first time there."

As I answer Mr. Patrick's questions, graphic images are flooding my brain, tiptoeing out of longtime hibernation. Two days later things got more involved. He gave my friend Tessa a note for me. It was sealed, but, of course, Tessa was perplexed as to why my former teacher was giving me a card. She actually seemed a bit jealous, like maybe she liked him or something. It said that he couldn't stop thinking about me. He wrote poetically about my dark hair and smile and how he felt nervous around me. He ruminated on my olive-toned skin and praised my curiosity about literature and life, and had no doubts that I would go on to be a writer myself, which was an incredible compliment coming from someone with a doctorate in English literature. I'd never been told things like this by anyone in my entire life. The only boys I knew were my cousins or kids from my neighborhood. They couldn't write anything like that if their life depended on it.

It was like I was lit from within. I couldn't stop smiling. I'm sure I looked like a lovesick fool. He drew a little picture of both of us with little hearts, like a comic strip. I found it incredibly charming. He didn't sign it, but anyone could recognize his distinctive handwriting. At the bottom he asked if I would meet him after school. Because I took a long bus ride home, he figured we had an hour to spend together and then he could drive me most of the way home to make up that time. I made an excuse for not getting on the bus and instead walked down the main road to Starbucks. He met me there shortly after I arrived and asked if I wanted to take a drive. Although I was a bit scared, I wanted to, so I said yes. I knew we couldn't sit at Starbucks together while I was in my school uniform, surrounded by Windemere parents who often stop there after doing pickup.

He asked if I had been to Griffith Park. When I said no, he said we had to go, and so he drove us there and we parked in a quiet wooded area. He asked if I would please call him Gregory when we were off campus. At Windemere we always addressed the faculty properly. I had never called an adult by their first name. Ever. So I felt like I was special or a trusted confidante, and that I wasn't imagining this thing I was feeling. Because we were so far from Windemere, and alone, it was safe to explore whatever was happening. We kissed a lot. Even though I knew it was very wrong, I was somehow able to push that out of my mind in the moment. Maybe it was my naiveté or really thinking Dr. Copeland and I were meant to be together. We had already crossed the line, on several occasions, so it felt like I might as well see what this was all about.

We were both aroused, but I was a virgin and sex was not an option. I don't think I even understood the mechanics of sex at the time. He touched my breasts, underneath my polo shirt, and I couldn't believe it was happening. It felt surreal because it was him. I had very little experience with boys, let alone a grown man, but I wasn't scared in the moment. It wasn't a dark alley with a stranger, you know, what girls are typically afraid of. I felt that Dr. Copeland would respect my boundaries if I wanted to stop, but I think I felt overwhelmed by the physical sensations and also the emotions. This was my favorite teacher, and my crush, and I now felt closer to him than ever before. In some strange way, I felt safer with him than I would have with a random boy my own age because I trusted him completely.

Then he unzipped his pants. I had never seen an erect penis before and couldn't fathom what you were supposed to do with it. I think Dr. Copeland knew I was inexperienced so he said, "Just touch me the way you would want to be touched." Looking back, that sounds kind of creepy, but in the moment, I felt like he was being patient and gentle. I had heard awful stories about boys who shoved girls' heads toward their penises for oral sex during hookups. So this felt more consensual and slow. I didn't know what to do and I didn't want to do the wrong thing, so he began masturbating while touching me. He rubbed the outside of my underwear, beneath my skirt. Within a minute or two he had ejaculated. I remember he cleaned up with napkins he found in the glove compartment.

I thought Dr. Copeland would lecture me about not saying anything to anyone or how I should act normal at school, but he never did. It was as if he trusted me enough or thought I was mature enough to know these things. Looking back today, though, I think he truly believed he would not be caught. He acted like a nice person, but was always a bit full of himself. I think so many years of adoration from his students and Windemere parents had definitely gone to his head. He seemed a bit brazen and often stared at me on campus. One time, I remember him pulling me out of science class for a couple of moments just to tell me he was thinking of me. The romance swept me away, easily. He said our connection was Shakespearean. He loved to say things like that, and I loved to believe them.

I told him I had never had an orgasm and he said he wanted to be the first person to give me one. I had no idea what it would feel like and I was curious. My parents never talked about sex and I'm the oldest of my siblings. I remember once telling my mom that Tessa was on birth control pills and she was disgusted. Her facial expression alone was enough to make me think that sex, or anything that came with it, was bad. So, of course I felt like I was doing something wrong by being interested in the subject. And I didn't have a computer at home, so it's not like I could do my own research. I was essentially in a vacuum.

Dr. Copeland drove me downtown where I could take a direct bus to my neighborhood. He was chatty on the drive over and I was quieter, but that was normal. He said next time would be even better. I remember that he encouraged me to masturbate at home, but that was unthinkable as I shared a room with my siblings and was rarely by myself. Also, in my culture, I was led to believe that masturbation could cause pregnancy. I was so clueless about basic biology and how reproduction even worked.

A few days later he found me during an office hours period in the hallway of the Upper Campus building and had a mischievous expression on his face. He said he wanted to take me off campus and I should meet him down the road. I agreed, even though I was nervous someone would see me walking off campus in the middle of the day. I met him by Starbucks again and got in his car. Since we only had forty minutes or so before the next period, he drove me to a big parking lot. I worried that we could run into a Windemere parent in that parking lot, but it was actually pretty empty.

He told me he couldn't control himself around me. That he thought about me all the time and couldn't wait to be alone with me again. It was as if we were two characters in one of the many novels we read for his class. I figured this was what love felt like. I was exhilarated. I felt a little more confident this time and I initiated kissing, which pleased him. I could see the outline of his erection in his pants as he put his hand under my skirt again and this time he removed my underwear. I didn't know what was going to happen, but I knew we weren't going to have sex right there in the parking lot, in broad daylight, and I didn't want my first time to be like that.

He stimulated me manually, with his fingers, and I did the same in return. I think he enjoyed his role as the teacher outside of the classroom as well. I'm not sure if that's because he was emotionally immature and related more to me than a woman his own age, or if he was trying to replicate the excitement he must have felt as a teenager. I guess it doesn't matter either way. I reminded him that I was a virgin. I remember my aunt calling one of my fourteen-year-old cousins a 'little whore' after being caught with tampons in her bedroom. In my family, girls who used them were viewed as promiscuous. I was so paranoid that someone would be able to tell that I'd let Dr. Copeland touch me, as if there'd be an invisible stamp on me or something, so I didn't feel that I could go any further even if I wanted to.

Before going back to campus, we went into a drugstore together. He bought me a soda and some gum. No one even gave us a second glance. Maybe they thought he was my dad, even though we don't look anything alike. Then he drove me back to Starbucks and I walked the rest of the way up the hill. I was late to my next class, of course, and could barely focus in my other ones, but otherwise the day went on as normal. I remember thinking I was a great actress, and that maybe I should go out for the school play, because no one ever suspected a thing.

I remember feeling deeply ashamed later that evening. I prayed to God so hard for forgiveness. I decided things had gone way too far and I couldn't do this again. Now that I knew what real arousal was, it felt extremely dangerous. I could tell that things were only going to progress further and I started getting scared of where that could lead. The guilt was because I was complicit in the situation. It's not like he forced me to do anything or threatened me. I willingly left campus with him both times. If I told my parents, they would be disgusted with me, and I would be forced to leave Windemere, which would probably end my plans for college. I didn't want that.

I knew if I told someone at Windemere, they'd be legally required to report it to the police. I had a friend who worked at a daycare center after school so I had heard about mandatory reporters. I didn't want him to go to jail or be fired. No matter how misguided it seems now, I had a lot of affection for Dr. Copeland at the time. I wanted to just handle it between us without it becoming a big deal. I didn't want him to be ripped away from his family and I didn't want to be sent away from mine.

I remember talking to my mom that night. I was washing the dishes and she asked me something about school and I talked back to her, which was not common or acceptable in my household. I remember feeling so angry with her for failing to protect me, even though she knew nothing about the situation and it's not like I was forced at gunpoint to do these things with Dr. Copeland. It wasn't a rational thought. A child's brain is not rational. Late that night, as my little sister slept in the twin bed next to mine, I wrote a confession to God. I actually still have it today. I told Him my whole story. I wrote, "I'm telling you this in secret because I can't tell anyone else." I begged for His forgiveness for my sins. I promised I would never do it again and reminded Him that I was a caring, nice person. I wrote, "I can't break my parents' heart. Please don't make me break their heart." I was basically a mess inside. I cried a lot back then.

The next day, I waited until Dr. Copeland's English class let out and then I approached him. He looked happy to see me, but immediately knew something was wrong when he saw my body language. I said something along the lines of not being able to go off campus anymore. That I was scared and I didn't want to have sex because I was too young. I also told him I didn't want him to get in trouble, or be forced to leave Windemere. I was genuinely worried about what would happen to him. His face changed entirely. It was almost like he had been wearing the mask of a kind person all this time and now he looked a bit sinister. He said he was extremely disappointed in me, which of course made me feel terrible. He told me he loved me and that I was ripping his heart out. I believe that was an attempt to guilt me into changing my mind. I can't see how it would be possible that a grown man who had traveled the world and spoke of enjoying fine wine could be in love with a naïve fifteen-year-old girl. As much as I wanted to believe that he loved me, I knew in that moment that it wasn't true.

People joke about teens being dramatic, but his reaction was over the top. He was hurt and upset. And angry. The disdain he had for me in that moment was palpable. He said he was wrong about me being so mature and special. Then he asked me to leave the room like I was a student who had been caught cheating or something. I felt like less than nothing and burst out crying as soon as I got outside. Looking back now, it's infuriating. The fact that I had to shoulder the blame and responsibility, all alone, makes me want to scream. I was fifteen.

As Mr. Patrick scribbles on his legal pad, I lose my composure for the first time since I walked in the room today.

"How could I have possibly been mature? How could he blame me for what happened? He is not a good person. He is not worthy of sympathy and understanding. The real him is the person who kicked me out of the room like I was an animal. And I know I am not the only one this happened to. *You* know I'm not the only one this happened to."

"I'm sorry, Eva. We are all sorry for what you have gone through."

"Mr. Patrick?"

"Please call me Michael."

"Michael. Don't be sorry. Just make this right. I beg you to make this right."

Chapter Eight

Jane

From: Sasha Sokoloff
To: Jane March
Date: May 10, 2016 at 3:25 a.m.

Subject: Gregory Copeland investigation

Hi Jane,
I hear you are looking for me. Here I am.
Sasha

From: Jane March
To: Sasha Sokoloff
Date: May 10, 2016 at 7:19 a.m.
Subject: Re: Gregory Copeland investigation

Sasha,

Thanks for getting in touch. I work with Caryn, who wrote the piece that got this ball rolling, and she has met with another former student who also had a relationship with Copeland. I don't know anything about your story, but if you'd be interested, I'd love to put you in touch with Caryn so that you could all talk or meet up sometime. I think you're stronger if you band together. I'm also in the midst of writing a reported piece about the investigation. If you'd like to talk to me for that story I'd be most grateful, but there's no pressure either way.

Jane March

"How did you do it?" I cradle the phone receiver between my ear and shoulder in the exact way that my chiropractor instructed me not to do.

"Wait a second." Ben pauses for dramatic effect. "Are you telling me that a Pulitzer Prize–nominated journalist is asking me, a lowly college admissions consultant, for investigative reporting tips?"

"Very funny, but I'm serious. How did you get her to email me?"

"Well, I thought a lot about what you said last time we talked."

"And?" Ben knows I have no patience so I don't know why he insists on drawing things out.

"And I told you I knew one of the Windemere board members. I thought she'd be sympathetic to the cause and I guess I was right."

"What did you say to her?"

"I simply told her the truth: that a trusted ex-colleague who happens to be a world-class journalist was trying to track down one of Copeland's victims so that she could facilitate an introduction to Caryn and the other Jane Doe."

"She must like you," I tease.

"Hardly. But she has a young daughter who may have Copeland in the future. It didn't take much convincing, but, of course, I can't tell you her name."

"That's fine."

"I don't even know the name of the victim who emailed you. The board member simply passed on your email address. It wasn't difficult, Jane, so don't give me too much credit. It was more about timing. I believe she had heard one of the victim's stories earlier so she was pretty shaken and raw about the whole thing."

"Well, can I at least buy you a drink sometime?"

"*Really*, March?"

"What, you want a full meal? You know we just had another round of pay cuts."

"No, I'm just surprised that you'd want to see me."

"Why?"

"I don't know. After I got laid off I never heard from you until you called me the other day."

"Well, it's been busy." I stall, taken aback by the confrontation. "You know me, I work all the time."

"Everyone's busy, March." There's an awkward pause in the conversation. "Look, I don't want you to change your mind. Let me know when and where, and I'll be there."

"How about the Filipino place you mentioned? Say, eight o'clock? That way you won't have to fight traffic."

"But you live on the Westside and I work on the Westside. Would it be easier to meet out this way?"

"You told me to tell you when and where, so I did, and now you want to make your own suggestion?"

"God, March, I forgot how much I love it when you put me in my place."

I'm now grinning like a fool and can feel Caryn staring at me from her cubicle, eager to know whom I'm talking to. "I have to go. I'll see you at eight."

"It's a date. I mean, not a date date, but a date, like, we have a planned engagement."

"Ben."

"I know, you have to go."

"I'll see you later."

"You got it. You've always got it."

Ninety seconds after putting the receiver down, Caryn is standing over me with a broad grin.

"Hi, Jane." She draws out the two syllables as if she's

learning to speak for the first time.

"What can I do for you?"

"I don't mean to be nosy, but I was just curious as to why you're blushing while making a morning work call."

"I'm not blushing." I am unable to control my fair skin's proclivity to turning all shades of pink at any hint of emotion.

"Okay, you're not blushing. But you were smiling. A lot. And you don't smile that much, Jane. You smile even less than I do."

I'm eager to change the tone of this conversation. "I have some good news for you. The person I was talking to is an old colleague. He was able to get Windemere's Jane Doe to email me so she could get in touch with you and Eva."

"Are you serious?"

"Her name is Sasha. She's going to email you."

"Today?"

"I just emailed with her about an hour ago. Of course, all of this needs to stay confidential, even from Eric, for now."

"I can't believe you did this."

"I didn't do anything but make a call. Just listen to her and see if she wants to meet up at some point. I don't know anything about her story."

"How old is she?"

"I have no idea. You'll have to find out all the details. I'm also scheduled to meet with Eva at her home in the morning, after her kids go to school."

"I'm so glad she didn't change her mind." Caryn's shoulders immediately descend a few inches.

"I believe she met with the investigative committee yesterday, so she'll probably have a lot to say."

"Is she going on the record?"

"We're going to use a pseudonym for the story, but yes, she's fine being quoted."

"I wonder what the committee is going to think of that. I mean they're obviously going to know it's her."

"I don't care what the committee thinks of it. The public has a right to know. They're doing their investigation, but I'm doing mine, too."

"Thank you, Jane."

"Don't worry about it. Copeland's the one who needs to worry about it. I need to get back to work, so just let me know how it goes after you talk to Sasha."

"I will, but I definitely won't bother you after eight o'clock."

I shake my head, but can't help but let out a small laugh.

Ben may not have been able to tell me his board member contact's name, but he needn't worry because she has decided to email me.

From: Xhana Stein
To: Jane March
Date: May 10, 2016 at 4:12 p.m.
Subject: Referred by Ben Lecours

Hello Jane,

I'm a Windemere board member and I hope you don't mind me getting in touch. Sasha mentioned that she emailed you earlier today and I'm glad I could help facilitate the introduction. I can't imagine going through something like this alone, so if these alumnae can find some solace with one another, then that would please me. Since the investigation is ongoing, it's not exactly appropriate for me to be talking to a journalist, even off the record, but Ben said I could trust you with my life, and I'm willing to take him at his word. There's more to the Copeland story than what you are aware of, and I'd like to talk to you soon, if possible. Of course, this needs to stay between us.

Sincerely,
Xhana Stein

From: Jane March
To: Xhana Stein
Date: May 10, 2016 at 4:16 p.m.
Subject: Re: Referred by Ben Lecours

Hi Xhana,

I'd love to talk to you anytime that's convenient. I can assure you that your identity will be protected, whether you decide to talk off the record or on, as an unnamed source. I could meet with you as early as tomorrow, if you're free, or my cell is listed below if you prefer to talk by phone.

Jane March

P.S. Thank you for giving Sasha my email.

"Do you know how many women are running around Los Angeles at this very moment wearing clip-in extensions made from some Indian woman's hair? It's practically a crime that you have this thick mane and always wear it up." Caryn appears to be legitimately outraged.

"Did it ever occur to you that that's *why* I wear it up? I don't have time to blow it out. It takes a good thirty minutes. It's easier to just wear it back." I haven't told her yet about the unexpected communiqué from Ms. Stein because I don't want to give her false hope. Sources can change their minds, especially once they know a story is being written.

"Well, I think you should wear it down tonight." She surveys me with the trained eye of an art appraiser.

"Fine." I pull my bedraggled hair tie out. A travel-size product appears suddenly from Caryn's oversize handbag. She looks at me for the green light so she can begin doing her thing. "Don't you need to get home? It's already seven."

Caryn ignores my question, and alternately sprays and scrunches my naturally wavy hair. "This will give you those sexy beach waves." From what I can see in the compact mirror, it doesn't look bad, but I'm not ready to give her the satisfaction.

"Do you have any jewelry? Like a bracelet or something?" Caryn is in her element.

"It's hard to type with a bracelet. And they make noise during interviews."

"Yeah, but you could keep one separate and put it on for after-work engagements."

"Caryn, if you think I have the time or energy to keep a separate bag for bracelets that I *might* throw on after work, then you don't know me at all."

"I saw you wear a bracelet once. It was one of those wood bead ones that white girls who do yoga like to wear. One of my Pilates instructors wears so many at a time that they're halfway up her forearm like a vise. She thinks you can achieve enlightenment through accessories."

"Well tell me how you really feel. And by the way, that was a gift from my neighbor. I got her mail for a month while she was in Bali. On a yoga retreat." We both laugh because Caryn's stereotyping proved right, at least this time. "You don't find all the primping stuff exhausting?"

Caryn laughs. "Do you think it's not feminist to wear makeup and do your hair and wear cute clothes?" She lowers her voice to a whisper. "You know, because sexism and the patriarchy."

"I don't know about that. For me it's more of a time issue

rather than a commentary on beauty standards or gender-based expectations. I've just never been a flashy person. I don't need people looking at me. I'd rather my work speak for me rather than a certain type of makeup or beauty trend."

"It's not like you need a full makeover. I just want you to feel good for your date."

"It's not a date, Caryn."

"It's dinner at eight o'clock at a cool downtown restaurant."

"It's a thank you to an old colleague who did us a favor."

"Is he straight?"

"Yes."

"Is he single?"

"I guess. I mean, he's not married, but I don't know what he does with his free time." I can't help but laugh recalling how reserved Caryn once acted around me. Now that almost everyone's gone home, we're practically having a slumber party in the office.

"I bet *he* thinks it's a date."

"How would you know?"

"Well, I'll be waiting to find out. I can tell you that much."

"I think it's time for you to go home. You're well over your hours this week."

"Just text me 'Yes' if it ends up being a date. I won't tell anyone."

I'm relieved to have a few moments to myself after I see her pack up her things and go.

"Wow, look at you." Ben catches me off guard near the hostess stand as I reply to a last-minute email from Eric. "You look fantastic." He kisses me on the cheek and I almost jump from the sensation of a man's facial hair against my skin. He definitely noticed my new look, and I know it would please Caryn.

"You're looking well, even though you're starting to resemble the Eastside hipsters I thought you despised." I forgot about his light brown eyes and the small scar on his eyebrow.

"Ah, yes." He strokes his chestnut-brown beard. "It's just laziness, not a fashion statement."

"I made a reservation." I scan the room for the disappearing hostess who wouldn't seat me until Ben turned up.

"I feel special."

"Don't." I immediately regret uttering the word. "Sorry, that came out wrong."

"I think she's heading this way." He tracks the petite hostess with his eyes as she moves from the back of the restaurant, which is filled with blond wood and a bustling postwork crowd that's eager to wash the day away with a few Filipino beers and *lumpia*. "I guess this place is the spot."

"Are you two ready to be seated?"

"We are," we chime in unison.

After being placed at a snug two-top, the wiry server, who claims his name is Rocket, appears with a spiel about the restaurant's non-GMO, fair-trade grains that are imported from various islands in the Philippines. We order a couple of beers before making some polite chitchat as though we barely know each other. Since I'm starving, I suggest we figure out food before we get into catching up.

Ben opts for the sweet and spicy sausage with pickled vegetables and "garlic crumbs," which is a new one, even for L.A. I pick a chicken and green papaya dish that's simmered in ginger broth and we decide to split one of their artisanal rice dishes.

"You know eating white rice is a crime in this town." Ben's tone is conspiratorial. "It feels like we're doing something naughty."

"Is this how safe and boring L.A. has become? A bland grain is considered a rebellion."

"You should hear the women I work for." Ben leans in

closer. "They think you're a heathen if you don't make your own almond milk or cold press your own juice."

I roll my eyes. "Remember Alison from copy? She acts as though white flour was anthrax. It's not a good day when she's around and the food team is up to something in the test kitchen."

"Honestly, I'm more amazed there still is a food section. I heard the *Daily* may be up for sale again soon."

"We don't know what's going on and we're on staff. I'm not sure I'll survive another owner. It's already been, what, three in the last five years? With layoffs each of those years?"

"But where would you go?"

"Maybe I'll join you. I wouldn't mind billing three hundred dollars an hour and moving out of my shitty one-bedroom apartment."

"C'mon March, you're only happy when you're chasing a story. You're too good for the elite high school college admission world. You wouldn't last a week and I mean that as a compliment."

"What about you? You're not too good for it?"

"No, frankly, I'm not." He sips what's left of his first beer. I never realized Ben held me in such high regard. When we worked together we weren't close. We always got along in a chummy coworker type of way, but I don't recall him ever complimenting me or trying to get to know me beyond staff meetings or mandatory company-wide events. In fact, this is probably the only time I've sat down and shared a meal with him one-on-one.

"Well look, I really need to thank you for what you've done in regards to the Copeland story," I say in between sips of beer. "I don't know if she told you, but Xhana Stein reached out to me today. We're going to talk soon."

"No shit?"

"She said there's more to the story."

"Of course there's more to the story." Ben's eyes light up like how they would when he was on a juicy assignment at the

Daily. I suspect he doesn't get this type of thrill in his current line of work. "From what I can tell, there's zero oversight. It's the school and the board. It's unlikely that the board even knows what happens on a day-to-day basis. There's no district or state government interference."

"Depending on how the conversation goes, we could be looking at a series of stories about Copeland."

"Have you told Caryn?"

"Not yet. I need to see if Ms. Stein shows up first."

"I don't know her well, but I have no reason to believe she wouldn't show up and be totally credible. You know, she was an attorney before she had kids and decided to be a stay-at-home mom. She's sharp as a tack."

"The LAPD has already opened an investigation and Windemere is doing its own internal investigation, but I don't trust them to do the right thing. I'm hoping a reported story will put pressure on them to get it right."

"Can I ask you something, Jane?"

"Since when do you call me Jane?"

"Well, we don't work together anymore, and tonight you look like a Jane."

"I'll take that as a compliment as well."

"What is it about Copeland? Why are you so involved?"

"What do you mean? It's my job."

"Don't get me wrong, no one can investigate a story like you, but this isn't exactly your beat."

"Caryn's my intern, and I wanted to help. It only makes sense that I would report the story, as I know all the background and players. And Eric assigned it to me."

"I'm not saying it's a conflict of interest, but you are going above and beyond for this girl."

"Someone has to."

The server returns with our aromatic dishes and another round of beers. I feel relaxed for the first time in weeks. The conversation flows with ease. There is laughter and flattering candlelight and lots of eye contact. When I get up to use the ladies' room, he stands.

"You got yourself a real man there," says a woman from a nearby table as I make my way to the back of the restaurant.

"He's not my man," I politely explain.

"Girl, I've lived in this city for twenty-three years and I've never seen a man stand for a woman like that. If he's not your man, I suggest you make him your man. And quick." She high-fives her friend and I smile because she's right. Ben was always polite and well mannered, even in the office. It must be his Southern upbringing.

As I return, Ben stands again. I can't help but look at my new friend three tables back. She is silently cheering with two fists in the air. Ben notices the distraction. "Am I missing something?" He looks confused. "Do you know her?"

"I think you have a new fan."

We finish up our meal, impressed that it lived up to the online hype, and the server presents a dessert menu. Ben gives a short speech about how a meal isn't really a meal unless there is dessert. I'm satiated, but could definitely enjoy a bite or two of something sweet. He suggests we share the *leche flan*, a decadent caramel custard, and it's exactly what I would have picked.

"It's so refreshing to be around a woman who likes food. And before you ask—yes, that's definitely a compliment."

"Are you on the whole dating carousel of women who agree to dates, but don't actually eat at dinner?"

"Not exactly. But it doesn't take a sociology degree to know that a significant number of women in this town won't eat. And if they do, it's often with lackluster enthusiasm."

"What's that Fellini quote? 'Never trust a woman who

doesn't like to eat. She is probably lousy in bed.' "

"Are you trying to tell me something?" He looks 90 percent teasing and 10 percent hopeful.

"I think I've just had two beers." I feel my face flush with embarrassment.

"Are you sure you'll be okay to drive? Because I could take you home, or call you an Uber."

"I'm fine. By the time we get the check and I get back to the *Daily*, I'll be dead sober."

"You're more fun when you're not." He is sporting a mischievous grin. I'm not sure if he's referring to this evening or past events. A few years ago there was an unfortunate moment at a work happy hour near the office. I hadn't eaten much and got properly shickered. I only know this from being told, as I have no memory of it myself, fortunately, but after most of the office crew left, I made a move on Ben on the patio of a cheesy sports bar. He rebuffed me and we never spoke of it again.

Although I told him he didn't have to about five different times, Ben insists on walking me the few short blocks to my car. It's an unusually clear night and the sky is lit up with all of the high rises' office lights that are still on. Go home, I silently say to those people, although I've been one of them far too many times over the years. Loud groups of all kinds of people are on the streets, pouring out of bars and galleries and bookstores, and the city feels alive. It's a far cry from my mostly white hometown, a place where the biggest news is the opening of a new Walgreens.

Ben looks up at the *Daily's* Art Deco building, part of the downtown skyline. "I can't lie. I miss this view."

"You know it wasn't personal. You are a great reporter and a good person. Layoffs are awful, even for the people who are still there."

"That means a lot coming from you, Jane." He steps closer

toward me. I feel the tension building and hope I remember how to do this. "If I'm being honest, I've missed this view too."

"I had no idea." Before I can say anything else, his full lips are on mine. The kiss only lasts for a few seconds, but it's enough to awaken the nerve endings and get my adrenaline going. We say our goodbyes and he gives me a hug, enveloping my body with his long arms.

"I've wanted to do that for a long time." His smile is wider than I've ever seen it before. "I never thought I'd have the chance."

"Really?" is all I can muster.

As soon as I get in the car, I lock my doors, turn the engine on, and glance at my phone before I hit the road. A text from Caryn, sent at 10:02 p.m., is waiting for me: "So???" I'm still on a euphoric high when I write back one word: "Yes."

Chapter Nine

Eva

"Jesse," I call from the doorway.

"Are you leaving now?" He's winded from working out in the garage. With the twins and his work schedule, he rarely has time to go to the gym anymore, but I'm glad he's willing to lift weights next to our minivan. Every bit of savings helps.

"Yes." I give him a quick kiss before I head to Caryn's parents' house in fancy Hancock Park for the big meeting. "Do you mind if I take your car?"

"Sure, go ahead." He hands me his keys.

"I feel a bit self-conscious pulling up in my mom car."

"You mean your hot mom car."

I take a second to appreciate his broad shoulders and defined legs. Since Copeland's been on my mind lately, I often do double takes looking at Jesse, who is classically handsome, in shape, and a good man. My husband is now about the same age as my former teacher and the physical difference is striking. It's hard to believe I was ever attracted to Dr. Copeland under any circumstances.

"Is it, like, strange meeting another woman who went through something so similar? It's kind of weird to think you and this random chick shared a guy." He shakes his head and shoulders like he's trying to rid his body of a ghost.

"The entire situation feels unreal, but it honestly feels better knowing I'm not the only one. I think it's helped me with a lot of my guilt."

"Do you know anything about this woman?"

"No, nothing. Jane was involved in getting this alumna in touch with us. I still don't fully understand how it all went down. Everything has happened so fast since my initial email to the *Daily*."

"Well, I'm sure she's more nervous than any of you. Just keep doing what you're doing."

"Thanks, babe. My stomach is doing gymnastics, but I know I'll feel better once I meet her, and Jane and Caryn will be there too. I trust them."

"Call me on your way back so I know you're okay."

"Okay, I will. Love you."

"Love you more."

Before I start my journey, I type in the address Caryn gave me into Google since I know I'll need directions. Instead, I see several real estate website listings that estimate the property to be worth fifteen to eighteen million dollars. I'm sure if a neighbor is watching, they'd say, "Why is Eva sitting in the driveway with her mouth hanging open?" I reflect for a minute. Am I ready for this meeting? I say a quick prayer, connect my iPhone to the stereo so I can listen to anything but Meghan Trainor, and get on the road.

Even though I've been in this area before, nothing prepared me for the grandeur of Caryn's parents' home. As I pull up to the circular driveway, marred only by a weathered sedan that I assume is Jane's, I take it all in: the massive rounded archways, expertly manicured garden, and scent of orange blossom that is so strong it makes me wonder if the Rodgers have the scent misted out from some secret place.

A uniformed housekeeper answers one of the majestic double doors and leads me inside the expansive Spanish-style estate. On the way to one of the terraces, where we're meeting, I pass a chef's kitchen, butler pantry, family room, and library. I will later learn that there are three stories, six bedrooms, a wine cellar, movie theater, fitness room, and saltwater pool and hot tub. The walk-in closets are probably bigger than my entire bedroom.

We're just minutes from grittier Hollywood and Koreatown, but in Hancock Park it feels like you're on a movie set or something. Everything looks perfect. Homes are set far back from the street, power and telephone lines are buried, and there's plenty of classic 1920s California architecture.

"Eva, hi." Caryn bolts out of her seat to greet me.

I give her a hug. "Your home is amazing."

"Thanks. I can't take any credit for it, but my mom will love you for saying so. She did all the interiors."

"It looks like a house you'd see in a magazine."

Caryn looks a bit sheepish. "It's been published, extensively."

"Oh my goodness. That's incredible. Is that your mom?" I point to the sizable portrait that hangs in the nearby living room.

"That's her."

"Wow, she's stunning. I see where you get your beauty from."

"She'd probably adopt you." Caryn laughs. "All she wants to hear in life is that she's beautiful and has an equally beautiful house so you'd be her new favorite person."

"Is that portrait from when she was younger?"

"She commissioned it, like, two years ago from some painter she met at a charity event. Going to charity events is what occupies most of my mom's time."

"Oh. Well, that's wonderful she's so engaged. I wish I had more time to volunteer." I'm not sure if I've complimented or insulted Caryn in her home.

"She's a lot younger than my dad. He met my mom at an

event here when she was Miss Korea. I think she was all of twenty years old. Two years later, they had me."

"What does your dad do?"

"He's a diplomat," Caryn says, "and a businessman. He was more than twice her age when they met. Thanks to a combination of Asian genetics and leading dermatologists, my mom still looks twenty-five, and my dad looks like her adoptive grandfather." I want to laugh but don't. "Between work and travel, he wasn't around that much while I was growing up. My mom always joined him on trips, not so much for companionship, but because that's her job."

I nod empathetically, but I really have no clue what to say. My mother worked six days a week, sometimes holding down two jobs at a time.

Jane, Caryn, and I catch up briefly while we wait for the guest of honor.

"What was she like?" I ask Caryn, as I know they recently spoke on the phone.

"She was a bit all over the place. A little flakey if I'm being honest."

"How so?" Jane is immediately suspicious.

"Just that we were supposed to talk at ten, then one, then four. By the time we actually spoke I think it was after ten in the evening."

I hope Sasha is a credible person. It wouldn't be in our interest to have someone who is unreliable involved. I always like to see the good in people, so I'm hoping Caryn's experience was just because Sasha was busy or nervous.

"It was a quick call; a bit awkward as you can imagine, but she was down for showing up today, so that says something."

I realize it's twenty minutes past the time we were meant to meet here and Caryn hasn't received the typical "I'm running late because traffic" text that so many Los Angeles residents employ throughout their day. So we talk more, about non-Copeland things, and it feels nice.

By the time the doorbell finally rings, forty-five minutes later, I realize that it's not a bell that sounds, but descending notes from a classical piece of music that I cannot place. I went to a few fancy homes while at Windemere, but nothing like this. I can't wait to tell Jesse all about it when I get back.

Elsie, their housekeeper, appears. "Excuse me, Miss Caryn. Miss Sasha is here."

We all stand up at attention as though the president has walked into the Oval Office. My own feelings of insecurity about fitting in at Caryn's house dissipate immediately upon shaking Sasha's spiderweb-tattooed hand. I don't know why it didn't occur to me to Google her, find her on Facebook, or look her up in the old yearbooks. I definitely wasn't expecting this.

"I'm so happy to meet you." I stretch out my hand. She reeks of smoke and mumbles something resembling a thank you, but evades eye contact. I wonder if she feels uncomfortable in such a grandiose house until I remember that she went to Windemere. She probably comes from plenty of money like Caryn.

"So how do you want me to do this?" Sasha asks, running a hand through her multicolored hair, which is partially shaved on the right side.

Jane begins. "I assume you know Caryn's story, from the article."

"Yeah." She purses her lips. "It's fucked up. I guess I can't say I'm surprised."

"Whatever you feel comfortable sharing with us is fine, or you don't have to share anything and we can just chat. It's really up to you."

"I've already met with Windemere's so-called committee, and told them everything. They immediately called LAPD, so I have the joy of retelling the story again to some fat detective who will probably get off on hearing all the gory details."

"Your identity will be protected, right?" Jane asks. "I mean with the committee. Did they guarantee you that much?"

"So they say. Is that what they told you?" Sasha looks in my direction. "You know, because you also had 'contact.'"

I wonder how much Jane has told her about me. Even though I'm somewhat relieved to know I'm not the only one, I'm a private person who wouldn't discuss things like this with even my closest friends. It feels strange and almost violating to think that several people at this table know some of the most intimate details of my past. "I spoke to the committee and they assured me confidentiality. Ever since I read Caryn's article, I've felt compelled to do whatever I have to do to make this right."

"Nothing will ever make this right." Sasha folds her arms across her chest. I wonder why she came forward if she doesn't think there's a benefit to getting him charged by LAPD or at least fired from his job. "I don't trust the committee. They're all Windemere lap dogs. They have kids who still go to Windemere or they're the administration at Windemere. How the fuck are they going to be impartial?"

"I thought Michael Patrick was impartial and just wanted to get the whole story for the record." I don't want to sound defensive. I want to encourage her to continue with the process, whatever that may be.

Sasha looks at me directly for the first time and I take in the sprinkle of freckles across the bridge of her nose and her wide-set eyes, which are messily lined in black, like the way a cool French girl would do it. She's stunning if you can see past the piercings, hair, and attitude. She reminds me of a pinup girl, albeit a punk rock pinup girl.

"I wish I could be as naïve as you."

I feel a small stab to the heart.

"I don't have experience talking to investigative committees or the LAPD, so if that makes me naïve then I guess I'm naïve."

Sasha looks like she's going to say something else to me, but then changes her mind and addresses the group. "Look, I'll save you the boring lead-up since you've all been through it—the compliments, the hand on the thigh, bonding over literature—well except for you, Jane." Jane shifts in her seat and recrosses her legs. It's clear that Sasha's not ready to trust any of us on face value. We're going to have to earn it.

"What year were you?" Caryn asks.

"Class of two thousand. The millennium." She extends her hands for dramatic effect. "When we were in kindergarten, there was so much excitement about us being the Class of 2000. Like we were from the future or were going to all be living on Mars or something. I remember the entire kindergarten class wearing these matching red T-shirts with rocket ships that said 'two zero zero zero.' It all felt so fucking hopeful."

"How old were you when you met Dr. Copeland?" Jane asks.

"Fifteen."

"So was I," Caryn says. I think the same to myself. He must love fifteen for whatever reason. I try to think back to that year, who I was and what I was doing before I got involved with Dr. Copeland. I remember worrying about the PSAT exam, and being crushed that I wasn't allowed to go to our annual school dance with the nearby all-boys school. Most Windemere girls, like my friend Tessa, who was assigned to be my Big Sister, were far more confident than I was. They thought nothing of public speaking or starting a new club on campus. They knew those esteemed hallways and classrooms well and never questioned if they belonged at Windemere. They had always been surrounded by vaulted archways and archaic pin ceremonies and state-of-the-art science labs.

It was common to see my classmates win national awards

or appear on local news segments because of an important achievement. We had regular guest speakers, ranging from famous authors to CEOs of major corporations. My classmates, some of whom were daughters of famous musicians and NBA players, didn't seem particularly impressed, as most of them had been around these kinds of people for their entire lives. My friend Colleen's dad ran a film studio, so going to her house for a movie actually meant choosing from Academy Award screeners. I was still singing in the Windemere choir back then, eager to one day understand the feelings and emotions behind the lyrics I'd practice over and over again. I thought about trying out for the school play, but I was so shy. It didn't help that a couple of girls from my cohort already had film credits from their child acting days. Singing was the one time I felt comfortable and like I fit in. All of that stopped after sophomore year.

"It's hard for me to even say this shit out loud." Sasha plays with one of the many heavy silver rings on her fingers. "I had planned to go to my grave with this one."

"I completely understand," I say. "I never told anyone either."

"After I read Caryn's story, and learned that Windemere was actually investigating, I figured I had to do something. I know there are others out there, I mean, obviously." Sasha looks in my direction. "Windemere should have protected them."

"I've been hearing from more students over email," Caryn reveals. "They are mainly stories like mine, where there was an inappropriate flirtation or a touch on the thigh or whatever, but then it stopped there for different reasons. It's like he had a playbook with one play."

"What pisses me off the most is how he was never worried about being caught." Sasha stares at the high ceiling for a moment. "He's such an entitled, arrogant prick. He has to be held accountable. He has to admit this happened."

"I think I can speak for the group when I say that our main goal is that he can never teach girls or young women ever again." Jane's confidence is enviable.

"I wouldn't mind if he suffered worse than that." Sasha's smile is as broad as the Cheshire Cat's. "He deserves to suffer."

"How long were you involved with him, if you don't mind me asking?" Jane asks.

"A few months total. I was quiet and bookish, and he definitely used that to his advantage. I never had a ton of friends at Windemere, just a few girls over the years. In all fairness, I never really gave anyone a chance. At the time, I thought I was smarter and more worldly than everyone there. I couldn't relate to most of the girls in my year who had sensible crushes on Daniel Radcliffe and Lil' Bow Wow. Because I didn't get any positive reinforcement at home, I was sort of my own biggest fan. Copeland made it out like he was so attracted to my intelligence and my unique way of thinking. My developing teenage body was just a bonus, I'm sure."

I shake my head in disapproval. To think that Dr. Copeland had previously been with an unknown amount of other students makes me feel nauseous. He always acted like what we were doing was so unusual and special when in reality, I was nothing even close to special. I wonder if he even remembers us all. Did he keep a journal or some sort of system? Does he remember every detail of every encounter or is it just a blur of short gray skirts and freshly straightened teeth and white ankle socks?

"He was so popular on campus and people knew he was a flirt, but I never thought he crossed the line with anyone but me." Sasha looks down at her lap and it's obvious that she's still in pain. "I was so fucking stupid."

"You were fifteen," Jane reminds her. "He was the adult, your teacher, the chair of the English department. From what I've been told, everyone—students, other teachers, administrators, the board, the community—loved him. You had every reason to trust him, and to believe the things he told you."

Even though I'm hearing the words come out of her mouth, it's hard for my brain to reconcile that just two years before I met Dr. Copeland, he was having a full-blown relationship with Sasha, who I don't remember ever seeing on campus even though we overlapped for part of my time there. I'm eager to look her up in my old yearbook, if I can find it, to see if I even recognize her.

Sasha looks down as she continues. "The hardest part for me is that I enjoyed many of our encounters at the time. I mean, as gross as it sounds now, I got off on the whole thing. He lavished me with attention, which was all I needed to continue making the biggest mistake of my life. I thought maybe we were tortured lovers like Romeo and Juliet, or that the universe wanted us to be together for some reason. He promised me all kinds of crazy things, like leaving his wife, us having kids, and reading poetry to one another while road tripping to Big Sur. I was so ready to escape all the fucked-up stuff at home that I lapped that shit up, big time. I think that's what I struggle most with, the fact that I truly cared for him, and regularly sought out his attention. For the longest time, I was convinced that I seduced him and not the other way around." Caryn and I are both nodding as she speaks. Even though our stories aren't exactly the same, they're similar enough.

Tattoos aren't my thing, but Sasha has beautiful script imprinted on the inside of her forearm. I couldn't make out the writing earlier, but now I see it says, "Even for me life had its gleams of sunshine." I discreetly search the phrase on my phone, under the table, while they continue chatting, and see that it's from *Jane Eyre*. I first read the novel in Dr. Copeland's class and I suspect Sasha did too. Literature warns us about the arrogance of men but we so badly want to believe otherwise.

"Can I get you a drink?" Caryn asks, realizing she never offered Sasha one.

"Do you have any vodka?" I do my best not to judge even

though it's one in the afternoon.

"Sure."

"Just straight is fine."

Caryn brings a crystal lowball glass over, filled halfway. Sasha takes a large gulp as though she's been in a desert all day and was just offered a cup of water.

"Don't worry, I'm doing the no car thing these days. It's a long story."

I feel strange asking Sasha to share any more gory details, and I'm not sure I even want to know them, to be honest, but there is one question burning in my brain. "Why did it end?"

"After a few months and a lot of 'contact,'" she says, using air quotes, "I had definitely fallen in love with him. It was messy and I knew it couldn't end well, but I was shocked by the way he treated me after I had a pregnancy scare."

"Jesus." Jane grimaces. She's rubbing her forehead with her thumb and fingers as if that's going to erase what she just heard.

"I was six days late, and told him so, and his entire personality shifted. His wife was pregnant at the time, and he acted like I had somehow tried to trap him. Like it was my dream to be a sixteen-year-old mom. My own mother would have murdered me if she knew I was pregnant. No matter how into him I was, I never wanted his baby, then or in some parallel universe where we could be together. I wanted to graduate from Windemere with everyone else, and go to college and have a good life."

I feel woozy hearing all of this, but Sasha's not done. "I couldn't believe how cold and mean he was to me, at school and off campus. It was almost as if that was his real personality and everything else was an act, rather than the other way around. It terrified me that this sensitive and emotional man, who claimed to feel torture that we couldn't be together out in the open, was now treating me like I was unworthy of even an ounce of compassion or concern."

"I'm so sorry," is all I can summon, even though I want to tell her how this sounds and feels so familiar. In an attempt to settle my stomach, I sip the Perrier that was put out.

"I'll never forget taking a pregnancy test, alone and terrified, in the bathroom of that shitty McDonald's near Windemere. Thank god I wasn't pregnant, but the scare was so bad that it shocked me into reality. I was totally overwhelmed and had no one to talk to or confide in. It felt like an avalanche, all the anger and rage I felt that I had to keep bottled inside."

I notice Caryn's eyes are watering.

"I no longer saw him in the same way and actually began to despise him. I decided I hated him, but you know hate and love are basically the same thing. They both require huge amounts of emotion and thought and time. What I really wanted to feel was indifference, to just not care about him in the slightest. But that was impossible. I had to get up each day and go to school, not knowing if that was the day I'd cross paths with him in the hallway, or see him at an assembly. I figured transferring schools at that point would be as traumatic as staying. The whole scenario fucked me up for a long time, mainly because it was all a secret and I never told anyone until last week."

Caryn sits up straight. "Because of you and Eva, he's going to be punished. This can't be swept under the rug. It's too late. The media is all over it. Windemere is investigating, finally, and now the police are involved. I wouldn't be surprised if he is arrested after you give your statement to LAPD."

"I fucking hope so." Sasha taps her empty glass with a black fingernail. "I hope his life blows up into a million little pieces."

"I wanted to ask you something." The group turns to look at me, which makes my face heat up a few degrees. "Did he ever talk to you about his family? I think that's where most of my guilt comes from, especially now that I have my own children."

"He spoke about them all the time," Sasha explains. "His daughter was three when we met and like I said before, his wife was pregnant, with Jack, when I was with him."

"I've looked them up before. Before the story broke, I mean." Caryn looks embarrassed by this revelation, but I can't blame her. I'm surprised I didn't think of it myself.

"And?" Jane looks like an impatient mom who just found out her daughter hasn't been telling the whole truth about something.

"Sophia is a freshman at Pepperdine. She looked like a normal, happy kid. Lots of friends. Nothing out of the ordinary. Jack had a few Instagram posts, but he plays football and looks a lot like his dad—only young and ripped. Now, because of my essay, I guess, their accounts are set to private, but they are still online."

I'm tempted to ask if Caryn has any photos or screen grabs, but then I realize it won't be helpful. I need to stay focused on the task at hand and not worry about his kids—otherwise I might not go through with everything. After some awkward silence, Caryn ends the meeting.

"Thank you all so much for coming over." She turns to Sasha. "You obviously didn't have to and we all appreciate it and everything you're doing to help."

"We have a weird little club here. I guess it's better than going it alone."

"You can reach out anytime." I hand Sasha my colorful business card.

"Thanks." She grabs her keys and removes a pair of oversize vintage sunglasses from one of the many pockets of her military-style jacket.

"Before you go, is there anything else you wanted to share with us that we didn't cover?" Jane asks. It's clear Sasha is eager to get out of here and hop in a taxi to who knows where.

"Just one thing: I wanted to tell you guys that he also told me I was so unique and special—like a rare rose," she adds. "Dude needs to get a new fucking line."

Chapter Ten

Caryn

"**J**ane, you have to see this." For once, she walks over to my cubicle instead of the other way around.

"What is it?"

"Some parents started a blog defending Copeland."

"You're joking."

"Look."

I watch as Jane's eyes scan the blog's content.

We are an anonymous group of concerned Windemere parents— past and present—who have compiled several reasons why Dr. Gregory Copeland is thought to be innocent of these egregious accusations that are swirling around our community.

First, according to various anonymous sources we've spoken to, the three girls who have gone on the record with the investigatory committee and the LAPD are all friends with one another. Because of their existing friendship (two of the so-called victims even attended Windemere at the same time, and could be best friends for all we know), plans were made to collude to harm Dr. Copeland. Maybe he made them mad when they were his students. Perhaps he didn't write them a strong enough college recommendation letter. Or maybe they are using Dr. Copeland as a cover for the real abuser (this is a very common phenomenon). Who knows?

Secondly, there are no signs that these alumnae have been sexually abused or assaulted. Oftentimes victims of sexual abuse have serious physical problems, and signs of struggle. Sometimes they become promiscuous. If these supposed victims were so traumatized by their time at Windemere, then why did all three of these women graduate on time, attend college, and go on to live normal lives?

Thirdly, why did the two latest victims come forward so many years after they attended Windemere? While Caryn Rodgers, who chose to go to the media rather than the school administration or the police, may believe her experience to be true (and no one will ever know the truth unless there was security footage of this supposed meeting at a coffee shop near campus that could be released—highly unlikely so many years later), it seems all too convenient that suddenly victims have come out of the woodwork to corroborate her assumptions about Dr. Copeland.

As you may know, the Rodgers family wields influence and power in Los Angeles and beyond. Perhaps Caryn or her family even bribed these friends of hers to back up her statements. Is it just a coincidence that Caryn Rodgers is an aspiring journalist who interns at the Daily*? Was she under pressure to "take down" Dr. Copeland or Windemere for some sinister reason? That's what the real investigation should be about. Why now? What is her true motive?*

Lastly, we all know Dr. Copeland is a wonderful man and excellent teacher who has received fantastic reviews from his students. He has educated our kids for more than twenty years and changed the lives of countless students—for the better. This is nothing more than a modern-day witch hunt. It truly breaks our hearts to think that some people are fine with ruining this man's life. Even if he is found to be not guilty of any of these baseless accusations, it will be a stain on his career and will haunt his family—especially his two children—forever. We must put a stop to this.

If you have any information about these "victims," or

about the case in general, please contact LAPD. We will continue to update any information we have so watch this page.

"That is some serious denial right there." Jane shakes her head in disbelief. "That is really something."

"And people wonder why victims don't want to come forward," I mutter under my breath.

"Well, these parents are in for a rude awakening, even if they don't want to believe it. I wonder if it's a group or just a lone wolf posing as something more substantial."

"It could be Copeland for all we know." I say this even though I know it couldn't be true. He always loathed computers and technology. I'd be shocked if he knew how to publish a Facebook post, let alone a blog.

"I don't think he'd be that stupid, would he? I'm sure someone in our IT department could at least find the IP address of the publisher of this blog."

"I wonder what he's thinking. Like, is his life now a living hell filled with meetings with lawyers and wondering how he's going to earn a living after he's fired, or is he in denial too, and thinks nothing is going to happen and he'll just go on teaching?"

"I guess we'll find out, eventually." Jane furrows her brow and rereads the copy again like a detective searching for a clue.

"Maybe your boyfriend knows something."

"Caryn, he's not my boyfriend."

"You sound defensive." I love seeing her squirm. "You must like him."

"I am never letting you do my hair again." Even though I'm standing behind her, I can see she's smiling.

"I put a little volume in your hair. You did everything else."

Jane swivels to face me. "I'll ask Ben if he's heard anything about this blog."

"Do you think Copeland's wife kicked him out already?"

"I don't know why she wouldn't. At this point, it sounds like he's a liability, in addition to being a criminal. I can't imagine his daughter's friends or their parents would be okay with him being around."

"Sometimes I wonder if Dr. Copeland and his wife were ever really in love, like in the beginning they must have been, right?"

"Who knows? People get married for all sorts of reasons."

"Do you ever want to get married?" Even though we work side by side a few days a week, I never ask Jane personal questions like this, and she doesn't offer up any details about her life outside of whatever we're working on.

"When I was a kid, I did."

"And then what changed?"

"Life changed, I suppose."

It's clear from her folded arms that she doesn't intend to go down this road with me now so I drop it.

"What about you?" I'm surprised she's continuing this nonwork, non-Copeland-related conversation.

"I'm sure that's what's expected of me, but I have other plans."

"You're so young, Caryn. The world is at your fingertips. You are so far ahead of the game. You're not an 'aspiring journalist.' You are a journalist. You have clips, and a profile now, thanks to the essay and your work at the *Daily Trojan*. You could become a speaker or a professional activist."

"I just want to write."

"Well you can do that, too." I wonder if this is what having a big sister is like. "You can do all of those things and anything else you ever wanted to professionally. And you could still get married. It wouldn't invalidate the other things in your life. Your parents have had a long marriage, right?"

"Yeah, but I wouldn't call it a great romance or anything.

It's more transactional." Jane looks puzzled. "My mom is on an allowance, and I'm pretty sure her entire day is spent shopping, going to lunch, and doing beauty treatments, or whatever, to distract herself from thinking about anything too much."

"Like her relationship, you mean?"

"From thinking too much about her life. She doesn't talk about anything serious or deep. There are no gray areas in her world. She knows her role and what is expected. Her life is about maintaining her long hair, being skinny, staying pale, making the house look nice, and attending events at the behest of my father. Sometimes I think of her more like his employee because being a wife is the only job she's ever had. She gets a cut check from my father every two weeks."

"I guess some women want that kind of life."

"I'm sure she had hopes and dreams as a kid in Korea that went further than sharing a bed with a wrinkled old man."

"Of course. Well, it sounds like there's a lot to unpack there."

"Why do you think I've been in therapy since I was thirteen?" I laugh so she knows it's okay to laugh.

Jane is spending the afternoon and evening working on her Copeland story and I'm not going to bother her. Old friends and distant ex-Windemere classmates are having a field day with the news, and I know she's interviewed some of them by phone already. Several alumnae have written me impassioned emails and cards, addressed to the *Daily*, while others have tracked me down via social media. I can place these missives into three groups: the ones who are compassionate and concerned about my essay and the investigation, the ones who are cruel and in complete denial that anything actually happened to me or any others, and the ones who agree that they knew something was "off" about Copeland, but they also have heard "things" about me. The people in the latter camp hurt me the most, but I ignore them.

Even though I've done my best to stay off social media, particularly Facebook, I still see things. A few Windemere girls tag me in their posts because they want me to see their snide remark or alert me to a pointless thread where my credibility is questioned and the truth is nowhere to be found. It's an amazing thing to witness. My profile is set to private and I even changed my online name so I'd be harder to track down, but the Windemere crowd is always able to find me. A current student's father sent me an email that began with sympathy and admiration for my "impressive courage," but concluded by saying that he could see why it would be hard to keep things professional around me and wondered if I'd be interested in grabbing a drink sometime to "talk things through." I haven't heard from anyone in the administration or faculty. I thought at least one teacher would say something, anything, to me, but the silence has been deafening.

Of course there are plenty of random people reaching out as well. Men in places like Kentucky and Ottawa and women from Connecticut and the U.K. all have feelings and opinions they feel compelled to share. These messages are more vulgar, and littered with spelling and grammar mistakes, but fall into some version of "you were asking for it," "nothing happened to you," or "get over yourself." I managed to create an email filter that sends most of these messages straight to my trash folder, but some still manage to get through, and on days when I feel like punishing myself, I look in the trash. I'm not proud.

The story has been bandied about for days on a men's rights activist's blog with "Bro" in its title. These readers are concerned about allegations that have not been proven in a court of law. They often write to tell me I am ruining this man's life. They also write to say that most sexual assault and rape accusations are false. They don't cite studies or crime statistics from police agencies. They just *know*. "Think of his children," one man implored yesterday. These people make me so incensed that my heart rate can easily get to 140 beats per minute within seconds. This idea that an occasional false accusation is a more serious problem than thousands of actual instances of abuse or assault or rape enrages me like nothing else. They write to tell me they'd fuck me so hard that I wouldn't be able to type anything afterward, which doesn't make a lot of sense from a physiological standpoint. These men don't know the first thing about the violent truths of being born female.

I won't tell my parents about these men because they would force me to stop working at the *Daily* altogether. Because my dad pays my tuition and owns the house I live in, he still has plenty of control over me and my mother will never stand up to him under any circumstance. She would rather pray about it and say it's in God's hands. And since Phillip is still a minor, they can threaten cutting off my access to my own little brother. They've done it before and it crushed me more than any slap across the face from my mother.

After I get my work done, I wave to Jane and head home for the day. I still have reading to finish for my Comparative Lit class and laundry that's piled up. I would typically send it out since a good amount of my stuff is dry clean only and because my dad would pay for it, but lately I've been enjoying doing it myself. Grace had to teach me how to do it properly since a lifetime of housekeepers didn't prepare me for independent living. She even found these dryer sheets that you can use for silks and other delicate fabrics.

I'll never forget the look on my first roommate Kat's face when I told her that my mom never taught me how to operate a washing machine, and that I wasn't sure she knew how to use one herself. "Didn't she worry about what you were going to do once you were living in the dorms?" Kat's earnestness was refreshing. Since my parents' home was nearby, I figured I could just drop it off and have Elsie do it. This continued during my sophomore and junior years as well, after I moved out of campus housing.

When Grace gets home from school, I'm standing over the couch, folding clothes. "This is . . . unexpected."

"Very funny."

"If this newfound passion for laundry continues, you're free to do mine too."

"I don't enjoy it *that* much."

"We're just lucky we don't have to go to the Laundromat." She throws her bag on the sofa. "I did that my whole damn life." I've never been in a real Laundromat so I don't say anything in return.

"I also made some dinner."

"I'm sorry, but where is Caryn? Have you seen her?"

"I think it's pretty good, too. You can see what you think. I already ate."

"I have to call my sister real quick, but I'll try it after that, thanks." Grace looks through a few pieces of junk mail. "Who was just here?"

"What do you mean?"

"As I was pulling up, I saw a man walking down our front steps."

"A delivery person? No one knocked or rang the bell. I've been right here."

"No. He was wearing slacks and a button-down shirt."

"Maybe he realized he had the wrong house."

"I think he left when he realized I was pulling up in the driveway."

"That's strange." I peek out the living room curtains but all I see is a young woman walking her corgi.

"Just be careful, Caryn. I know the Copeland story is getting bigger because of the investigation. Sometimes things like this bring out all kinds of weirdos."

"Yes, I know."

"Is everything okay?"

"It will be. I think they're getting close to finishing the investigation."

"Do you know stuff you're not telling me? About other victims?"

"Yes, Unnie. There are others. I met two of them." Grace's jaw drops and she covers her mouth with her right hand. "Sorry. I'm not trying to hide it, I'm just trying to process it all myself. I don't want to breach their privacy, but I should be telling you because you're my only real friend."

"What are you talking about? You have tons of friends."

"I do?"

"What about Alex and Farai? Or the newspaper staff at school?"

"I haven't heard from them since my essay came out. I think they're ashamed of me."

"How could they be? You're a hero, not someone to be ashamed of."

"Well, you and Jane are the only ones who check in with me. My therapist asks me questions, but that's because she's paid to do so. My parents have not even called me since the day the story came out. They said I had embarrassed the family and made them look like they didn't do enough to help me. My mom texted me this morning and asked what she did wrong to deserve a 'stupid, ungrateful' daughter like me."

"I'm really sorry to hear that, Caryn."

"It's okay. I guess I'm not much fun to be around these days. All I do is work and go to school and hang out in my bedroom."

Grace perks up like someone who's discovered money in her pocket. "You also go to Pilates."

"Can you imagine if I died tomorrow? Caryn Rodgers was born in Los Angeles, California, where she attended the famed Windemere School for Girls and University of Southern California, where she was a reporter for the *Daily Trojan*. One time, she tried to do the right thing. And she also went to Pilates.'"

"Caryn. That is so morbid."

"Is it? I could die tonight. You could die tomorrow. Isn't that why people are always posting those 'live in the moment' memes? Because life is fragile and can be taken away at any moment?"

"You're acting weird."

"You just called me a hero and now I'm acting weird? Maybe I've been weird this whole time and you're just figuring it out now."

"Caryn." Grace is looking at me like I'm a stranger who just wandered into the house.

"I don't know what you want from me, Grace."

"I don't want anything from you."

I sigh. "Look, I'm just joking around. Go call you sister; I have work to do anyway."

"Okay, but please talk to me anytime and don't push me away because you're stressed or tired or scared. Just know that I always want to talk to you, no matter what."

I feel like a toddler on the verge of a meltdown. Going against my first instinct to lash out or say something sarcastic, I try to be more like Grace. I hear Susan's voice in my head telling me that I need to accept help and not carry the weight of the world on my shoulders. "Thank you, Unnie. I honestly don't know what I'd do without you." I should probably go give her a hug, but I offer a closed-mouth smile instead, and she gives me the same in return.

Chapter Eleven

Jane

*T*eacher Leaves Elite Girls' School After Alleged Student
Affairs and Inappropriate Conduct
By Jane March

A popular Windemere School for Girls teacher and department chairperson left his current job amid a current investigation that he pursued inappropriate relationships with teenage girls ranging from flirtatious emails to full-blown sexual contact.

Windemere School for Girls has released multiple statements via email assuring families that they are immediately addressing allegations against one of their teachers. The Daily has learned that the teacher is Gregory Copeland, who taught English at Windemere—Southern California's oldest all-girls private school—for 18 years.

Citing a commitment to transparency, Windemere said it immediately notified the Los Angeles Police Department and Child Protective Services after learning that two victims had recently come forward with allegations of inappropriate physical contact with Copeland more than a decade ago. The school has hired attorney Kim Holder, a partner at the law firm of Jacobs & Wells LLP, to lead an independent investigation.

Jane Doe 1 and Jane Doe 2, who agreed to speak with the Daily *on the condition of anonymity, were empowered to tell their stories after reading an essay published in the* Daily *by Caryn Rodgers, a 2012 graduate of Windemere. They told the* Daily *that*

Copeland was so beloved by the Windemere community that it was challenging to come forward at the exclusive and expensive school, which costs $38,000 per year to attend.

Both women, now in their thirties, have been interviewed by the school's Special Investigative Committee, made up largely of board members, as well as by LAPD.

"The only reason I came forward now was with the intention of protecting other girls from Dr. Copeland's predatory behavior," Jane Doe 1 told the Daily. *"My greatest regret in life is not speaking up sooner. Perhaps naïvely, I assumed I was the only one who had these experiences. It makes me sick to think that he has been doing this for an unknown number of years."*

Copeland, a Shakespeare specialist known for his outgoing personality, made his teenage students feel special and sophisticated, "all while complimenting them on their intelligence and physical appearances," said Elizabeth, a 2002 graduate. (All of the women who agreed to speak to the Daily *did so under pseudonyms.) "He was so popular on campus even though everyone knew he crossed the line at times and could be openly flirtatious in the classroom. 'Naughty' would be a word I'd use to describe him."*

Back in 2010, after Rodgers provided Windemere with emails exchanged between Copeland and herself and comments he had made to her privately, administrators told him to have no further contact with her and requested that he attend counseling sessions.

She alleged that he placed his hand on her leg at an off-campus interview for Windemere's school newspaper, and behaved inappropriately in emails and on campus. Rodgers's parents grew concerned that the school was taking no real action, but they were assured that this was a first-time offense and that the school was watching him closely.

Copeland did not respond to the Daily*'s repeated requests* *for comment.*

According to interviews with his former students from Windemere, Copeland was a charming and passionate teacher who often treated his teenage students as adults. "I don't think any of us were surprised to hear these allegations, sadly," said current Windemere student Valerie. "However, I also don't think anyone thought it was this bad."

"My sexual relationship with Dr. Copeland went on for months in between sophomore and junior year at Windemere, and I never told a soul," Jane Doe 2 told the Daily. *"This man managed to convince me that we were artists and tortured lovers who did not need to play by the rules. He took advantage of every insecurity I had and I would have done just about anything for him." Their relationship ended when Jane Doe 2 believed she could be pregnant. "It doesn't get much worse than thinking you're pregnant by your married English teacher," she said. "It was terrifying to see the person I loved and trusted turn on me like that. I was instantly persona non grata because of that pregnancy scare—he was done with me."*

The former and current Windemere students interviewed by the Daily, *including Jane Doe 1 and Jane Doe 2, have not spoken publicly about Copeland until now. Two alumnae stated that they complained to Windemere about Copeland's unprofessional behavior well before Rodgers was a student. Many others have said they heard rumors about "bad behavior and a preoccupation with certain girls each year."*

Six different women, who were all former students of Copeland, have told the Daily *similar stories of private conversations culminating in physical contact, namely a hand on the knee. Rebecca, a 2004 graduate, said, "Touching my leg was clearly a test. He wanted to see what he could get away with. When I pulled away and made a face, he lost all interest in me."*

A 2011 alumna said, "His modus operandi is to make

girls feel like enlightened souls. Through poetry and romantic literature, he makes you feel like you're on his level. Then he gets really personal once that bond is there."

Sheila, a 2014 graduate, said that Copeland crossed the line on numerous occasions by sharing personal details of his marriage with his teenage students. "Looking back now, it seems insane that he would tell us negative things about his wife," she said. "At the time, I think most of us felt flattered that he trusted us with this personal information, but now I'm just disgusted. If he was so unhappy, then he should have talked to a therapist."

Some Windemere alumnae and their parents are wondering why the school didn't do more to address Rodgers's complaint and why someone who was known to have crossed the line on numerous occasions wasn't fired.

Windemere Head of School Ann Erickson told the Daily *she could not comment on an ongoing investigation, but that her students and their safety are of "paramount importance."*

My story on Windemere has been online for all of ten minutes before the comments start rolling in:

Are you aware that Ann Erickson's salary is $425K? Does that seem right? She was clearly more concerned with padding her own bank account than protecting these innocent girls!

The timing seems very suspicious. Why are victims suddenly coming out of the woodwork when they've been silent for more than a decade?

I will never give one penny to Windemere from this day forward. I can't wait for their next solicitation so I can tell them what I think.

Why didn't your story go into the fact that one of the Jane Does is known to have serious mental issues? I'm not trying to discount what these women are saying, but you need to present ALL of the facts.

These allegations happened so long ago—move on with your lives and stop playing the victim.

Gregory Copeland and his family go to my church! I feel sick!

I'm very sorry for what these women dealt with, but they made a choice. If they are smart enough to get into a school like Windemere, they should be smart enough to know that there are consequences for reckless behavior!

His poor wife and kids. They are the real victims.

If you know anything about Windemere, then you know that Copeland was a bit of a Svengali. He often pitted girls who liked him against one another. I think it was entertainment for him. Had no idea it went farther than psychological games or I would have said something.

Let's not forget that these are totally unproven allegations. Until he is found guilty in a court of law, this is all meaningless. If this teacher is found not guilty, these women will still ruin his life.

Teachers' unions and employment contracts have strong protections against firings. Unless a teacher is caught in the act, a teacher cannot be fired by the school or school district (I'm speaking of public districts). Things in private schools are very different. In my school district, if emails were provided when you reported this teacher to your school administration, the teacher would have been removed from the classroom by the district and been asked to report to the district offices for the amount of time it takes to investigate the case. There, the teacher would still get paid for sitting at a desk reading the newspaper or playing games on his cell phone. If the allegations were true, the teacher's tenure might be terminated with the district and he would have to deal with the legal system. If there are no emails (or other proof of the teacher's inappropriate relationship to you) when you reported his actions to your school's administration, then my district would have done the same as Windemere, which is to allow the teacher to continue teaching, send him to counseling, and put an official memo in his personnel file detailing the accusation. If the teacher continued to be written up due to similar reasons, then the district might investigate. More likely, he would just be moved from school to school, with each administration offering different excuses. This is known as "passing the trash." In my experience, the system is rigged—and not in favor of the student.

I am ashamed to have Windemere on my resume. The name has been forever tainted, in my opinion.

I always promise myself I won't read the comments—and yet. Ben has been trying to see me, but I've been too busy. I text him to say that I'm meeting Xhana Stein this afternoon, and that I'm free afterward if he wants to grab a bite. "I'd like more than a bite, but I'll take whatever you're offering. I haven't stopped thinking about you." I'm flattered and eager to fully understand how we got here, as it all feels surreal to me. I also remind myself to enjoy it. This is the best part of dating, when your friends and colleagues don't know, when there's no talk of commitment or expectations. When you still have hope for whatever this is or could be.

Caryn's not in today, but I email her the story link. I wonder if my new source will have seen my piece before we meet up. I hope it doesn't scare her off now that things are heating up.

"Ms. March?"

"Hi, yes." I stand to shake her hand. "Please, call me Jane. Have a seat."

"I'm Xhana." She has a firm shake. "A lot of people are thrown off by the X, but it's pronounced just like Shawna."

"Thank you so much for meeting with me. I wasn't sure how you'd feel after my story." I motion for the waiter to come by so she can order a drink.

"We knew the media storm would be reignited once Dr. Copeland resigned, so no one was surprised. But I think I can speak for the board when I say that we were shocked by how many Windemere students had similar experiences." She sets her phone to silent, but leaves it in plain view. "How did you get so many of them to come forward?"

I sip from my iced green tea as Xhana places an order for a soy milk cappuccino. "It wasn't very hard. Many of them wrote to the *Daily* as soon as Caryn's piece first ran. Some of them contacted Caryn directly. If I had more time, I would have interviewed others. Has the committee heard from other students aside from the Jane Does?"

"Are we off the record?"

"Yes."

She looks around at the few occupied tables near us to make sure they aren't Windemere people. "Then yes. I would describe it as a flooding: emails, calls, letters, and in-person visits. Many of their stories are credible. Others are, let's just say, a little hysterical. Some of the parents appear to be on the verge of nervous breakdowns. Of course it's all anyone can talk about." I nod along, encouraging her to keep talking. "The teachers are going through a lot as well. Some of them clearly had no idea what was going on, and they are personally hurt to discover that they have been working alongside him for so many years. Others suspected something was not right about Copeland and have shared various anecdotes, although they never knew the whole truth. Two female teachers have used the investigation to push a theory that male teachers like Copeland have easier times with students because of flirting, teasing, and banter, and they want to address this issue going forward."

"How are you holding up? I imagine this is stressful for everyone involved."

"Surprisingly, I'm doing fine. I don't know if Ben told you, but I used to be a lawyer. I've seen some ugly cases in my day, but this one hits extraclose to home."

"Of course."

Her cappuccino arrives with a heart designed into the foam. "I've only been on the board for the last two years, so I never knew Dr. Copeland beyond exchanging pleasantries on campus. Fortunately, my daughter never had him as a teacher. She's just in eighth grade."

I shift in the uncomfortable wooden seat. "Where is the committee in their investigation?"

"We're wrapping up. We've interviewed more than forty people at this point—victims, teachers, administrators, and of course, Ann Erickson. We have a pretty clear picture of the findings, although there could be more victims, of course. Everyone comes forward in his or her own time. Some, like the Jane Does, are empowered by seeing others speak their truth. Other victims may wait a bit and see how the victims are treated before stepping forward."

"And others will never come forward no matter what."

"We have accepted that as a possibility. I think Copeland chose to resign because he realized this was not going away. There was simply no way to contain the story once the media jumped on it. We're a tiny school on a hill in an upscale residential neighborhood. The spotlight is not comfortable for anyone."

"A tiny school with a $56 million endowment."

"I just meant that we have less than six hundred students total. Even though Windemere is considered among the best in the nation—and has a ridiculously large endowment—we still fly under the radar in terms of national media. Even the city, at large, is unaware of us."

"Well, I'm eager to hear anything you're willing to talk about. You mentioned that there was more to the story than what's been reported so far."

"Yes." She bites her lower lip. "It would be wise to look into Copeland's time at Adams, where he was before Windemere. I heard rumblings that his departure there was abrupt. Why was that?"

"Is that in Thousand Oaks?"

"Yes, it's a private K through eighth grade, not a high school. But that's not all."

I raise my eyebrows in anticipation.

"Your story mentioned two alumnae who said they told the school about Copeland's inappropriate behavior, but internally, Windemere has always denied any wrongdoing. I think they thought any fallout from Caryn's essay could be managed, especially as she didn't name Copeland or Windemere."

"But of course everyone figured it out anyway."

"It's amazing how fast news travels these days. But in our first committee meeting, everyone acted as though the bigger accusations against him, like the ones from Sasha and Eva, were shocking. And maybe they were to the board members, but I don't believe the entire administration is shocked. I think others have heard rumblings over the years."

I sit up taller and feel a rush of excitement. "Are you implying there's a cover-up going on?"

"Not exactly." She looks around again before continuing. "I think the board is genuinely disturbed by what they've heard and they're prepared to take action to ensure that this never happens again."

"That's good to know, but what is it that you're trying to tell me?"

"I believe that Ann Erickson, Windemere's beloved Head of School, knew about the prior students' complaints. I don't know for sure if they knew Copeland had trouble at Adams. But I do believe that they downplayed the complaints against him over the years to the point where they were hidden from the board altogether. At no point did Ann or anyone on staff say, 'We had several students say he was creepy or inappropriate.' In fact, when Caryn's story came out, the administration casted her as a bit of a drama queen and suggested she was seeking attention or trying to make a name for herself."

"I've worked with Caryn for months now and would not agree with that assessment of her personality."

"The lack of empathy for her was what sounded a bit of an alarm for me. I wondered why they would paint one of their alumnae that way. That's what had me the most suspicious. It's a bit maddening that no one on staff has said anything along the lines of 'we really screwed up here.' "

"So what you're saying is if they had done their proper research about Copeland or believed the first girl who reported his bad behavior, none of us would even be sitting here today."

"Correct." The oversize mug looks cartoonishly large in her diminutive hands.

"How do you know all this if you're newish to the board?"

"We talked to so many people for the investigation: past administrative employees, people involved in record keeping. One of them, an old assistant of Ann's, recalled several instances of students complaining about Copeland. However, these official complaints never ended up in his file. Only Caryn's complaint is in his file and it was not taken very seriously, as you know."

I sit back in my seat and fold my arms. "That's outrageous."

"It is. That's why I'm talking to you. I'm afraid the committee isn't going to do the entirely right thing here. I mean, they're going to take action and spend an untold amount of money to ensure to the best of their ability that it never happens again, but I don't think they're going to report every single thing we found. I'm not sure 'full transparency' is a phrase that can exist at a school like Windemere. I wouldn't be surprised if they try to whitewash things. They have a brand to protect after all. Some of the megadonors are threatening to withhold donations if the story gets worse."

"Why would Ann Erickson cover up for Copeland in the first place? It's not hard to fire a teacher at a private school. Does he have something on her?"

"I believe she didn't think the complaints were all that serious. I mean, no one walked into the Upper School office and said, 'Copeland raped me.' The complaints were more along the lines of him being inappropriate, flirtatious, or mean. The former assistant recalled a student saying she felt targeted by him, not in a sexual way, but that he picked on her."

"From what I was told by the students I interviewed, Ann cares deeply about Windemere girls. Everyone had positive things to say about her."

"It's true. That's what's been so hard. It's bad enough to find out we had a wolf in our midst, but Ann has always been revered, so it's also the disappointment and shame of knowing that she had the power to investigate him many years earlier."

"Are Ann and Copeland particularly tight? Does she know him well or have a particular fondness for him that obstructed her judgment?"

"I wouldn't say they're close. They know each other well as they've worked together for so many years. I think Ann dismissed any allegations in her mind because perhaps she didn't want to believe them or didn't feel like conducting an investigation that would draw attention to the school. He also had stellar teacher reviews from the students themselves. I'm sure you've heard how well liked he was on campus. Perhaps she figured a few complaints over nearly two decades wasn't a big deal when everyone else seemed downright enamored."

The waiter approaches to see if we need anything else, but I wave him away. I don't want her to stop now. "Is there a transcript of that interview with the ex-assistant or anything I could use?"

"I don't have access to materials from the investigation, but I know what I heard in the room. I'm hoping you can dig around and get to the bottom of things yourself. I want to believe we are doing the best job for Windemere, but I don't know." Her eyes cast downward upon saying this.

"Is there something else you wanted to share?" I've been doing this long enough to know that the answer is yes.

"This really needs to stay between you and me." She exhales. "I don't have any real proof of this, but they hired a PI to dig up dirt on the girls, and their associates."

I feel like my face is on fire. "Forgive me if I don't look surprised. And they're hardly girls anymore. Eva and Sasha are in their thirties for Christ's sake."

"I'm not sure what, if anything, has been found, or if they are going to leak anything. God, I hope they wouldn't be that evil, but I just don't know. I heard rumblings that they're going through a parent so that it can't be traced to the administration. I'm honestly terrified that something could happen to impede the LAPD's investigation, or that the Jane Does will change their mind because of some kind of intimidation."

"I think they're savvy enough to recognize that Windemere is capable of just about anything. This is the reason they never came forward before. They always knew it would be their word against his, their word against Windemere's, their word against a criminal justice system where prosecutors get to decide if a crime is worth pursuing. They didn't have control then and they barely have it now."

"Were you a lawyer in your past life?" Her laugh releases some of the tension she's clearly been feeling, but before I can answer, her alarm begins to buzz. "Oh shoot, I have to get going; it's time for pickup."

She places a five-dollar bill on the table for her drink, and I stand to shake her hand. "I appreciate your time and hope we can speak again."

"I hope so too." She looks relieved to have gotten this off her chest and begins gathering her stuff. "Oh, one last thing. Do you know who Ann Erickson is married to?"

"No. Should I?"

"Her former teacher. It's an open secret. She was nineteen when they met. He was a distinguished professor at UCLA, and left his wife for her, but I believe he's long retired and in poor health. But they've been together for thirty-plus years so it's the real deal."

"Well that is"—I search for the right word—"fascinating."

Once I get back into my car, I write down as many notes as I can think of. Normally, I would go right back to the office to get to work, but I want to see Ben. I've managed to surprise myself with how often he's crossed my mind since the other night. Plus, it's after school hours and I know I won't be able to reach anyone at Adams until the morning. I text him and he says he'll meet me as soon as he finishes up with a student.

"Since it will be nearly five, what do you say to a drink in Brentwood?"

He writes back immediately: "A dimly lit bar with you? Yes."

I arrive before Ben and sink into one of the cozy black leather booths. It's quiet now, but the mahogany-trimmed room turns into a lively spot for the over-forty crowd as the night goes on. It's not my typical scene, what with the fifteen-dollar martinis and all, but several of my Westside sources enjoy coming here and the food is always good.

"I always thought this was the place you'd come if you were having an affair." Ben has appeared while I read a news story on my phone. He slides into the booth and kisses me on the cheek. Before I can say anything, a middle-aged woman has appeared asking what we'd like to drink.

"A glass of rosé would be great."

"I'll take a Balvenie. The twelve, please."

"You got it, darling." She winks at him.

"The older ladies must love you. I imagine some of the moms enjoy being around you."

"If they do, I wouldn't know. I'm just one of the many contract laborers who are helping to get their kid from point A to point B. I imagine I occupy a place in these women's minds somewhere between the gardener and family therapist."

"It's refreshing to see a waitress that age. I'm always shocked when I'm served by someone in L.A. who's in the profession as their actual profession."

"That's part of the charm of this place. Ever since I turned forty a few years ago, I feel strange going into most bars since they're filled with twentysomethings. I don't want to be the creepy old guy. So, how did your meeting go?"

"She was great and to the point. Thank you, again, for your help. I'm not sure we'd be this far without you."

"I hardly did anything except vouch for you, which isn't hard. Xhana's definitely one of the good ones. From what I've seen so far, she cares about her kids and treats them as actual people rather than trophies or pawns. What has the response been to your latest piece?"

"It didn't get as much play as Caryn's story, of course, but we had a ton of comments and sharing on social, according to Eric. More importantly, I think it will force the board into more transparency. We're going to see it through until we know the full story."

The waitress serves us our drinks and we clink glasses. The first sip goes down so easy that I'm tempted to finish the entire glass inside of thirty seconds, but my maximum is two drinks on a weeknight, so I decide to pace myself. Ben inches closer to me. "I told you I couldn't stop thinking about you."

Another couple is seated on the other side of the room and paying us no attention so it feels like we're the only ones here. "I've thought about you, too."

Was Ben always this handsome? I always thought he was kind and funny, but I never saw him as sexy until now. I give him a quick kiss because I know it will break up the nerves I feel in my stomach. He smiles and I realize I can see his dimples underneath his beard.

"Would you lovebirds like to order something to eat?"

My eyes widen in embarrassment, but Ben doesn't miss a beat. "They have really good meatballs. And the Maui onion rings are sort of life-changing."

"Either is fine with me."

"Then we'll take both." He hands over our menus. "Now, back to you thinking about me. In what instances were you thinking about me and what were you wearing at the time?"

"Ben."

"I'm just teasing you. I know how busy you must be. If I can be so much as a passing thought in that mind of yours, then I'll take it."

"There's something I've been wanting to ask you." I break eye contact out of embarrassment. "The other night, you made it seem like you were interested in me before our dinner. If that was the case, why did I not know that? And I have a follow-up question after that."

"It's not a presser, Jane." He laughs. "You can ask me as many questions as you like. I can't think of anything better than being grilled by you." There's an awkward pause as we both recognize that there could be something better we could be doing right now.

"Are you going to answer my question?"

"I've been interested in you since I started at the *Daily*. Since the first meeting in Eric's office when Celia said, 'Ben, this is Jane March.' " I'm in disbelief as I'm certain this is not the typical reaction most men have when meeting me. I know I can come off as cold or abrasive at times, and I'm far from a flirt. "I had read your stuff for years. I don't know if I told you that at the time. I had enormous respect for you as a reporter, but I never knew what you looked like. I'd never heard your voice or seen the way you'd spar with Ethan when you knew you were right about something. I don't think we spoke much at first, but it wasn't long before I saw you in action. I liked everything I saw and heard."

"I'm flattered. A bit confused, but flattered."

"After a few weeks on staff, I asked Eric what your deal was. He said, 'Her deal is that she's the best and brightest writer we have. She's out of your league.' "

"Out of your league?" I can't help but laugh because it sounds preposterous. "Of course Eric wouldn't want two of his staffers dating or hooking up. It wouldn't be good for the paper."

"It wouldn't have been good for the newsroom. When I moved to L.A. to accept the job, I left behind someone who I was with for many years. We decided she would stay behind and very quickly, we realized it wasn't going to work doing the whole long-distance thing. So the last thing I was looking for when I started at the *Daily* was a relationship. I would have loved to get to know you better, you know, outside the office, but I had too much respect for you to put you in an uncomfortable situation. If I had thought you had any interest in me, then maybe it would have been different."

"Wow."

"Now, what's your follow-up question?" He puts his hand on mine for a moment, rubbing it softly, and I feel excitement travel throughout my body.

"What about that night at the sports bar when I was hammered?"

"I wasn't sure if you remembered." He's grinning now. "That was the first time I saw a different side of you—a more relaxed and playful side. We were throwing darts and playing that hook 'em game, remember? I'm not sure what came over you, but trust me, I was more than happy to be the object of your drunken affection. It gave me a kernel of hope that you liked me in some small way, whether it was entirely subconscious or random luck."

"But then why did you push me away? That's what I was told, anyway."

"Because I wanted to earn it myself. I didn't want to have some meaningless make out session with you on Grand Avenue. I wanted it to be different. You didn't seem like a woman to just hook up with once or twice."

"I'm glad. I was always so mortified by my behavior that night that I think I avoided socializing with you after that out of sheer embarrassment. I guess that's why I didn't do a better job of staying in touch once you left."

"When you called me about the Copeland story, I was excited to hear from you. I always hoped to see you again. I often asked about you when I'd talk to some of the guys at work. I guess they never mentioned it. You have no idea how nervous I was walking into that restaurant last week."

"Why would you be nervous?"

"Because it was you. Don't you get it? You're Jane March. I'm still a little nervous."

After being treated as an average person—someone you'd

take or leave—for much of my romantic dating life, this new feeling of admiration and appreciation is more than welcome. I just hope he's not too disappointed when he realizes I won't live up to this idealized image he has of me.

After we finish our drinks and stop picking at the appetizers, I signal the waitress to bring the check. Ben walks me out to the small parking lot around the corner. The sun has begun to set, so everything is cast in a magical golden light that makes the world seem okay for about an hour each day. I fiddle with my car keys, knowing that I don't want to say goodbye just yet. He kisses me and asks when he can see me again. I ask him if he wants to follow me to my place, warning him that it may be a bit messy. He looks happier than a kid on Christmas morning.

Chapter Twelve

Eva

"They're finally asleep." Jesse tiptoes into our room and gently closes the door behind him. The girls, who for the first six years of their lives preferred that I and I alone put them to bed, are now insistent on their dad being the one. Because I hate feeling left out, I've been known to eavesdrop on story time from the hallway, falling deeper in love with my husband with each passing night as I hear him act out various storybook characters and lead them in their bedtime prayers. I can't recall more than a few instances of my own dad tucking me in at night. Dads weren't all that involved when I was a kid, not like they are now.

Ever since Caryn's story came out and I became involved in the Copeland case, I cherish the girls' bedtime, which can last up to an hour depending on how much pushback he gets, because it gives me some time to think at the end of the day. With Jane's new story, things are starting to feel more heightened, like the stakes are greater. I've never been quoted in a newspaper before, let alone the largest one in Los Angeles, and I certainly never imagined I would be under these circumstances. The detective I'm working with at LAPD believes there's plenty of evidence for the district attorney's office to bring charges. For all the complaints about city bureaucracy, I'm shocked by how fast everything is moving.

I never stayed in touch with any Windemere girls after the first few years out of high school, so I'm not sure what their reaction is to Jane's story. I suppose I could go online and see, but the victim advocate at the police station suggested that we avoid internet comments. Within my own Facebook network of friends, filled with former colleagues, extended family, and other moms I've met through the girls' school, I've seen the story—and plenty of outrage—posted. It's a dreamlike feeling to watch several people you know openly discuss Copeland and Windemere as a current events topic. Most of my acquaintances online have no idea that I attended the famed school, and I never bothered to list that particular fact in my About section as I've always been a private person. I imagine the shock they would feel if I announced that I was Jane Doe.

Jesse worries about me a lot, especially because I haven't told my family or close friends the truth about my involvement with Copeland or about my participation in the investigation. One of my girlfriends from childhood, Pamela, saw Jane's story and immediately forwarded it to me to see if I knew anyone involved. I wrote back something noncommittal and along the lines of "That's awful." I hate to lie, even in these extraordinary circumstances, but I am simply not ready to come forward or risk being outed to the entire internet. I like to think I could trust my friends and family, but it doesn't feel right yet.

Whenever this is all over, I'll make a decision about coming forward to some people, but I can't have the entire peanut gallery in my head right now. I've always been the dutiful daughter, older sister, doting wife, and loving mother. Since I was a kid, I let others tell me who I was supposed to be and how I should behave. It's taken until now to realize that I need to take care of myself, first, so that I may be strong enough for whatever is to come in the near future.

After brushing his teeth, Jesse joins me in our bed so we can start our own nightly ritual of watching something from our DVR. I notice he's been picking lighthearted comedies and game shows lately and I wonder if it's because he's trying to protect me from seeing something upsetting. While I appreciate the thoughtful concern, it's also impossible to prevent me from seeing stories—fictional or real—that will remind me of my own reality. Teacher and student relationships, sexual assault, court cases, procedural cop dramas—they're all over the place.

He gets into our queen-size bed but stays on his side. I turn to face him but he keeps his eyes facing toward the television. "There's something that's been bothering me."

"What is it?" I sit up.

"I know you're going through a lot of stuff with all this Copeland shit, and I'm really sorry about it all. If I could make it disappear somehow I would, but it's kind of scary to me that you kept this to yourself all these years." He finally looks me in the eyes. "That you could essentially lie to me."

I scoot closer toward him and put my hand on his thigh. "I wish I told you sooner too."

"It just makes me wonder what else you could be hiding. It's messing with my head a bit that you could keep such a big secret. I've known you for ten years."

I'm taken aback by what he's implying, but don't want to overreact or get emotional right now. "I'm not hiding anything from you. I was so ashamed of that time at Windemere and never wanted to change your image of me."

"But I'm your husband. You should be able to tell me anything."

"I'm sorry, babe. I promise you this is it. There is no other secret or revelation you don't know about."

His expression softens and I'm relieved. "I have an idea." I rub my hand over his flat stomach. "But it doesn't involve TV." His eyes quickly light up. It's rare that I initiate sex, but that doesn't mean I don't enjoy it. With my small business and the responsibilities that come with being the mother of twin girls, I'm usually too exhausted at the end of the day to think about intimacy.

Before Jesse's work schedule changed, we could often enjoy time together in the midmorning, when I'd be more awake and the girls were at school. I'm careful to never let too much time pass as I think sex is a powerful way of staying connected, literally and figuratively. Maybe I learned it from Copeland's talk of his own troubled marriage. Regardless, I'm thankful that we're still so attracted to one another after all these years.

"Are you sure, babe?" He looks surprised as I toy with the waistband of his sweatpants.

"Of course I'm sure." Jesse is irresistible as far as I'm concerned.

"That's the smile that gets me every time." I turn on my side, facing him, and he rubs his hand down my waist and over my hip. "You could be in dental commercials, you know that right?"

"You told me that on our first date." I nuzzle into his neck and kiss the sensitive spot right behind his ear.

"I had never seen a smile like yours before. Most girls I grew up with had no real reason to smile. You were different, always seeing the good in people, the good in me."

"A person would have to be blind and deaf to not see the good in you."

I slept well last night. That hasn't been the case since Dr. Copeland became a central focus of my day-to-day life again, so I'm grateful. I feel rested and ready to tackle the day: getting the girls ready for school, handling drop off, picking up groceries for the week, and making a new batch of cards this afternoon. Jesse got up before me, when it was still dark, so he could get a quick workout in before heading to the cable company where he works in IT.

"Babe?" he calls to me from downstairs.

"Yeah?"

"Your phone is blowing up." He hands me my iPhone, which has several missed calls and a bunch of texts. My brain immediately goes to the worst-case scenario. I'm convinced that someone has died or there's a serious issue at the girls' school, but I quickly realize that's not the case.

"Good Morning," reads a text from Caryn. "I wanted to be the first person to tell you that Copeland was arrested early this morning. I will never be able to properly thank you for what you've done. I'll be around this afternoon if you want to chat."

And from Jane: "My source at the DA's office said they're charging him with multiple counts. Bail is going to be high—in the hundreds of thousands. He'll be arraigned this week. You, Sasha, and Caryn deserve all the credit. Congratulations."

Even though I'm thrilled by the news, and expected it could happen at some point, I'm still caught off guard and lose all control of my emotions. I drop my phone and Jesse picks it up and hands it back to me. Tears are flowing fast and I feel like I can't catch my breath. I don't know how I thought I would react to this news when it came, but it certainly wasn't like this. "They arrested him" is all I can say, stunned to hear the words aloud, even though they came from me. The girls scamper around upstairs, so I ask Jesse to finish helping them get ready. He sighs like this is a lot to ask, but heads toward the staircase. I don't want them to see me like this, so I go outside and start walking briskly, away from our ranch-style house.

I text Jesse to let him know that I'll be back in a few minutes. I just need to compose myself. I don't want the girls to worry about me. The last thing a child should be doing is worrying about their mother, especially at this age. How could I possibly explain it to them without doing permanent damage? "I can take them to school today," he writes back. "I just need to know you'll be okay. I don't want to leave you like this. I want to talk to you." I attempt to compose myself, but I feel like the wind's been knocked out of me. Neighbors are probably starting to wonder what I'm doing out on the street, without a dog or workout clothes, aimlessly wandering around. "I promise I'll be okay," I write. "I just need ten minutes, maybe twenty, and then I'll be back."

When I return home, I'm surprised to see Jesse's car still there. He should have already left if he was going to get them there on time. I take a deep breath and walk inside the house, through the garage. He's standing in the kitchen and pouring a cup of coffee. "Where are they?"

"I asked Tracy to take them this morning. I told them you weren't feeling well and I had a meeting to go to. She's going there too and she always said if we were stuck to give her a call."

"Thank you." I can feel my eyes are already swollen from crying. "I didn't know I would be this emotional. I thought I'd be happy and dancing around or something. I've never helped get someone arrested before. No one mentioned how it might feel."

"I don't know what to think either. There's no handbook for something like this."

"The best way I can describe it is like an onion. There are a lot of layers and they're being peeled away over a period of time as I learn new information with each passing day. I think I have a lot more anger than I'd like to admit."

Jesse steps closer to me and wipes the newest batch of tears away with his thumb. "I'm not sure what to say. I want to be there for you, but I'm not sure I have any answers. Maybe you should talk to someone at church?"

"Maybe." The idea of bringing this to our pastor is unappealing. I don't want to be told right now that I need to forgive Copeland or understand him. I'm too angry and raw, even though this happened so long ago. "LAPD has a victim's advocate. I could give her a call."

"I don't know how to fix this, but I bet a professional does." Jesse pours himself a glass of juice I made from our orange trees in the backyard.

I don't think he'll ever understand that this isn't something you fix or heal because you talk to someone for a few hours. Especially now, when there's so much we don't know. Are we all going to be in court together? Is Copeland going to plead guilty to avoid the spectacle and attention that comes with a trial? Will the media intensify now that he's been arrested? I have so many questions. "You should get to work. I'm sure I'll talk to the other girls today and I'll feel better after that. This whole thing is a process."

"We have a big meeting at ten, so I better get in there. I'll be swamped most of the afternoon, but I'll see you later."

I kiss him goodbye and am relieved to have the house to myself. I finish my coffee, take some more deep breaths, and write back to Caryn and Jane. I go online and search "Gregory Copeland" into Google, but nothing new pops up.

Although I feel a type of closeness to Caryn, and am comfortable talking to Jane, Sasha is the one I need most right now. She hasn't replied to the group text from earlier this morning, but it's possible she's not awake yet. It wouldn't surprise me if she didn't keep traditional hours. None of us are clear on what she does for a living, if she lives with someone or alone, or if she has anyone to talk to if needed. I try my best not to judge people, but from our brief meeting, it seemed obvious that she was not in a great place.

The other day, I managed to find my old Windemere yearbooks in a dusty box in the garage. Sure enough, I found a seventeen-year-old Sasha in one of them. I'm not sure why I can't remember her on campus, as I'm pretty good with faces, but it has been nearly twenty years so I cut myself some slack. In the black-and-white thumbnail photo, she's edgier and cooler-looking than the rest of the girls in her class. While others on the page look as though they were captured smack in the midst of their awkward adolescence—braces, acne, baby fat, insecurity—Sasha has a mysterious expression on her face that resides somewhere between a scowl and a smirk. I've looked at the picture on five different occasions and each time I notice something different about her. It said she played the violin and preferred being "surrounded by books instead of people."

Although I don't know much about Sasha beyond what she's told us, it's clear that we're living in different worlds. We don't share any physical or personality traits from what I can tell, and where I was naïve in high school, Sasha looks like someone who was experienced. Her eyes manage to pierce the page, like she's daring the camera to do something. I can see how she could captivate a grown man, even though that grown man should know better. I decide to text her, because I want to talk to her about Copeland's arrest, and because I'm getting scared. There are things I want to say to her that I don't want to talk to Jesse or our pastor or a therapist about. She is the only person I know on this planet who is going through the same exact thing as me.

By the afternoon, Jane's latest story is online and will run in tomorrow's paper. "It'll be above the fold," she writes in her email to me, which I gather to mean that the story is important enough to run on the front page of Los Angeles's biggest newspaper. I'm not sure what to think about that.

Ex-Windemere School for Girls Teacher Arrested on Sex Charges Involving Former Students
By Jane March

A former English teacher at Windemere School for Girls, a private all-girls high school in Los Angeles, was arrested Tuesday on felony charges of sex crimes involving two former students at the school, authorities said.

Gregory James Copeland, 50, was arrested Tuesday

morning and released hours later on $320,000 bail. He faces nine counts each of oral copulation of a person under 18 and sexual penetration by a foreign object of a person under 18.

Copeland allegedly initiated a sexual relationship with two different 15-year-old students beginning in 1998 and 2000, respectively, according to a district attorney's office statement. He is scheduled to be arraigned Thursday in downtown Los Angeles.

Two victims came forward to police in May after sexual harassment allegations against Copeland surfaced in an essay by another former Windemere student that was published in the Sunday magazine of the Daily *in April.*

Copeland, who worked at Windemere for nearly twenty years, could not be reached for comment Wednesday.

"Windemere expresses deep sympathies for the victims of the sexual misconduct that has come to light," said a statement by the school. "We have no further comment at this time."

In May, Windemere assembled a Special Investigative Committee after numerous alumnae of the elite school reported misconduct by Copeland. Citing "a commitment to transparency," their findings are expected to be shared with the Windemere community.

Copeland faces more than 12 years in state prison, the district attorney's office said.

The Los Angeles Police Department's sex crimes unit is investigating the case. Detectives said Wednesday that they interviewed two other alleged victims, but one incident happened too long ago to file charges and the other occurred outside the state of California.

Chapter Thirteen

Sasha

S till groggy and a bit sore from last night's impromptu living room dance party, I open my front door to find two older ladies with Watchtower pamphlets in their hands. "Are you fucking kidding me?" I slam the door in their faces. Anyone who rings your bell at eight in the morning, unsolicited, deserves nothing less. I shuffle back to bed, relieved to find that I am alone, and manage to go back to sleep for a few more hours thanks to a black eye mask and headphones that block out the noise of the city waking up. It's just past eleven in the morning when I finally see the news about Copeland's arrest.

One thing worse than starting your day with a pair of Jehovah's Witnesses is being in a group text that never ends. Leave it to Caryn, the millennial of our weird little group, to have initiated a chain that is now twenty-eight messages deep. The other night, in a drunken haze, I renamed the group conversation The Roses. I read the first few messages before selecting the Leave This Conversation option, the single greatest iPhone invention since the forward-facing camera. I notice that Eva has texted me separately several times with a worried tone, so I write back with the thumbs-up emoji to placate her, and tell her I'll talk to her soon. I can't deal with all of this for at least a few more hours.

I throw on a pair of yoga pants, even though I haven't done yoga in years, grab the weathered pack of American Spirits miraculously left behind in the kitchen, and step into the alleyway. As soon as the cigarette touches my lips, before I've even lit it, I feel calmer. I play with the lighter in my right hand for a moment before forcing the spark wheel with my thumb. I've loved this ritual since high school when I'd sneak out of the music room and puff away behind the building. I remember smoking in front of Dr. Copeland after one of our many trysts, and he was so disappointed in me. His little lecture about well-being was rich considering he was the one committing crimes several times a week. In one second, I have a flame that ignites the tobacco, nicotine, tar, and cigarette paper into smoke that I suck into my lungs where it's quickly absorbed by my bloodstream and tissue. Because it's the first one of the day, I catch a little buzz; a feeling of lightheadedness and tingling spreads throughout my body.

A minute later, a ruddy homeless man approaches with a mangy dog and an unsolicited opinion. "You're too beautiful to be a smoker." I turn to face the other way. "I want to see you smile, baby girl. C'mon, just give me one smile then I'll leave you alone." It's not enough to have religion brought to my door, apparently, now there's concern for my health in a litter-filled alleyway.

I turn back around to face him. "Please forgive me." I put on a convincing act with sad eyes. "But I don't feel like smiling or taking life advice from you. Perhaps you should consider working on yourself before telling a complete stranger how to behave." His tanned face is dumbstruck, as most women, including me at times, are too scared for their safety to ever challenge a man in public. He keeps walking before shouting "cunt" back at me. I haven't been up an hour and it's already a shitty day.

After two cups of coffee and a couple more cigarettes I'm ready to face the rest of the world. My hair's greasy, but there's no point in washing it as I'm getting it colored today. A friend who I go-go danced with back in the day has opened her own hair salon and she's been begging me to check it out for months. She's even willing to do it for free if I let them take some photos afterward.

Because of said photos, I figure I better at least slap on some concealer to hide last night's damage and I use a few eye drops to brighten the whites of my eyes. I now look at least 10 percent healthier and that's as good as it's going to get for now.

The East Hollywood salon is fifteen blocks from my apartment so I decide to walk, with headphones. I have no appetite; snorting Adderall will do that to you, but I'm thirsty and my voice sounds hoarse so I part with a dollar fifty and grab a bottle of water at the liquor store downstairs.

"Where you been?" asks Ari, the regular guy behind the counter.

"I have no money is where I've been."

"What about your mama? You came in here with her before."

"That was a long time ago. I'm not even sure where she is—we don't really talk anymore. Her newest husband made it clear that he'd only marry her if I wasn't part of the picture."

"Damn, that's cold."

"It's nothing new for her. It's always been this way. Men before women and children."

"Don't you got a sister or brother?"

"Nope." I peruse the candy section with my eyes, but won't be hungry for hours.

"You can always work here." He lets out a hearty laugh and gives me the once-over. "You'd probably be good for business."

"I'll keep it in mind." He pushes my money back and smiles. "I'm going to write you the most amazing Yelp review, I promise."

"No fucking way." Carla feigns shock upon seeing me walk into her small salon. "The elusive Miss Sasha actually showed up."

"Nice to see you too." I give her a kiss on the cheek. The exposed air ducts, ironwork fixtures, and concrete floor give the place an industrial vibe that I'm digging.

"That's a dope jacket." Carla fingers the buttery leather. "Stolen, borrowed, or thrifted?"

"Paid in full, thank you very much." The reality is I took it from a photo shoot because the stylist I was working for that day treated me like shit and the photographer tried to get me to fuck him in the bathroom.

"Good for you." She runs her fingers through the hair that's left on my head. "What do you want to do today?"

"I was thinking about going dark again. You know, to match my soul."

"You can't bullshit me. I know you're a big softie underneath it all."

"Don't tell anyone, especially him." I point to her assistant, Jorge, a heavily tattooed twentysomething who has sharper cheekbones than I do.

"You can do just about anything, but please don't fuck my assistant." She gives me a knowing smile.

"Can I get you something to drink?" he asks, making eye contact via the mirror. "Water, coffee, soda?"

"I'd love a glass of champagne." Carla gives him an approving nod and a couple of minutes later he's back with a glass of bubbly. "Won't you have one? To celebrate your opening?"

"I'm a boring sober person now." She begins mixing the bowl of color. "I always thought the world was against me, like no matter how hard I tried, I just couldn't catch a break. Turns out it was just the booze and way too much coke. I think I've gotten more done in the last eight months than in the last eight years."

I roll my eyes, but decide against teasing her because she owns her own business and has a new husband while I'm part of the gig economy and still accepting money from my grandmother when I really need it.

Jorge, defying stereotypes about men in hairdressing, is eyeing the black lace bra that's showing through the sides of my vintage Clash muscle tee. He hands me a black robe to put on over my clothes. I smile at him and he quickly disappears, embarrassed that I caught him.

Wearing black rubber gloves, Carla applies the dark color to my hair with a little paintbrush that's cold against my scalp. As she works the formula through, I realize this is the most intimate thing I've done in ages. Previously numb nerve endings are waking up, releasing what feels like dopamine into my body. I'd like to take a nap in the corner.

"Look how your eyes are popping." Carla stares at my face via the mirror. "You look extra-Russian now. God, I'd kill for those eyes. What did Jay call you? The green-eyed monster?" Even though I look like a punk rock kewpie doll at the moment, she's right. My eyes are practically jumping out of their sockets.

While the color sets, we catch up a bit. She accuses me of being impossible to track down and getting too skinny. "Curves are finally in, didn't you hear?"

I ask Jorge for more champagne. "I walked, okay?" I can feel her judging me even though she doesn't say anything.

"So what's going on with you? Have you gone to any shows lately?"

"Not really. It's been more hermit vibes lately."

"Well that's good, right?"

"I had a few people over last night, but things ended early because this ridiculous couple started fighting, like literally hitting each other, and that killed the mood."

"That sounds stressful. How are *you* doing?"

"You know, just living the dream." When it's clear I'm not going to elaborate, she brings me over to the sinks to wash the color out. I lower my head into the neck cradle, and Carla begins the rinsing process. Joy Division's "Love Will Tear Us Apart" plays overhead and I close my eyes to avoid being sprayed by the water's mist. She shampoos my hair, massaging my head with her strong fingers, and I start feeling sad. I want a smoke, a drink, and a Xanax, in that order.

"Since when are you so quiet?" Carla feverishly dries my hair with a towel before pulling out a hairdryer. "Usually you don't shut up."

"I just have a lot of shit going on today." It isn't a lie. Jane and the others want to meet up tonight to discuss Copeland and I'm not looking forward to it.

"Well let's at least get your hair looking right." She sets the dryer to high. "We'll snap a few pics for our Instagram and you can get back to your day. Remember when we modeled for that guy?"

"If you mean do I remember amateur photo shoots with cheesy props, bad lighting, and a total perv photographer, then yes."

"Oh he was harmless."

The salon's not exactly packed, but she's come a long way from the days of us posing as modern-day pinups. There's only one photo I ever kept from those days because it's the only one I ever liked. I'm sitting on the floor, wearing a sixties baby doll dress and thigh-high tights that rolled down from the top. My tits are squeezed together, offering a hint of what lies beneath, and the dress's long bell sleeves cover the majority of my tattoos. My hair, which was cut into a severe bob at the time, brushes across enough of my face to hide the bad makeup job. I was probably twenty-three or twenty-four, but I could still pass as a teenager in those days.

I jump in an Uber, running late, and head to the designated meeting spot, a loungy bar in Koreatown. They wanted to meet on Larchmont but I hate that entire village. I was able to plead my case by pointing out that we'd be discussing adult subject matter and Larchmont is notorious for being patronized by kids and families.

To my surprise, I'm the first to arrive, so I order a vodka soda and a shot of vodka, which I throw back quick. Two guys who look like they're waiting out traffic after work attempt to engage me in conversation. They introduce themselves and I tell Tom, the more forward one of the two, that I'm waiting for someone.

"Who would ever keep someone like you waiting?"

"A for effort." I turn to face him. "I'm sorry to tell you, but I don't go out with guys named Tom anymore. And I really am meeting someone." I grab my drink and turn to go find a discreet table that will accommodate the four of us. Tom immediately rises from his bar stool. "Are you going to be escorting me?" I ask. He steps closer, coming toward me like he's going to tell me a secret I didn't ask to hear. I am way too sober for this invasion of space and feel my body tense up as some sort of natural protection. His breath smells like bourbon and it makes me want to gag.

He gets inches from my face. "You're fucking sexy." The bartender makes eye contact with me, silently communicating that he's there if I need him. Tom tilts his head to the side and looks me up and down like he's inspecting an exotic car. "I bet you're an angel underneath it all."

" 'You must neither expect nor exact anything celestial of me—for you will not get it, any more than I shall get it of you, which I do not at all anticipate.' " I've found that quoting Brontë is the quickest way to shut a man up, at least for a few moments. Before he can respond, I feel someone tugging at my bomber jacket.

"I almost didn't recognize you." Eva looks wildly out of place in her chambray button-down shirt and ankle-cut mom jeans. She has to get on her tiptoes to give me a hug and I ask if she wants a drink. She gets a club soda and I lead her away from the bar, away from them.

"You're not going to say thank you?" Tom shouts out once I'm a few feet away. I pretend I didn't hear him over the music and chatter.

"What was that about?" Eva's eyes are on him as she sits down.

"Nothing. Just some guy. How are you?"

"I'm okay, a little nervous, to be honest. I like your hair."

"Back to black, for now at least." I tuck part of my long bangs behind my ear.

"Caryn texted me to say she and Jane were running a bit late because of traffic."

"God, is there anything more boring than talking about traffic?"

Eva looks confused, wondering if I've insulted her.

"I don't mean you're boring," I add.

"Well they should be here soon. So what have you been doing? We haven't heard much from you."

"I don't have a car anymore because my nightmare ex took it when he decided to go back on tour with his old band, so that complicated things for me."

"Oh, I'm sorry to hear that."

"It's fine. He ripped my heart out, so he may as well have taken my car, too." I gnaw on my drink's short black straw. "I was working as a stylist's assistant but that required driving all over town and being on time for shoots, so now I'm doing odd jobs here and there."

"I was going through my old Windemere yearbooks the other day, and I saw you in one." She smiles as I grimace.

"I burned my yearbooks the day after graduation, so I haven't seen mine since then." Even though I desperately wanted the education, I was more than ready to be done with Windemere, which I blamed for everything that my life had become by graduation day. "Did I look crazy?"

"No, you looked beautiful." Eva's smile is so bright white that it's practically purple under the dim lights. "It said you played the violin."

"Yeah, B.C." Eva looks confused. "Before Copeland. Once everything happened I could no longer concentrate or focus on music. I hated him for taking away my ability to enjoy one of the things I was really good at. I got a lot of my confidence from playing, but after Copeland, I would play a certain note and just burst out crying in front of people. It was mortifying. Eventually I just stopped playing."

Eva goes to place her hand on top of mine as a gesture of comfort or relation, but I quickly move it away. "Sorry" we both say simultaneously.

"Maybe you could start playing again. I'm sure it's like riding a bicycle. One of my best friends works at a music store in Pasadena. She could probably hook you up."

I think how lucky Eva's daughters are to have her as their mother and give her a closed-mouth smile. "Did you play anything at Windemere? Sports or music?"

"I sang in the choir sophomore year, but then stopped. I really wanted to join the swim team as I always enjoyed being in the water, but my parents vetoed that because I needed to get home to watch my sisters."

I want to ask her more questions, but I know the dynamic duo from the *Daily* will walk in at any moment. Eva asks how I feel about the arrest and I explain that I'm pleased, but thought we'd at least get a heads-up.

"It definitely took me by surprise," she says. "I was much more emotional than expected. For a while I was amped about coming forward and you know, doing the right thing, but now I'm feeling a lot of different emotions."

"I'm sure I would be too if I weren't medicated. Antidepressants can have a kind of numbing effect." She eyes my drink and I know what she's thinking.

"Hey." Caryn appears, almost breathless, and Jane trails

behind her, eyes glued to her phone. They exchange hugs with Eva as though they are all old friends from the same Girl Scout troop and look at me like a wild animal they're not sure if they should approach. I get up and give Caryn a side hug and Jane a head nod. They make meaningless chitchat for a few minutes as if we don't all know why we're really here. In an attempt to break the ice, I comment that we're an odd-looking group.

"What do you mean?" Eva asks. "We could just be a group of colleagues."

"I've never seen an office like this."

Jane laughs. "Well, it's dark enough that I'm not sure anyone would notice or care. The reason I wanted us to meet is because I wanted to share some things with you before they come out tomorrow." Caryn looks relaxed; she must already know whatever Jane is going to share. I hate that they know more about everything than I do when I more than paid the price of admission. Eva is unconsciously rubbing her thumb and forefinger together like she's trying to start a fire. I wish she would have a real drink so she could calm down.

"We're listening." I motion for the waitress to stop by our table.

"A source from Windemere got in touch with me because she believed there was more to the story than what had been reported or admitted to by the school. I hope you understand that I can't share who that source is, but I can tell you that they are credible."

"What did they tell you?" Eva is biting her lower lip.

"They suggested that there had been complaints about Copeland way before Caryn."

"I think we figured as much," Eva says, "but that helps us, doesn't it?"

"Absolutely." Jane sits up straighter. "I haven't been able to confirm this on the record, but I'm working on it."

"Is that the bombshell news?" I ask.

"The other item that was shared was to do with Copeland's employment history."

"I assumed he went to work at Windemere straight out of graduate school." Eva's voice is shaking at this point.

"I always thought the same." Caryn blinks, hard. "I couldn't recall any instance of him mentioning working at another school. In fact, I think I even asked him about it during the interview for that stupid profile."

"Well he did. He taught English and was a soccer coach at Adams, a private K through eight in Thousand Oaks, for a few years. He actually attended the school himself during middle school."

This is all news to me. When I knew him, he spoke about his public school education and never mentioned that he was a privileged brat like most Windemere girls. "I thought he only liked teenage girls." I feel like I might throw up, but I continue on. "I hope you're not here to tell us he did something to some kid."

"Not that I'm aware of. But he was fired. The administrator I spoke with said several students had complained about Copeland, including one female who said he flirted with her, and a male student who said he got into a physical altercation with him."

"Wait, I'm not following," Eva interrupts. "A K through eight means the oldest student would be thirteen or fourteen. Are you saying he got physical with a boy under fourteen?"

"That's what's in his file and why he was finally fired. So there was a clear pattern of misconduct from early on in his career. I'm working on talking to their Head of School. His assistant believed he would go on the record because he's been following the Windemere case and 'was horrified,' according to her."

"I didn't think I could have a lower opinion of this man." Caryn has lost at least a shade of color from her face. I guess she didn't know what Jane was going to say.

"What we need to find out is whether or not Windemere knew this and hired him anyway."

"I'm shocked." Eva shakes her head. "If these things happened at Adams and were true, why would he even be allowed to teach at Windemere?" I want whatever it is Eva has that makes her this bewildered. Her naïveté is something to behold. Has she been living in the same city and on the same planet as the rest of us for all these years?

We eventually say our goodbyes. Eva has to get back home to her kids, Caryn has an exam tomorrow, and Jane must be boning someone because I saw the way her face lit up every time she got a text. She doesn't have much of a poker face for an award-winning journalist. The last thing I want to do is go back home, alone with the thoughts in my head, so I decide on one last drink. Maybe Tom wants to pay for it.

Chapter Fourteen

Jane

The sound of chirping birds who live in the Chinese elm tree outside my apartment wake me at sunrise and I realize I forgot to turn my white noise machine on last night. I look over and see Ben's back rise and fall with each breath. I don't usually sleep well with someone else, but had no trouble last night thanks to a progression of wine, sex, and laughter. I tiptoe out of bed, careful not to wake Ben who looks so innocent, as all men do when they sleep.

I close the door behind me and silently curse the floorboards for their noisy creaks as I head toward the living room where I find some of my clothes from last night. I check the morning's headlines on my laptop and think that the world would be a different place if everyone was high on this feeling. I eye a stack of hardbacks authored by friends and colleagues and realize that I'll never get around to them if I keep spending all my free time with Ben. But I quickly remind myself that one should always choose in-person adventures over reading about someone else's. And how long can it go on like this anyway? Eve Babitz said, "All art fades but sex fades fastest," and I've yet to disprove this.

After a few minutes, I head to the galley-style kitchen, which is really more of a storage area as I don't have the time or interest to cook, and pour myself a glass of water. Yesterday's mail is on the counter: a reminder that it's time for an oil change, a postcard from my high school's reunion committee saying that tickets are now available online, and a contract from my new speaking agent. I put the paperwork in my bag so I can look it over when I'm more coherent and plop back on the hand-me-down leather couch I scored when my neighbor moved to Phoenix for work. While I'm engrossed in today's print edition of the *New York Times*, I hear Ben stirring in the bedroom.

He makes his way down the narrow hallway, rubbing his eyes. "I thought you left and I felt used."

"Good morning." I close the paper and set it down. "I can make you coffee or tea or cereal. For anything else, you'll need to hit up that café where it takes ten minutes to get a dry muffin made with flaxseeds." He curls up next to me and starts kissing my neck, which takes me by surprise as he told me he wasn't a morning person.

"You can't sit here like this, reading the paper while the morning light hits you like that, and expect me to want coffee when I could have you instead." His smile turns devilish as he takes my hand and leads me back to the bedroom.

"This all feels dreamlike" is all I can manage before he devours my décolletage. "Most men aren't aroused by the sight of women reading the paper."

"They don't know what they're missing." He pulls back from kissing me, his hands still around my waist. "You know, I could get used to this, Jane."

Further convinced that morning is the most underrated time of day for sex, I scan my emails while Ben showers. I flag the most important ones so I can deal with them as soon as I get to work, and see one, from Windemere via Caryn, that gets my full attention. I read it quickly.

"Hi Sasha," I type before forwarding the email since I know she's no longer on Windemere's master email list. "Here's the latest and greatest from L.A.'s most prominent girls school. I hope it offers some sense of peace or feeling of progress. We'd love to see you or talk whenever you have time."

I assume she's heard that Copeland pled not guilty during his arraignment last week. We've texted her but received no replies. As I've told Caryn and Eva before, Sasha's credible but not reliable.

Dear Windemere parents, alumnae, and friends,

Several months ago, the Board of Trustees (the "Board") formed a Special Investigative Committee ("SIC") to undertake an independent investigation of matters arising out of reports of misconduct by a former teacher, Dr. Gregory Copeland ("Copeland"). The Board and SIC retained outside counsel from Chatham, Gilchrist & Wendler LLP to conduct that independent investigation, which has now concluded. A final report has been presented to the Board and in the interest of transparency, we want to share its summary and the conclusions of the investigation.

The SIC investigation revealed a disturbing pattern of misconduct by Copeland, including improper physical contact, communications, and, in some cases, harassment, involving several former Windemere students. The investigation also identified mistakes in judgment by Ann Erickson, Head of School, in responding to past allegations of misconduct. Finally, it revealed the need to improve School policies, procedures, and training, as well as to increase Board oversight.

On behalf of the Board, we offer our deepest apologies to the victims and their families, both for the inappropriate actions of Copeland and the manner in which the School initially responded to them. We also apologize to our broader community of students, parents, alumnae, supporters, faculty, and staff who care deeply about our students and the School.

Beginning of the SIC Investigation

In the spring, the School and the Board became aware that a 2012 Windemere graduate, Caryn Rodgers, had written about inappropriate communications and conduct by Copeland that occurred during the time that she was a high school student in the Daily. Following Caryn's article and the subsequent media coverage, a number of former students stepped forward and reported similar or related conduct by Copeland.

Upon learning of Caryn's article, the Board held an emergency meeting and called for a thorough examination of these complaints. The SIC was formed and authorized to retain an independent investigator, attorney Kim Holder, a partner at the law firm of Jacobs & Wells LLP.

Scope of SIC Investigation

Ms. Holder's team spent several hundred hours on the investigation, interviewing alumnae, parents of alumnae, current and former Windemere teachers, staff, administrators, Head of School Ann Erickson, prior Board Presidents, and prior legal counsel. They searched all available emails, personnel files, and related materials.

Findings Regarding Copeland

The SIC investigation validated and confirmed the serious concerns raised by Caryn and her parents in 2010, and again in 2016; it also uncovered additional misconduct, some of which was previously known by the Head of School and some of which was not. The SIC investigation found that Copeland on many occasions attempted to engage students in improper conduct, often using his position of authority to initiate improper discussions and invitations for further contact.

During the course of the SIC investigation, a separate alumna contacted the School and reported that Copeland had engaged in inappropriate physical conduct toward her over a decade ago, while she was a student and minor at the School. The LAPD and the district attorney's office have conducted an investigation, with our full cooperation. That same week, an additional victim came forward to report an inappropriate physical relationship with Copeland during her sophomore year.

In 2004, a different student reported to the Head of School improper harassing behavior by Copeland. The Board first learned of this report during the course of the SIC investigation. At the time she reported it, the student's complaint was not fully investigated by the Head of School, who incorrectly questioned the veracity and motive of the student's allegations regarding Copeland. The decision not to fully investigate the student's complaint represented a serious error in judgment by the Head of School.

In 2010, Caryn raised with the Head of School specific serious concerns regarding Copeland and provided to the Head of School copies of email correspondence from him. The emails sent by Copeland to Caryn were clearly inappropriate, as recognized by the Head of School. However, the Head of School did not fully investigate Caryn's concerns, and she failed to reevaluate the related allegations made in 2004.

Moving Forward
The School issued a newly expanded Student Antiharassment and Antibullying Policy, which has been distributed to all students, parents, and employees. It expands and clarifies the definition of "harassment" and instructs students on how to report such acts. The School's IT department has recommended improvements

to the electronic communications policies and updates to our retention and forensic capabilities, which are in the process of being implemented.

The School has scheduled eight one-hour sessions of student training and education specifically related to sexual harassment and bullying, which have been initiated and will continue throughout the year. Recent articles in the New York Times, Boston Globe, *and other widely read publications have brought attention to the pernicious problem of sexual assault on college campuses, and the School feels that extensive training on this subject is critical to make sure our girls are prepared to protect themselves, now and in the future.*

Shared Responsibilities
It is clear from the SIC investigation that the Head of School did not fulfill several crucial management and oversight responsibilities. The Board is indebted to Ann Erickson for her significant contributions and twenty-three years of dedication to Windemere School. Nevertheless, Ms. Erickson has submitted her resignation to resign effective September 30, 2016, and the Board has agreed to accept her resignation. We are working together to ensure that the transition to a new Head of School is accomplished in as smooth and orderly a manner as possible.

Conclusion
While there have been numerous requests for Windemere to publicly discuss specifics of the aforementioned cases, we do not believe it would be right to do so. The matter is now in the hands of law enforcement and will be resolved via the legal system. We are confidant that Windemere will continue to thrive as it has for nearly one hundred years. We hope that together we can build an open and healthy campus culture.

Sincerely,
Rachel Wasserman, President, Board of Trustees
Ann Erickson, Head of School

For weeks, I've been trying to get an interview with Ann Erickson. I've sent numerous emails, left multiple voice mails, and even tracked her down at home before being promptly hung up on. I knew the chances were slim to none, as people in her position are far from candid once the shit hits the fan, but since the news of her stepping down broke last week, I decided to try reaching her one last time.

Xhana said in an email that the board is devastated, but more than willing to sacrifice Ann since someone had to take the fall. Ben said the parents of his Windemere clients were experiencing a range of emotions, from relief to rage. Even though I'm going to continue to cover Windemere as a news story, I'm done interviewing students, alumnae, and parents, for now. There are other important stories to be written.

I don't know if it's because today marked the release of the board's official report, or because I was eager to put Windemere behind me until the next phase of the case, but I was not expecting this.

After the first ring I pick up the phone. "Jane March."

"Ms. March, this is Ann Erickson. I believe you're familiar."

Cradling the receiver between my shoulder and ear, I save what I was working on and open a new Word doc, so I can transcribe our conversation in real time. I feel my heart rate spike immediately, adrenaline shooting through every inch of my body.

"Yes, of course. Thank you for the callback. I must say, I'm surprised to be hearing from you now."

"Before we proceed, I'd like to make sure this conversation is completely off the record."

"Of course. I'd prefer to conduct an in-depth interview, but I will take what I can get."

"Thank you. My lawyer would kill me if he knew I was talking to *you* of all people. I know you've been busy covering the story as it unfolds, and I will say, it has been covered quite fairly."

"I'm pleased to hear that."

"Of course I wish there was no reason to be writing these stories about Windemere."

"Well, we're in the same boat then."

After some awkward silence, Ann explains that she'd like to offer me her perspective.

"I've made my peace with the decision to leave, although I will miss everyone with every ounce of my being." She sounds drained from the many years of being a surrogate mother to six hundred girls each school year. "I have a new normal to get used to."

"The students and graduates I spoke to had glowing things to say about you." I'm not sure why I feel the need to comfort this woman. "And I know many people in the Windemere community are disappointed that you chose to resign."

"I appreciate that. I'm not sure I had a choice in the matter. It was the right thing to do after the investigation, and what most people don't know is that I was looking to retire in the next year or two because my husband has some health challenges."

I want to ask her how old she was when she met her husband, if they flirted or went on secret dates while she was his student, or if it was something done out in the open. I feel a nagging need to know if her own happily-ever-after with her former teacher is why she didn't think what Copeland was doing was that big of a deal.

We speak briefly about the hiring of Dr. Copeland. She maintains that she never knew about his troubled past at Adams, and said she was also a victim of his charm and charisma.

"Having grown up in the private school world, he

immediately understood Windemere. His eyes brightened when we spoke of his dissertation research on Shakespeare's sonnets and we just hit it off right away. He had a lovely wife and they were churchgoers." Jamal, one of our new interns, stops by my desk with mail for me and I mouth a quick thank you to him. "I'm sorry to say that we did not check into his background more thoroughly. I had a friend from my book club who taught with Copeland at Adams and she had wonderful things to say about him. I thought he almost seemed too good to be true, and so we hired him."

"What about once Copeland was teaching at Windemere?" I mute the call for a moment so I can take a sip of water.

"I could show you years of evaluations where he received higher marks than any other teacher. I know you're well aware of how competitive Windemere is, even nationally. He was a star in our eyes, and perhaps that gave him more credibility than he should have been afforded."

"From my research, it seems that there is a culture of not removing bad teachers. Not just at Windemere, but a nationwide pattern, whether it be public or private school. Would you agree with that statement?" I really want to ask her what she thinks about women who are complicit in men's abuse of girls, but I don't want to scare her off the phone.

"Yes, I would," she says, slowly, as though she's counting her words.

"Why do you think that is? I believe the official term is 'organizational loyalty.'"

"I've had a lot of time to think about these issues lately. I believe, at least in my case, that I was being willfully ignorant. Perhaps I didn't want to think this could be true, as it would reflect badly on all of us, including our hardworking students." I'm surprised she's taking some responsibility. "I know the committee found that there had been other complaints about Copeland— ones that didn't end up in his file. I wanted to explain to you that this was not done for sinister purposes. Even though we are a leading institution with plenty of funds, we were often in over our heads. Today, administrators are trying to keep their students alive. Between the eating disorders, anxiety and depression, divorce, and general teenage drama, there is always something going on. Of course we want the best for Windemere girls, but there were certainly times where things fell between the cracks, or administrative paperwork was obviously ignored."

"But didn't you realize after a few students made these complaints that there could be a pattern going on? Wasn't Caryn's initial meeting with you pretty cut-and-dried with the email records and all?"

"I don't remember the other complaints." Her tone has turned curt and defensive. "They may have been made to others in the administration, I really don't know. So many years, and thousands of students, have gone by. I don't even remember Caryn's story exactly the way she does. For example, I didn't remember anything about him kissing her in the classroom. If I had known that, I believe I would have acted immediately. Yes, there were inappropriate emails, but they didn't reach a threshold of a fireable offense in my mind."

I know I need to tread carefully or she'll simply hang up the phone. I stop typing and focus on what I need to ask. "Some people believe that you or the administration didn't want to make waves since so many of these girls' parents are subsidizing the school, not just in the form of tuition, but in generous donations as well. I believe Caryn's parents have given over a hundred thousand dollars over the years, in addition to tuition payments."

"I've been a mandated reporter for decades now, Ms. March. If I truly believed Caryn was being abused or harmed in some way, I would have been forced, by law, to report that. Dr. Copeland apologized to me profusely over that incident and convinced me that it was isolated. I suppose I didn't want to draw any negative attention if it wasn't necessary, if it could be contained. I honestly didn't think something like this could happen at Windemere, right under our noses. If I did, of course I would have reacted more harshly."

"One thing that's been so perplexing as I researched this case and others like it, is that there are so many educators—ones who are good, moral people in the rest of their lives—letting this kind of thing happen."

She cuts me off before I can continue. "I understand what you mean, Ms. March, but that was not the case at Windemere." Her terse tone makes it clear I've struck a nerve, but she continues. "Were mistakes made? Yes. Could we have done more? Of course. But I will never endorse a belief that we let this happen or knew about it and ignored it. We did the best we could at the time."

There is one more thing I need to ask her since I'm guessing it will be my last chance. "I appreciate you calling and just have an additional question." I hear an audible exhalation, but she doesn't say no. "How did it all go down with Copeland? Did he resign of his own free will or did you ask him to?" There's a long pause. "All off the record, of course."

"A lot of people have asked me if I believe that he's a sociopath. I guess they assume you'd have to be one to misbehave for so many years without any known remorse. While he may not have the type of conscience we expect from our fellow citizens, I can tell you that he certainly had remorse. Unfortunately, it was for himself and not the girls." I let her keep talking while I take everything down like an amateur court reporter.

"I don't think he believed he did anything all that wrong. He repeatedly called the transgressions 'bad decisions.' He made several mentions of how mature these particular students were, and how he often felt seduced by them and not vice versa." My left brow automatically rises. "He felt very much like the victim of a witch hunt. I guess that's not all that surprising, but as the investigation went on, and he realized that he couldn't continue to lie or manipulate his way out of this, he was overcome. There were several outbursts on campus, and he became so agitated in my office one afternoon after LAPD had paid a visit that he knocked over an antique globe that was a gift from the ambassador to France."

"Is that when you gave him his walking papers?"

"The investigators made it clear to me that charges were going to be brought. I let him know that he should leave, on his own accord, before he was taken away in handcuffs. I was shocked when he said he and his wife were going to get out of town for a while. I thought women only stayed with men like that because they had no way out. Marie makes plenty of money."

"Thank you so much for your time. It has been nothing short of enlightening."

"I just ask that you consider the Windemere girls when writing any future stories."

"That consideration is why these stories need to be written."

Chapter Fifteen

Caryn

Six Months Later

Acourt clerk fiddles with paperwork while I try not to pass out from nerves. "Jane." I grab her hand. She squeezes it in return. I haven't felt this terrified in many years. Even Jane, the award-winning reporter who's normally unfazed by anything after years covering murder trials and corporate criminals in this very building, is taking deep breaths while staring at the California flag that sits to the left of the witness stand. My internship ended a few months ago, but the courthouse is just blocks from the *Daily* offices. It's surreal.

The judge enters the courtroom wearing the black robe you've seen a thousand times on TV and in movies. It's my first time in a courtroom and I'm shocked by how small it is. We're seated close to the bailiff, a member of the Los Angeles County Sheriff's Department, who has a tape dispenser on her small desk that's in the shape of a black stiletto heel.

"Case number BE 734330, People versus Gregory Copeland," says the Honorable Timothy Nelson.

My awareness of everything and everyone in the courtroom is suddenly heightened. I can hear every time someone in the four-row gallery clears their throat or shifts in their seat. One disheveled man in the row in front of me is playing a game on his phone as if he's in a waiting room at his dentist's office. A woman three seats down from Jane bolts out of the room for some unknown reason. The media is here too. I recognize a local reporter from KTLA who's been on TV since I was a kid, and other journalists and producers with credentials around their necks.

"Yes." Copeland's defense attorney, a short man in a sharp suit, sports a ring of closely cropped gray hair around his otherwise bald head.

"Appearances, please."

"Good morning, Your Honor. David Greenspan appearing with the defendant, who is present, out of custody." His white pocket square is as crisp as a new dollar bill.

"Shannon Orth, Deputy District Attorney for the people."

"I understand that the people and the defendant have reached an agreement as to a disposition; is that correct?" Judge Nelson asks.

"That is correct, Your Honor." Greenspan adjusts his wire-rim glasses. I wonder what Copeland is paying him. I wonder if they knew each other prior to this case and if he knows Copeland's wife. I wonder how much Copeland even told his attorney.

As the DA begins speaking, the court reporter types away furiously, unfazed by the packed courtroom or today's subject matter. I take inventory of the gallery. No one appears to be here on Copeland's behalf. No wife. No kids. No colleagues. Where are his friends or extended family? I remember he told me his students were his friends during the interview I did with him so many years ago. At the time, I didn't realize how sad and strange that sounded.

"Gregory James Copeland." Hearing the DA say his full name makes him sound even guiltier. "Is that correct? Is that your true name?"

"Yes." I haven't heard his voice in years. He appears to have gained at least thirty pounds since I saw him last and seems calm, all things considered. I ponder if he is perhaps medicated, as he was always an emotional man. We chose to sit a few rows behind him so he wouldn't notice me, not that it would matter if he did. My photos from the *Daily* and other corners of the internet have been blasted around the world because of the case. I'm sure he's seen it at least a hundred times. If you search my name online,

Gregory Copeland's case is all that comes up. My *Daily Trojan* stories don't stand a chance against Google's algorithm. I am forever going to be associated with this man no matter what.

"You understand the charges against you, specifically in the amended complaint BE 734330 as to counts 1 and 6, a violation of Penal Code Section 288A, subsection B, subsection 1, Oral Copulation of a person under the age of 18, and count 2, violation of Penal Code Section 289, subsection H, Sexual Penetration by a foreign object of a person under the age of 18. All felonies. Do you understand the charges?"

"Yes."

"Do you also understand that these charges are filed pursuant to an extension of the statute of limitations under both Penal Code Section 803, subsection F, and Penal Code Section 801.1? Do you understand?"

"Yes."

"Have you discussed both the charges and statute of limitations allegations with your attorney, including any defenses?"

"Yes."

"And as a result of those discussions, it is my understanding that you wish to enter guilty pleas today in respect to those charges?"

"Yes."

"You will be pleading to counts 1, 2, and 6. In exchange for those pleas, you will be sentenced to five years of formal probation. You will serve one year in the county jail. Do you understand the terms of the agreement?"

"Yes."

"Before the court will accept your plea, you first must understand and give up certain constitutional rights. You have the right to a preliminary hearing. You have the right to a court trial. You have the right to confront and cross-examine the witness against you. You have the right to use the subpoena power of the court at no cost to you. You have the right to present a defense and to testify as part of that defense. However, no one can force you to testify. You also have the right to remain silent in the right against self-incrimination. Do you understand each of those rights?"

"Yes."

"Do you waive and give up each of those rights?"

"Yes."

"Before the court will accept your plea, you must also understand the consequences of your plea. Again, you will be placed on formal probation, in this case, for five years. The court will impose certain terms and conditions of probation. If you violate the terms of your probation, the court can sentence you up to the maximum in state prison, which is five years on the count to which you are pleading. Once you complete the sentence, you will be placed upon parole or postrelease community supervision. If you were to violate your parole or postrelease community supervision, you could be sent back into custody. Your conviction will constitute a prior prison conviction within the meaning of Penal Code section 667.5, subsection B. Do you understand all of that?"

"Yes."

"Your plea here today will also mean you have been convicted of a felony. This condition can be used to increase or enhance any punishment you receive on future crimes. Because this is a 290 registerable offense, any future prison sentence you receive will be served pursuant to Penal Code Section 1170, Subsection H, Subsection 3, meaning you'll be actually serving state prison custody time. Do you understand that?"

"Yes."

"As a result of your plea here today, you can no longer possess, own, or use a firearm, as that would constitute a violation of your probation supervision or parole. Do you understand that?"

"Yes."

"Pursuant to Penal Code Section 290, because of your plea here today, you are required to register as a sex offender with law enforcement upon your release and within five days of moving to a new city or county. You must also update registration annually within five working days of your birth date; failure to register would violate your probation, mandatory supervision, or postrelease community supervision or parole, and may also be charged as a separate crime against you. And you understand that registration as a sex offender is a lifetime requirement?"

"Yes."

"Are you waiving your right to challenge the plea, to challenge pleas based upon the statute of limitations, and are you doing so freely and voluntarily?"

"Yes."

"Has anyone made threats or promises to you or anyone close to you in order to get you to plead?"

"No."

"Are you pleading because you believe it's in your best interest to do so today?"

"Yes."

"Your Honor, do you wish me to inquire any further?"

"No. You may take the pleas."

She reads count 1, Oral Copulation of a Person Under 18, a felony, as to Jane Doe 1—Eva, who's seated one row in front of us with her husband who has his eyes closed like he might be praying. I met him for a brief moment outside the courthouse and he was soft-spoken and kind.

"How do you plead?"

"Guilty."

I can't believe this is happening. Jane takes a deep breath, and I feel goose bumps all over my arms. Eva turns to us for a moment, her big brown eyes pooled with tears. Jesse hands her a tissue from his shirt pocket.

Before I know it, the DA has read count 2 and count 6, which concern Jane Doe 2. Sasha. She didn't want to come to court today and I can't blame her. She didn't say so, but I think she's paranoid about the media attention. Even though she has nothing to hide and knows it wasn't her fault, it's a lot to ask of someone who's still raw.

"Guilty on both counts."

Judge Nelson gets closer to his microphone. "The court accepts Mr. Copeland's pleas of guilty, finds him guilty as charged in counts 1, 2, and 6, based upon those pleas. Before we move on to sentencing, I understand there are victim impact statements."

"Yes, Your Honor." The DA moves toward the podium. "I would like to read a statement from Jane Doe 2, and then we will have a statement from Jane Doe 1." Eva starts to fidget.

The DA begins reading Sasha's statement, which none of us have heard until now:

For so many years, I've never mentioned what happened to me at Windemere. I didn't think anyone would believe me because in our culture, being a woman often means no one believes you until it is too late. So I tried to bury it deeper than the deepest part of the deepest canyon on earth. But no matter what I did, it would always rise to the surface, like an inflatable pool float you try with all your might to sink underwater and yet it keeps popping up. I was convinced that more harm would come to me than would to him.

With the help of alcohol and drugs, I could sometimes numb the pain for days at a time. I'd even have moments where I felt like a regular person, consumed by everyday problems rather than this dark secret. But every time I would see a news story about a teacher and a student having an affair, I would sink deeper into despair and wonder if Dr. Copeland was still doing that to other girls. This haunted me for years in quiet moments when I had no choice but to be alone with the thoughts in my head.

What started as a wink from him in class progressed to a full-on sexual relationship over an intense six-month period. Dr. Copeland convinced me that I was different, that I was the only one, so special that he would risk his entire career, marriage, and livelihood for me. The more time I spent with him, the less I was with my own circle of friends. Living this double life made me feel grown-up.

He had this fancy gold bookmark on his desk that said, "These violent delights have violent ends." I asked him once what it meant. He said Friar Lawrence was trying to warn Romeo about the dangers of falling in love with Juliet too quickly, and that it was one of his favorite lines from Shakespeare. But when I read the scene in context, it was clearly a warning that the star-crossed lovers would destroy each other, "like fire and powder."

Dr. Copeland repeatedly talked about societal norms and the arbitration of the age of consent. How it was only natural that we would be attracted to one another. He alluded to the fact that we could even get married once I turned eighteen. I'll never forget how many times he said it was a "mutual relationship" even though he was clearly in a position of power over me in every way imaginable. He loved to tell me I was an old soul, but I had just gotten my braces off the year prior.

Toward the end of our twisted relationship, I had a pregnancy scare. It shouldn't have come as a surprise, as he refused to wear condoms, citing a latex allergy. When my period was six days late, he was callous and defensive. He accused me of sleeping around when the truth was I lost my virginity to him, something I will always regret deeply. I finally realized that he didn't care about me and was simply using me for his own sexual gratification. I felt like an idiot.

He was one of the most popular teachers at Windemere and I was already a broken young woman who had suffered past sexual abuse at the hands of trusted family. Part of my anger now comes from the objective fact that he targeted his victims with precision and malice. Our pseudorelationship wasn't an accident or coincidence. It wasn't because of unbridled passion. He picked me for a reason. He knew my father had died when I was young and that I hated my mother, who I blamed for not protecting me in the past.

By age sixteen, after we ended our relationship, I was depressed, drinking heavily, and experimenting with marijuana and cocaine. By seventeen, I discovered cutting and bulimia. Things got so bad that I was hospitalized twice. By eighteen, I was failing out of school and behaving in ways I am too ashamed to revisit. I let boys and men do things to me because I believed I was worthless. I may as well have had a target on my forehead for any male who wanted to mistreat me. I was disassociated from my own body. I started getting tattoos and piercings, and often dyed my hair a different color each month. It was as if I wanted to be anyone but myself.

I alienated anyone good in my life and sabotaged opportunities to enjoy a better existence. In my mind, I was a horrible person who deserved to suffer. I was consumed with misplaced anger that I took out on myself. Because the sexual contact felt good most of the time, I blamed myself for wanting the attention and experience. I thought it was my fault for having these desires. Now I know there's no such thing as a mutual relationship when one person is a teenager and the other is a grown man with a Ph.D. and a family.

I am currently plagued with nightmares, anxiety, insomnia, and paranoia about my identity being outed online. The media attention, in particular, has been disturbing. I can't tell you how many times I have seen this story pop up on social media, and made the mistake of reading comments from strangers and people I know in real life who don't know that I'm Jane Doe 2.

While Windemere would like the public to believe that they have our best interests at heart, I disagree. The investigative committee heard my story and called LAPD, as they are legally mandated to do, but beyond that, they offered me zero support, condolences, or contact of any kind. Perhaps they saw me as an enemy, or someone who could potentially taint their world-famous reputation, but I felt even more alone because of it.

You cannot imagine the fury I felt when I learned of Windemere's disturbing pattern of ignoring allegations, misplacing records, and doubting the claims of their own students when they should have been supporting us. If Windemere had believed the first girl, everyone's lives would be different, and the school wouldn't have this stain associated with its long history. If I had come forward at the time, further incidents would have been prevented.

I'm pleased that Dr. Copeland is admitting to his crimes and receiving time in jail. However, his sentence will be far shorter than mine. I feel like I was sentenced to life at age fifteen. I have to live with this guilt and shame forever. I would have loved to be the person I was meant to be had I not ever walked into his English class.

Chapter Sixteen

Eva

I say a quick prayer and remind myself to breathe. Just breathe. I have barely processed Sasha's statement, and all that she has been through, and now it's already my turn. My heart is racing faster than I've ever felt before and I hope I don't faint before I even get started.

"I understand there is a statement from another victim?" the judge asks.

"Yes, Your Honor." Shannon gives me the nod.

"The cameras and audio are to be turned off," instructs the judge as I rise to speak.

I can't believe I am Jane Doe 1. How many Jane Does are there, really, when it comes to Dr. Copeland? Ten? Twenty? How many Jane Does are there in Los Angeles? In America? On earth today? Throughout the history of time? That's what I kept asking myself each time I wanted to back out of showing up today. My girls are at school right now, working on writing basic sentences and short narratives, their handwriting becoming smaller and neater with each passing day. One day, they'll learn about this, and I'm determined to do right by them.

"Good morning, ma'am." I love how authoritative Shannon is in the courtroom. When we've met in the past, to prep for the case, she acted more like a friend. Today, she looks sharp in her gray suit and crisp white shirt. Her strength is giving me strength.

"Good morning." I adjust the mic and stare straight at her, like she prepped me to do. The feeling of all eyes on me is unsettling.

I haven't been in front of so many people since I graduated from college and was asked to serve as a speaker at our commencement ceremony. I pray no one from the gallery is going to snap a photo of me or record my voice. Even though you're not supposed to, the bailiff can't possibly watch everyone. All it would take is one photo and a peek at a yearbook from my time at Windemere and anyone could put two and two together. There weren't enough Latinas to blend in. I wonder if Copeland is looking at me or if he is looking away. I will not give him the satisfaction of eye contact.

"I understand you would like to address the court?" asks the judge.

"Yes."

"Please go ahead."

I unfurl the statement I typed out a week ago on our home computer, careful to hide the Microsoft Word file so that my daughters didn't find it by mistake while playing Minecraft, and start reading:

"When I was fifteen, Gregory Copeland, my tenth-grade English teacher at Windemere School in Los Angeles, led me into an inappropriate relationship that culminated in explicit sexual contact. It happened over the period of so many months that I did not notice the escalation as it was happening. We would often chat for hours, about literature and poetry, and he had a positive impact on my writing skills. He opened my mind with the help of books and I truly believed he was interested in helping me as a student. I was too young and naïve to see what was really going on.

"He convinced me that we had a special bond, and while society said it was wrong, we should ignore the status quo and explore our feelings. I was completely inexperienced, as I was raised in a strict household and not allowed to date. Mr. Copeland pushed things a bit further with each meeting. Eventually I agreed to see him off campus, where I was simultaneously terrified and thrilled. He made me feel like a sophisticated woman rather than a teenager who earned five dollars an hour as the neighborhood babysitter. Anytime I expressed concern that we would be found out, or that he could potentially be fired, or worse, for spending time with me, he replied with arrogance. He was so convinced that he would never be caught.

"In the media and these court proceedings, I am known as Jane Doe 1, but I am also a wife, mother, and woman of faith. When I first read Caryn's article in the *Daily*, I was sick. I thought our time together served as a lesson, something he regretted and swore to never get involved in again. Her essay triggered within me a relentless need to protect other girls at any cost. I was determined to make sure his behavior stopped immediately. And while I am appreciative of the fact that Dr. Copeland chose to plead guilty to select counts, I do not believe he fully understands the consequences of his actions, so I would like to share part of my story.

"After the final incident between us occurred, in a parking lot of a Westside shopping center, I began a downward spiral when it came to my self-esteem and self-worth. My easygoing personality became closed off and empty. I felt alone and isolated even though I was surrounded by hundreds of happy Windemere girls. I had no interest in attending social functions anymore and felt like I could no longer relate to my peers.

"As I watched some of my classmates go on weekend dates with boys their own age, or develop crushes on their friends' older brothers, I became angry and resentful. I often cried myself to sleep at night and sometimes placed ice packs on my eyes in the morning so no one would notice the puffiness before my one-and-a-half-hour bus commute to Windemere each morning. I no longer trusted men outside of my family. It took more than a decade for me to have a romantic relationship.

"My schoolwork immediately began to suffer, something that I hope Windemere and other schools pick up on as a red flag going forward. I was always terrified of running into Dr. Copeland in the hallways or at school events. I would cringe anytime I'd hear a Windemere student profess her adoration of him, and was torn between warning them to stay far away from him and protecting my own privacy and safety. When I returned to school that fall, I tried my hardest to not let the past define my future. I wanted to be the first person in my family to attend college and I put all of my energy into making that happen. Thankfully, I did.

"I come from a conservative religious family and did not feel I could share this information with them or with our priest who I had known since he baptized me as a baby. I begged for God's forgiveness. Of course now I wish I had told a counselor, a police officer, a friend, anyone, but I honestly had no idea that anyone would believe a teenage girl from Duarte who received a hefty financial aid package. I felt loyal to Windemere and yet the School's past decisions were part of what caused my pain and suffering. Windemere spends so much time preparing young women to be thoughtful, independent leaders, but there isn't a paragraph in a brochure that tells you what to do if one of their faculty or staff members lures you into an illegal sexual relationship.

"I would like to thank everyone involved with bringing this case to fruition, including our wonderful DA, Shannon Orth. For most of you, this is an ending. The media coverage will come to a close, the investigation is finished, and the defendant has admitted his guilt and is being punished accordingly. Windemere will go on and eventually this story will be a footnote in the School's history.

"While I'm grateful for what is transpiring today, I would be lying if I said I had closure on this matter. There is no such thing as closure. It is still raw and painful. I continue to struggle with anxiety and social awkwardness at times. It has infected my marriage and is something I have to hide from my young daughters. I hate being dishonest when they ask me why Mommy is crying. I will deal with this for the rest of my life.

"In the months leading up to today, I have wondered if there is such a thing as justice for victims when it comes to cases like these. Even if criminals are caught and punished, does it ever take away the pain? As a Christian, I am told that I should forgive Dr. Copeland. Colossians 3:13 says, 'Bear with each other and forgive whatever grievances you may have against one another. Forgive as the Lord forgave you.' I'm sure people think that forgiveness would lead to salvation. It sounds tempting, but I'm not ready for that. I'm still furious. Furious on behalf of myself and other victims. Furious about a society that so easily casts doubt and blame on women as though we have nothing better to do than make up stories. Furious about the fact that men like this believe they are entitled to do what they please, regardless of laws, common sense, or decency.

"Dr. Copeland." I address him directly for the first time since I was a scared, shy teenage girl in a school uniform. "You are not forgiven."

His reaction is the equivalent of a blank canvas. There's nothing there.

"Thank you for your statement." The judge looks at me directly. "I know that can't have been easy to write or read aloud. I've heard many statements over the years and it never gets easier. I'm sorry for everything you have been through and wish you the best."

"Thank you." I walk back to my seat.

"Is arraignment for judgment and time for sentencing waived?"

"Yes, Your Honor."

"Is there any legal cause why judgment should not now be pronounced?"

"No, Your Honor."

"In accordance with the plea agreement, the court enters the following orders: imposition of sentence in this case will be suspended for a period of five years, during which time the defendant will be on formal probation on the following terms and conditions: he is to first serve one year in the Los Angeles County Jail. Within forty-eight hours of his release, he's to report to the probation office at the Ascot Intake Center. Mr. Copeland, you are to obey all laws and orders of the court, rules, regulations, and instructions of your probation officer.

"You are to make restitution to all of the victims in this case in an amount and in a manner prescribed by your probation officer, subject to a hearing, if required. You're to complete an approved fifty-two-week sex offender therapy course. You are to maintain a residence as approved by the probation officer, to keep that officer advised of your work and home addresses and telephone numbers at all times. You are to submit your personal property to search and seizure at any time of the day or night by any probation officer or other peace officer, whether or not they have a warrant, probable cause, or reasonable suspicion.

"You are to stay away and have no direct or indirect contact with the victims, Jane Doe 1 and Jane Doe 2, in this case. You are for the rest of your life to register with your local police agency as a convicted sex offender, pursuant to Penal Code Section 290. You are to submit to an AIDS test, pursuant to Penal Code section 1202.1 (A), and provide a DNA sample and print impressions. You are not to teach in the future in any capacity at a public or private school. Your travel will be restricted to Southern California by your probation officer. You are not to be alone with any minor females.

"Do you understand and accept these terms and conditions of probation?"

"Yes."

"The defendant is ordered to surrender to this court on February 6, 2017, to begin serving his sentence. Thank you all for resolving this matter."

"Thank you, Your Honor." Shannon gives me a quick smile.

"Thank you." Mr. Greenspan packs up his files.

It's over. Case closed.

Terrified of running into Dr. Copeland or reporters in the hallways or parking structure, we previously agreed to get out of the building as fast as possible and meet at the café next to the *Daily* offices, walking distance from the courthouse. Seeing as he's guilty and pled accordingly, I don't know why they don't haul him off to jail right now.

"I'm so proud of you, baby." Jesse strokes my arm with the back of his hand.

"Thanks." I feel the relief wash over me like a wave. It's finally over.

"He looked so smug sitting there. He looked like he enjoyed having the attention on him. There is something wrong with that dude."

"Well, I'm sure that's part of why he got into teaching in the first place. He got to hear himself talk all day, with all eyes on him, and it was probably a huge bonus that his audience was made up of teenage girls who adored him."

"Girls who conveniently stayed the same age."

"Well, he'll never be teaching teenage girls again."

"I just couldn't believe the way he just sat there. He never once looked down or held his head in shame. He had the opportunity to publicly apologize to you guys, to his family, or Windemere even, and he chose not to."

"It's okay, baby." I give him a quick kiss goodbye. "He wasn't sorry then and he probably isn't sorry now. I'm sure he's only sorry that he got caught."

Jesse decides to go grab lunch at a sports bar while he waits for me. He hasn't shown any interest in getting to know

Caryn or Jane, so it's probably for the best. I send Sasha a quick text to let her know it went well, and that I thought her statement was incredible and so beautifully written. I wonder why I haven't heard anything from her since she knew we'd all be in court today.

The café is deserted, much to my relief. The second I walk in and see Caryn and Jane waiting for me, I start crying. It's the culmination of everything: Caryn's essay, the interviews, our gatherings, and revisiting the darkest part of my past. Of course we'll stay in touch, I'm sure, but this is the last official meeting for now. We exchange hugs and congratulations and I notice Caryn has a lightness about her that I've never seen before. It's clear she's been crying, so her makeup looks imperfect for once, and that pleases me. She doesn't appear to be distracted by racing thoughts or how her hair looks. She just looks content. She looks like a beautiful young woman.

"You did it." Caryn hugs me so tight that I'm caught off guard. "You were absolutely incredible."

"If it weren't for you, I wouldn't even be here." I give her a maternal stamp of approval because I know how bad she needs it. "I have to remind myself that you're fresh out of college. I couldn't have done something like this while I was an undergrad. Not in a million years."

She shrugs her shoulders and smiles. She's finally proud of herself, and of us, too.

"You are a fantastic public speaker, especially under the circumstances. Not many people could do what you did today."

"Thanks, Jane. I was so blown away by Sasha's statement I could barely think straight. I had no idea she had all of that in her. It broke my heart, to be honest. I guess I had an inkling that she had a tough background, but to hear it all laid bare like that was tough."

"At first I wished she was there today," Caryn says. "I thought it would serve as the ending to a very long story, but hearing what she went through, I realized she is far too fragile to sit in a room with him."

"When I first met her, I was intimidated. It was like she was wearing armor, but now I see the truth. Where is her family or friends? She's never mentioned any support system. If I thought she'd let me, I'd love to be there for her. We have this huge connection on paper, but in person, or over text, she's always kept me at a distance."

Jane, who interviewed Sasha privately when we first met one another, is quiet. She probably knows things about Sasha that weren't even revealed in the statement, but she's too ethical to share anything with us. I decide to add her to my nightly prayers.

Over salads that we can barely bring ourselves to eat, we do a play-by-play analysis of the short courtroom proceedings, and then Jane brings up a final item she wants to discuss.

"Ben knows a prominent local attorney who represents sexual assault victims locally. He specializes in cases like these."

"What does that mean?" Caryn's left eyebrow is slightly raised.

"He thinks you and Sasha have a civil case to sue Windemere, for their negligence."

"I don't know, Jane. I was looking forward to putting this all behind me. Jesse, the kids, my little business, church—it's a lot to handle. I can't imagine a prolonged civil trial as well. There would be depositions that could go on forever."

"You don't have to decide today," Jane explains, "it's just something to think about. And I doubt it would ever reach a courtroom. I think they would be eager to settle and move on. I would think their lawyers have warned them that this is a likely possibility."

"I feel like we got some justice today," I say. "I wouldn't want anyone to think we were in this for a financial settlement."

"You did get some justice today. Others would argue that spending a year in prison is hardly adequate for having sex with a teenage girl when there are black and brown people serving twenty-five years for smoking pot. You know for every one thousand rapes, only around three hundred and fifty will be reported to the police. About sixty of those will lead to an arrest, then ten of those will be referred to a prosecutor and if you're lucky, five of those rapists will serve prison time with no real rehabilitation of any kind."

"Geez, Jane, I thought we were here to celebrate. Let her at least finish her iced tea first," Caryn says.

"We *are* celebrating. I'm sorry, but these are the facts. I just want you to consider your options."

"I need to talk about it with Jesse, and maybe Sasha, too. I'll get in touch with you after that if I want to speak to the attorney."

"The money could go toward your girls' education, or to helping others who have been through something similar. I don't want to be hyperbolic, but you could be talking about millions of dollars."

It would be nice to be able to send the twins to private school, not Windemere, obviously, and to not have to worry about college tuition, but that amount of money sounds terrifying. Suddenly receiving millions of dollars is what breaks up families and leads to all kinds of trouble.

"Jesse's been working so hard and while we're getting by, we don't have much as far as a savings or future plan. The idea of some extra money is tempting, but I don't know what the real cost will be. I could change my mind, but right now I feel satisfied that he's going to jail and can never teach again."

"I would never undermine your victory today," Jane continues. "Most men like him are never caught, never arrested, and certainly never tried. You've saved countless girls from ever having to so much as meet him. I would just urge you to not let Windemere off the hook so easily. If they had done their research about Copeland and taken those prior complaints seriously, then things could have been different for everyone."

"I know. I promise I'll think about it."

Chapter Seventeen

Jane

One Month Later

*E*x-Windemere School for Girls Teacher Begins Jail Sentence for Having Sex With Teen Students
By Jane March

A former English teacher turned himself in today to begin serving a jail sentence for having sexual relationships with two female students while working at the private all-girls Windemere School for Girls in Los Angeles.

Gregory James Copeland, 50, of Santa Monica, was sentenced to a year in county jail last month on charges that he engaged in sex acts with two 15-year-old girls more than a decade ago.

Copeland was charged with nine sex abuse counts and faced up to 12 years behind bars, but in a deal with prosecutors, he pled guilty to three separate counts.

As part of his sentence, Copeland was required to register as a sex offender and complete at least one year of sex offender therapy. He was placed on five years of probation, during which he is barred from teaching or being with any female minor under the age of 18.

"I hope you sort out what it is that led you to this courtroom," Judge Timothy Nelson said before ordering Copeland into custody.

One of the victims has filed a lawsuit against Windemere. "The civil lawsuit will prove that Windemere knew about Copeland's bad conduct and predatory behavior for many years and did nothing about it," said lawyer Nathan Nguyen.

He expects more victims to come forward due to the publicity from the case. "We now know that Copeland engaged in similar misconduct prior to joining Windemere. They knew, and hired him anyway."

Although Windemere has already admitted to some of its failings after releasing findings from an independent investigation, the lawsuit alleges that the elite girls school would never have taken action if alumna Caryn Rodgers had not spoken out in the Daily, which led to additional victims coming forward and worldwide media coverage.

The lawsuit also alleges that Windemere's report from their Special Investigative Committee, which was emailed to all alumnae over the summer, is inadequate because it does not detail what Windemere knew about Copeland's employment history and glosses over the plaintiff's allegations as "an inappropriate physical relationship."

At the time the report was written, Windemere knew that the plaintiff was groomed to participate in sexually explicit activities that were serious enough to warrant charges by the district attorney's office. The Special Investigative Committee, which was primarily made up of the school's board members, interviewed the victim extensively in person several months ago.

The report mentioned that "complaints arose alleging sexual harassment and inappropriate behavior by other adults at the school," but failed to detail what they were. This led some in the Windemere community to threaten to withhold donations and accuse the school of a cover-up.

"It's all too familiar," Nguyen said. "Our schools often do the bare minimum until someone or something forces them to act. If they had done their due diligence in hiring Copeland, and believed their own students and investigated, my client would never have suffered the way she has, and we wouldn't be suing Windemere."

It's likely that Windemere—which has a $56 million endowment and access to a powerful coterie of lawyers—will fight back. In a recent court filing, their attorney, Colin McGowan, said, "The plaintiff exposed countless other girls to the risk of abuse by Copeland. Her negligence and carelessness contributed to the psychological injuries and damage alleged in the lawsuit."

Nguyen believes that the school is insinuating that the plaintiff is responsible for her own assault. "Windemere didn't protect my client back then, and they aren't trying to help her now. Since she told her story to the committee earlier this year, the school has been completely MIA as far as she's concerned, and now they are going to blame her?"

Placing blame on a student for a sexual encounter with a teacher was a common tactic, particularly by Los Angeles Unified School District, prior to being outlawed in California in 2015. A new law states that schools can no longer claim that children consented to sexual acts.

McGowan told the Daily, *"We are not saying that the plaintiff was negligent as a teen. The contributory negligence defense in our filing is standard procedure and related to events that occurred while she was an adult." He declined to specify what these events are.*

"It would be inappropriate to comment on this matter as it's now in litigation," said Laura Lundgren, a spokesperson for Windemere. Copeland's attorney, David Greenspan, said he was unaware of the lawsuit and declined to comment.

Copeland is expected to serve six months, half of his sentence, due to jail overcrowding. The other victim from the criminal case, known as Jane Doe 2, is not part of the lawsuit.

"Honey?"

"I'm coming." I made a last-minute decision to attend my twentieth high school reunion and Ben agreed to come with me.

I can't think of anything I'd rather do less than going to someone else's reunion, but he doesn't mind, and even thinks it could be fun. I am under no such delusion, but I haven't been home in nearly a year, and the guilt is palpable, especially now that my mom is approaching seventy. Ben and I did steal a romantic weekend in Palm Springs two months ago, our first trip as an official couple, but this weekend will be our first time on a plane together and the first time he meets anyone from my family, not to mention at least eighty of my former classmates. I may as well be back in high school the way I'm tracking all these firsts. But there are many worse things in life than feeling like a lovesick teenager.

I roll my bag to the front door and Ben takes over from there. I double check that I have our boarding passes, turn off the lights, and grab my jacket, as you never know what Northern California weather is going to do. It's not like Los Angeles where you can count on three hundred days of sunshine and a steady seventy-two-degree average. Novato in February could mean twenty-eight-degree nights or seventy-degree days. Located about thirty miles north of San Francisco, my hometown has around fifty-four thousand residents, comparable to the population of L.A.'s Westwood neighborhood, which is considered a small village.

We get through security fast and sit at the gate for a while, which gives Ben a chance to pump me for information. "I can't wait to hear embarrassing high school stories about you. Were you class president? Editor of the school paper? Were you on the debate team? If you weren't, that is a travesty. Never mind, don't tell me. I want to be surprised."

I give him a look. "We didn't even have a debate team. I was pretty regular in high school. I don't think there are many stories to be told."

"Oh c'mon, Jane. There is nothing regular about you. Please don't undersell yourself on my account. I can take it. You can tell me that you were a badass, breaking hearts and taking names."

"I definitely was not breaking hearts. I was more bookish. I mean, I went to parties and prom, but I think I was always daydreaming, hoping and wishing for more."

"More what?"

"More anything. To get out of Novato and see what the rest of the world had to offer."

"I'd say you checked that box a few times."

The flight is quick and easy. The woman sitting in the window seat of our row has clearly never landed at SFO before; she's holding on to the armrest so tight that Ben tells her not to worry and tries to distract her by being talkative. That's the thing about journalists; we can talk to anyone, anywhere, anytime. The plane hovers just above the water before hitting the runway that seemingly appears out of nowhere. The woman takes a deep breath and releases her hand; I'm relieved to see the blood flow return to her skin.

Our flight pours out into a shiny terminal with its own yoga room, unique art installations, local restaurants, and multiple compost and recycling bins. If California is the land of fruits and nuts, then San Francisco is its epicenter—only the fruits will be organic and the nuts will be fair trade.

It doesn't matter what professional success I have achieved, small talk at a reunion, or any similar gathering, will still be focused on two things and two things only: why I'm not married and why I don't have children. It doesn't matter that we grew up in a mostly liberal, nonreligious community, in the come-as-you-are Bay Area; there are still questions that need to be answered. It doesn't matter if Ben is a good guy or a bad guy or the right one for me. What matters is that I can be placed in a box. It makes them feel better about their own life choices. One of the things I love most about Los Angeles is the fact that people in the sprawling big city are too busy or self-involved to worry about your personal life.

We decided to get a hotel for the first night. It didn't feel right to introduce Ben to my mom for the first time late at night after the reunion, so we decided to spend time with her tomorrow instead. I haven't done the greatest job of staying in touch with people, but a few hometown friends have written me over the years and I try to check in on them every few months. It doesn't matter much to me that twenty years have passed, there's something about your childhood friends that feels permanent, even though you may have nothing in common now or go years without seeing one another. These are the people who knew you before you were you.

Ben takes a sports coat out of his garment bag and I accessorize my black dress with a matte gold bracelet. Caryn would be so proud.

"Wow, you're really wearing that dress." He eyes me up and down before pulling me toward him. "You're making me feel like a horny teenage boy."

I'm immediately reminded of the thing I hate to be reminded of most when I'm home. Though it's unlikely that the subject will be broached at the reunion, I figure I better give Ben a primer, just in case.

Because most of us were eighteen—old enough to vote, smoke cigarettes, or go to war—it wasn't difficult getting the okay from our parents to stay out all night on the last day of high school. My mother just asked me to "be smart" and to check in with her as soon as I woke the next morning. Billy, a friend we'd all known since we were in kindergarten, offered up his parents' place in Inverness, a sleepy bayside town surrounded by lush wilderness. Although it's a forty-five-minute drive west from Novato, it seemed well worth it to have a house to ourselves to drink, smoke, and celebrate our final days together before most of us went off to college in other parts of the state and country.

Back then, there was no greater allure than an opportunity to feel like a grown-up. The idea of freedom—from our parents, high school, sports, and daily chores—was so intoxicating that I'm not sure we even needed to bring alcohol. We had just finished twelve straight years of schooling—thirteen if you count kindergarten—and we were tired. Tired of writing essays, prepping for tests, and filling out college applications. As soon as the graduation ceremony was over, we said our goodbyes to our families. We'd see them in less than twenty-four hours, but we were going to enjoy our newfound adult status regardless of the time constraints.

Inverness sits on the west shore of Tomales Bay, practically on the San Andreas Fault, near the famed Point Reyes Lighthouse. Downtown has a general store, library, post office, a couple of restaurants, and some hotels and inns that draw tourists because of its hidden and remote beaches, hiking, and kayaking. Billy's parents' place, nicknamed the Henhouse because of its proximity to Chicken Ranch Beach, could sleep six, and so we assembled a group of eight, figuring the two extras could deal with a couch—or maybe we wouldn't even sleep at all.

The Henhouse didn't disappoint. The two-story craftsman home had a spacious living area, wood fireplace, and two large decks that overlooked an idyllic scene. The only house rule that Billy set was that we couldn't smoke anything inside, so we decided that the booze would go on the lower deck and pot and its accouterments—rolling papers, pipes, and one glass bong—belonged on the upper deck so the smell would travel upward into the low-hanging clouds. Situated on a quiet private road and surrounded by hulking redwood trees, the Henhouse may as well have been heaven. You'd never know you were an hour from the bustling and comically steep streets of San Francisco.

The night was fairly typical, except that it went on much

longer than any other high school party I'd been to. Instead of running out of beer or rushing home because of a curfew, everyone kept drinking until they passed out in one of the many rooms of the Henhouse. I never drank to excess, but I hadn't eaten much and was exhausted from the last week of school and all the corresponding events, so I was one of the first ones out. Sheila, who I'd known since preschool, lay next to me, babbling about how she wanted to hook up with Jason, but he didn't seem interested.

"Everyone's drunk," I said. "I'm not sure he's even seeing straight. You can try again in the morning." It's the last thing I said before falling into a deep sleep. At some point in the middle of the night, I woke with a ravenous thirst and stumbled out into the main living area in search of water. It was dark, but the curtains were open, and I could see thanks to the glow of the moonlight. Billy was sleeping on the chaise part of the sofa, while Kristin was splayed across the main part. I finally found the kitchen and drank water from a plastic red cup.

On my way back I heard a noise coming from the room next to mine. I thought someone was getting sick or making a muffled cry of some kind and so I tiptoed over, careful not to wake the others on the couch. The door was cracked open and I couldn't see much, but it looked like Dave and Aya were fooling around. I was surprised, because they weren't a couple or particularly attracted to one another, but I figured since it was the last night of school, it was possible they just decided to go for it. In the two seconds I stood there, I could just make out the shape of his head between her legs, which was farther than I'd ever gone with a guy, and she was making some audible, low-level moans. For all the stories you hear about boys wanting only one thing, I remember being impressed that he was pleasuring her, and not vice versa, and so I went back to bed.

In the morning, everyone was hung over, moving slow and offering monosyllabic answers. Sheila made pancakes for those of us who weren't sick, but mostly we were just tired from being up most of the night. We split into two different cars and made the drive back to our real lives, and our final summer together. Ten days passed before I heard that Aya was accusing Dave of raping her that night at the Henhouse. I don't know why, but I didn't speak to her directly about it even though I had known her since junior high school. I was too terrified of the allegation and what I saw (or thought I saw). The summer tore our social group apart. Dave was adamant that he never forced himself on her, although he couldn't remember key details of the night, and Aya disappeared to the East Bay, where she stayed with her aunt and uncle for the rest of the summer and refused calls from any of us.

"Consent wasn't part of our lexicon. Lots of kids got drunk and had sex. Sometimes there were regrets or embarrassment, but this was different."

"So what ended up happening?"

"She never pressed charges and eventually people dismissed it. Anyone I talked to felt confident that she was lying or simply ashamed that she had let this happen. I tried reaching her again after some time had passed and was told she didn't want to speak to me. I wrote her a letter and explained what I saw and offered to help her if she wanted to go to the police. I ran into Dave at a pizza shop two weeks before I moved to New York for school and asked him flat-out what happened. He said he couldn't remember every detail, but that in the middle of the night they started fooling around. He didn't have a condom and believed that's what she was mad about. The longer she stayed away, the more I started thinking that she was telling the truth."

"What did the others think? Did anyone else see anything?"

"No. I was the only one who saw them hooking up, or what I thought was hooking up. But maybe her moans were an attempt to say no or say anything. She could have been incoherent and not experiencing pleasure; I didn't discern the difference at the time."

"That's awful, I'm sorry you had to deal with that at such a young age."

"That's the thing. I never dealt with it. I still don't know the whole truth and I don't think I ever will."

"It sounds like Dave was hammered and had sex with a passed-out drunk girl. In his mind that isn't rape because for most guys, rape would involve a threat or weapon."

"But we don't know that for sure. Maybe she wanted to be in that bedroom with him, but changed her mind. Maybe he didn't threaten her but she felt like she had to go along with it because she didn't know what would happen if she didn't."

"She was surrounded by friends. Wouldn't she have just got up and left if she didn't want to be there?"

"Even with our male friends we have to ask, Is he dangerous? Is he going to hurt me? Will he freak out if I say no? Sometimes it's easier to let a guy do something you don't want to do if you think it means you'll be able to leave the situation physically unharmed. Saying no to a man is often when the real danger, begins."

"It's honestly amazing women still want anything to do with us."

"I don't need to tell you 'not all men,' but back then, date rape was a new thing. It just didn't seem relatable because most of us had never even been on real dates. Part of the reason we hung out in groups was to be safe."

"Are any of these people from that night going to be at the reunion?"

"Some of them could be, but Dave and Aya won't be there. Dave died in college in a terrible swimming pool diving accident. Aya never came back to Novato as far as we know. People tried finding her over the years and had no luck. Everyone else from that evening moved on and rarely spoke of it, but I've found it hard to move on. It's haunted me for twenty years. I've often thought about tracking her down, because I know how to find anyone, but I feel like it's not my right. She didn't want to hear from me then and I doubt she'd want to hear from me now."

"But now she's almost forty. Maybe she'd feel differently."

"I don't know."

"I'm so glad you told me this story."

"I wish I never had to. I wish it never happened. I wish I did something. I didn't know what to do as an eighteen-year-old."

"The reason I'm glad you told me is because I understand you so much better now. The way you are with Caryn, always going above and beyond, helping take down Copeland, and all the victims you've ever written about, it's all because of Aya. You ask questions for a living because of her."

I want to tell him he's wrong, but he's not.

Chapter Eighteen

Caryn

"Have you heard from Sasha at all?" I ask Eva over text.

She writes back immediately: "No. I gave up after a while. I don't think she likes me."

I compose an email to Jane and Eva. I tell them that Sasha hasn't replied to any of my texts or calls in the last two months, and remind them that none of us have talked to her since Copeland's plea. The reason I'm panicking today is because the unthinkable has happened: someone posted Sasha's name and photo to the private Windemere Alumna Facebook Group and said, "Can you believe Copeland went to jail for *her*? And now she's suing???" It was an unflattering amateur modeling photo where she appeared androgynous and angry. The image looked nothing like her; in person, Sasha's beauty is arresting, no matter how hard she tries to hide it. As soon as I saw the post I was enraged, knowing that being outed is her biggest fear and would crush her. Plus, she's not the one suing, Eva is. Sasha had no desire to join the civil suit because she knew what they would try to do to her. The page moderator eventually deleted the post a few hours later, but at least eighty-seven grads saw it, according to Facebook, and anyone could have taken a screenshot.

Over the next few hours, I receive six emails from fellow grads I'd been in touch with earlier in the year while I was still at the *Daily*. Some want to know if it's true that Sasha is one of the Jane Does, while others are concerned about their own identities being outed since they spoke to Jane for stories or to me for moral support. I promise them that they are safe, but refuse to confirm her as one of Copeland's victims. I am tempted to contact the vile woman who originally posted to the group, but I know if I react strongly, it will validate her accusation. She's of similar age to Sasha. Do they know each other, and if not, how would she know such a thing? I want to contain this before Sasha hears anything.

Of course Jane is the first to write back. She's in triage mode and sends me a host of instructions to forward to Sasha to help her secure her computer, social networks, and private information. She also tells Eva not to worry, because the DA or LAPD would never sell her out like that, and unless she has told anyone she is a Jane Doe, there's no one who would know. I can't possibly forward this information without alerting Sasha to the issue and so I don't. I text Sasha an innocent, "Hey, can you talk real quick?" and hear nothing in return. I rack my brain trying to think of any details she mentioned: where she worked, any friends she had, where exactly she lived, and I realize I have nothing to go on.

Jane says she's going to call a friend in the DA's office and try to get an address so we can request a welfare check from the police department. While we're waiting, I debate trying to reach Sasha's mom. She hasn't mentioned her, but I hear she's Russian and lives in West Hollywood. If Sasha knew I was considering this, I'm sure she'd despise me. While I'm waiting to hear back from Jane, I search Sasha's name to see if I can get a hit. A few tweets pop up, naming Sasha as one of Copeland's accusers. How could they possibly know? These aren't Windemere alumnae but men who don't even live in Los Angeles. I go through a few more pages of results until I find a blog that's dedicated to "the oppression of the American man."

Unbeknownst to me, they have covered the Copeland case since my essay came out. I'm skimming and scrolling as fast as I can until I come to a post that feels like a gut punch. Not only is Sasha's name and photo there for all the world to see, but the author writes about her as though her dream in life was to get to Windemere so she could seduce her paunchy English teacher and then get him jailed all in the name of misandry.

In the comment section, someone has outed her, leaving Sasha's name and address in Hollywood right there. Beneath that, anonymous commenters with names like Pigman1 and RapeCultureIsntReal debate whether she's "still fuckable" and another suggests that she looks "just like the type of girl who needs to be taught a lesson." I forward the link to Jane only, as there's no way Eva can benefit from hearing about this right now, and tell her we need to call the police. She calls me within minutes.

"Caryn, you need to calm down. I already called the DA's office and someone is going to go by her place today."

"But what if something bad happened and that's why she isn't replying? What if one of these men has it out for her? If you read the comments you'll see these men don't sound stable."

"The only reason I'm not worried is because she wasn't replying to us before her name was connected to the case." Jane's tone becomes more hushed. "I didn't tell you this, because I didn't want to upset you, but Sasha made it clear to me when I spoke to her about the civil case that she didn't want anything else to do with us. She wasn't mean about it, but just matter-of-fact. I got the sense that she did her part and she was done with it. You can't force someone to take your call."

"She doesn't have to be friends with us or feel a bond because of the case. But how is this legal that someone can put a sexual assault victim's info online for anyone to see it? What if one of those men contacted her? They linked to her Instagram account and everything."

"I'll call the DA's office again. Maybe we can get that post removed with a little verbal strong-arming. It looks like an obscure site with a few hundred readers. It's not too late to get it contained."

"Did you get my text?" Grace asks as soon as I walk in the door.

"I had a crazy afternoon and didn't see it." I scroll through and see the unread message.

"I can just tell you since you're standing in front of me."

"Sorry, Unnie."

"It's nothing big. Your mom stopped by."

"She did? That's weird."

"I think she was trying to be nice." Grace grabs an envelope from the dining room table. "I guess this came for you to their house. She said you're never around anymore and asked me if you have a secret boyfriend."

I roll my eyes. "Great, thanks."

"Is everything okay? You look like you're spinning out."

"I don't know, Unnie."

"Did you eat anything? Maybe you'll feel better if you have a snack."

"I gained six pounds in the last few months, so snacking is the least of my problems."

She rolls her eyes. "I'm sure that's muscle weight. You've been so diligent with working out. You still look slim as a knife."

I'm pleased to hear this even though I'm working hard, with Susan's help, to get my eating issues under control. Focusing more on others is helping me be less obsessed with myself.

It's not until the next morning—after a terrible night's sleep that involved me imagining every horrible thing that could happen to Sasha—that I even bother to open the envelope. Inside and scribbled in messy handwriting is a note addressed to me:

Caryn,

Sorry for sending this to your parents' place, it was the

only address I had for you because I don't think you're still at the Daily. I don't know which jail the piece of shit is at or I would have sent it myself. But please, I beg you, send it to him for me. I just want you to do this one thing. I need to know you'll do this one thing. I left it open so you would understand everything. I'm sorry. It's not your fault. Tell Eva and Jane and everyone I'm sorry.

There's an immediate pit in the bottom of my stomach. Terrified to read whatever is inside, I open the typed pages gingerly, as if trepidation is going to make this any easier.

Gregory,

Remember how you begged me to call you Gregory? I thought you got off on our age difference and I assumed you'd want me to call you Dr. Copeland, even when we were fucking, but you were actually twisted enough to believe we were equals, and so I started calling you Gregory after your repeated requests. As Dr. Copeland, you sounded important and accomplished—two things I so badly wished I were, too. As Gregory, you were just another guy. I should have realized that sooner. You were just another guy. Then maybe you wouldn't be sitting in a jail cell and I wouldn't be writing this letter. You are just another guy.

I've spent too much time over the years thinking about you. Was your kindness and empathy all an act? Was any of it—even a shred—real? What about your passion and emotion? Remember that time you cried because you said you loved me so much? You were like a teenage girl. Remember you said that I made you nervous? That being in my mere presence would make your hands tingle and your mouth go dry? Is that what you told all of your roses? You weren't big on originality, were you? Sometimes I think you are a full-blown sociopath incapable of feelings but highly capable of acting like someone with feelings. But I'll never know because I'd never believe a word that came out of your small mouth anyway.

When I think about you, I remember how you adored your little girl so much. I loved that about you. I wished I had a father to love me, but instead I had a stepfather who was just another guy, too. He was the benefactor of my education, but trust me, I paid. It was the worst kind of quid pro quo. I sometimes wonder, was your love for Leah sincere? If it was—if it is—did you ever consider how she would feel about your proclivity for teenage pussy? Do you think about how you've now robbed her of any semblance of a normal life? Girls are embarrassed of their fathers for all kinds of reasons, but you've done something extra. Something that would send a blond man with a doctorate in English to prison. Has anyone visited you? Do you still have a wife or friends? What does your LinkedIn page say now? I guess I could take a look.

When Leah turned fifteen, did you find yourself attracted to her, too? I don't mean to conflate your penchant for girls with incest, but I have to ask the question. Did you love going to her high school games so you could watch the cheerleaders with their rosebud tits and bright white teeth? Did their hair shine under the fluorescent lights of the gym? Did you ever read Leah's diary and become titillated? Did you know all of her childhood friends since they were little kids? Did they make you nervous, too? Did you wish you could hold their small faces in your mitt-like hands and tell them you were scared of how they made you feel? Did you even try to hide it? Or were you generous with your winks and smiles and eye contact? Were you the 'cool dad'? Did your daughter have friends spend the night? Did they know to be scared of you? Did they call you Dr. Copeland, Mr. Copeland, or Gregory? Did you watch them, wishing you could simply get them alone for a few minutes so you could tell them they were special? Extraordinary. Otherworldly. Sent from God.

You were excited to have a son. He was going to be a prince, an heir, a miniversion of you. I recall you talked about how you would teach him to play football and give him books by Kerouac and the Beat poets when he was old enough. You would raise a son who was well spoken, intelligent, and athletic. You claimed to love him before he was even born. Do you remember missing one of the ultrasound appointments so you could be with me instead? Do you remember lying to your wife on the phone, making up some excuse about an emergency at school, so you could instead take me to that most average motel in Santa Monica? As you parted my legs and worshipped my virgin slit with your mouth, I imagined your wife's legs being parted by her doctor for her examination. Does that turn you on or make you feel sick? Or do you feel nothing at all? I would do anything to be able to feel nothing at all.

We weren't speaking by the time Jack was born. You had already discarded me like a used condom (except you wouldn't wear a condom, remember?). Did you quickly find someone else after me? Because it couldn't have been your wife. With sympathetic eyes, Mrs. Goodwin told us that Marie had a tough pregnancy and recovery. Were you scared into being a good boy for a while? Did you tell yourself you wouldn't do it again? I thought about Jack sometimes over the years. I imagined what he would look like. Who he would become. His body would be hard in all of the places yours was soft. Maybe you had a body like his when you were in high school. I'm guessing you didn't though. Jocks don't get hooked on Shakespeare, as you know. He would have a million-dollar smile, inherited from your wife, and stand six-foot-two, dwarfing you. He could make a girl feel safe. He would outshine you. He would do the right thing if he saw injustice somewhere. Because he is his mother's son.

But he loved you and may still love you because you were and are his father. Sons need their fathers, even if their fathers are horrible people. To bond over things like March Madness and fishing trips and The Beach Boys and looking at girls. But sons are also in competition with their fathers, whether they love them or not. Did you ever read that article about Joe and John F. Kennedy and Marlene Dietrich? Why would a son want to go where his adulterous father had been before? Is it emulation or emasculation? You would say it's Shakespearean. Everything was fucking Shakespearean to you. Maybe it's biblical. "They trample on the heads of the poor as on the dust of the ground and deny justice to the oppressed. Father and son use the same girl and so profane my holy name." (Amos 2:7) I've known guys who were taken to whorehouses with their fathers as teenagers and young men. They didn't think it was that big of a deal.

You always hated technology. I imagine you scolding people for reading books on their Kindles or posting on social media when they could be writing in ink, in flowing cursive, in a leather-bound notebook. But technology makes it so easy for people like you. Now you can groom someone over text messages with emojis. Did you figure that out yet or are you still old-fashioned? Chatting on a device is not the slow burn of an in-the-classroom flirtation that I know tantalizes you like nothing else on earth, but it's easy and less time-consuming. It's like online shopping. You just see who piques your interest and add to your cart. I didn't know how easy it was until I tried it myself.

When I first contacted him, he didn't write back. I figured I needed to up the ante. The next time, I included some photos of my own. Within two minutes, I had a reply. Boys and men are so reliable that way. We started chatting back and forth. His messages were short, but lacked typos or typical slang and I liked that. He never asked how I landed on his profile or why I could possibly want to talk to a boy who's still in high school. When a guy's ego is being stroked, nothing else matters. It's the end of their curiosity.

It only took a week before he agreed to meet me. I was a bit disappointed that he wasn't a virgin. He told me about awkwardly losing it last year to a friend at a party in Santa Monica where people were trying to barge in the entire time. It's amazing any of us make it out of high school with the constant humiliation. I'm sorry if you don't approve, but I gave him a drink and we shared a joint. He looked older than I expected, but still younger than anyone I would ever be attracted to. His unlined skin felt smooth and his green eyes were intense and sad like mine. He was polite and waited for me to take the lead. He nervously smiled a lot. He said I looked twenty-five. We talked for a while about music and festivals before I went down on him. He didn't last long. He never mentioned you.

He tried to reciprocate, but I didn't want him to. I asked if he wanted to fuck me instead and he said yes, of course. I told him to lie down on the bed and found a condom in the nightstand drawer. I straddled his body, all limbs and long muscles and hormones. He was immediately hard again because that's how it goes when you're sixteen and a living, breathing woman is on top of you. He closed his eyes while I unfurled the latex. "How did I get so lucky?" he asked. I lifted the skirt of my dress up and pulled the top of it down. I kissed him. His lips were bigger than yours. Everything was bigger than yours. He told me he would think about this all the time, that he'd remember it forever. He grabbed my breasts, unsure what to do with them, and I moved quicker, up and down, suddenly wanting it to end. After he finished, he wanted to lay with me for a bit, but I felt claustrophobic and said it was nothing personal. I told him he would indeed remember it forever. I was positive of that.

And though he was kind and innocent, Jack was just another guy.

Chapter Nineteen

Sasha

"Hi, Miss Tracy," I call out to my neighbor. She hates me most of the time, but has been a bit nicer since I saved her dog from being run over last month. "Can I print something at your place? Just this once?" Her unit is sunnier than mine, and filled with hanging plants, but I haven't been all the way inside in over a year.

"Fine."

"It's just that Brad stole my printer when he left."

"You knew damn well that boy was no good." She clicks her tongue. "Can't trust a man with tight jeans and long hair like that."

"Why didn't you tell me? I'm always the last one to know these things."

"He didn't go to no job, was always out here smoking *something*, stinking up the courtyard. I never liked him. Neither did Mr. Chips." As if on cue, her Norwich Terrier jumps on my lap, eager for affection. "Maybe if you took that thing out of your nose you could get yourself a better man. Or get some rest. You look *tired.*"

"I haven't been sleeping well."

"Well, I hope your tired self is printing a resume."

"Very funny, but you'd miss me around here if I was at a typical nine-to-five. I mean, who would be on animal rescue duty and bring you your packages?"

"Maybe an office job would be good for you. You could

meet a man with a good job. Don't your mama want you to get married?"

"She's had three different husbands, so it's not like she can give me great advice about love and marriage."

"Three? Once was enough for me. In my day we had no choice. You have too many choices. Maybe that's the problem."

"Maybe so. Do you know any eligible bachelors?"

"Hell, no. I've been living here alone since 1987, and never been happier. You're still young, so you want to have fun with boyfriends and all that, but lemme tell you, there's plenty more to life than cleaning up after some man."

"I didn't know you were such an independent w-o-m-a-n."

"And proud of it."

I grab the papers from the printer and give Mr. Chips a final squeeze. "Thank you, Miss Tracy. You have yourself a beautiful day."

"We'll see about that."

I never thought that I'd spend the last day of my life running errands. After going to the post office, I stop at the ATM to take out what's left. I give twenty bucks each to the first ten homeless people I can find. This is an easy task, unfortunately, and most of their eyes light up upon realizing it's Andrew Jackson, and not George Washington, looking back at them, which brings me a rare moment of joy. Before returning home, I stop by the liquor store to see Ari and to buy a box of Milk Duds, my favorite childhood candy. The only real memory I have of my dad—the one I truly remember myself and not the ones that were implanted by a story or photograph—was when he took me to the movies and bought me Milk Duds.

In movies, when people die and go to heaven, they are somehow instantly reunited with their loved ones who also died and went to heaven. I held on to that for a long time until I could no longer do so. Plus, my dad was Jewish. He didn't believe in heaven and hell. He wanted to focus on this life. I debate making a phone call, but decide against it. I have a cousin in Glendale who is the only one always willing to help me, no matter how many times I borrow money or show up unannounced when I get too lonely. I know she would tell me to just make it through one more day, to go back to my psychiatrist, to come over and play with her kids. What I've never been able to explain to her, or to anyone, really, is how overwhelming and unbearable my inner life is. There is no amount of time or doctor visits or distracting activities that can solve what goes on inside my head.

There's nothing anyone could say to me right now that would make me think the world would be better off with me in it. I'm just so tired. Tired of the intense sadness and constant need to escape the pain. Tired of never having enough money and taking advantage of people's goodwill. Tired of waking up each morning only to feel dread. Tired of doing terrible things with and to my body. Tired of anxiety and not being able to sleep well for months on end. Tired of being tricked into having hope only to have it dashed within days or minutes. Maybe this was my destiny all along. Maybe some people aren't meant for this world. Maybe all of my molecules will end up somewhere else, somewhere they were supposed to be.

I plop onto the sofa where I promptly fall asleep for ninety minutes, long enough to have one final dream. It's the last day of high school, and I'm standing on the Lawn at Windemere, wearing my white polo and gray skirt. Even though we aren't supposed to accessorize with anything besides plain white socks and shoes, I'm wearing a black pair that say "Meat is Murder," a nod to The Smiths and my passing phase as a vegetarian. It's my final day. What are they going to do, suspend me?

Wherever I turn, girls are hysterically crying as if they've been told of impending nuclear war. I ask Susannah, one of the few classmates I can stand, why everyone is crying. "It's the last day of the last year so people are sad to leave," she says matter-of-factly. I start laughing like a maniac and she walks away from me in disgust. The intense female bonding and penchant for dramatics at Windemere are always entertaining, but this scene is ridiculous. They're acting as if they don't have email and cell phones and frequent school reunions. In the old days, you'd have to write a letter to someone you wanted to stay in touch with, wait for it to arrive, and then wait some more for their reply. It was so romantic.

Most of the senior girls drive themselves to school now, so the crowd begins to dissipate as people head toward the parking lot. I realize I'm left alone, waiting for a ride from my mom, and see Dr. Copeland walking by himself on the other side of the Lawn. I wave to him, but he doesn't react. This is the last time I will ever see him and so I start running in his direction. I try to call his name, to get his attention, but I'm unable to make any audible sound. Is there anything more terrifying than losing your voice, wondering if it will ever come back? I decide to scream at the top of my lungs, but nothing comes out and I start to silently cry. He sees that I am getting closer to him and begins to laugh at me. When I get within a few feet of him I stop in my tracks and turn the other way.

Like when I was a child, my mom is the last person to show up in the pickup area. I'm about to give up and start walking down the hill when I see her old Mercedes round the corner. I figure I better write on a piece of notepaper that I've lost my voice so she doesn't start screaming at me for not responding. I grab a notebook from my backpack when I hear her honk the horn. The blazing sun makes it hard to see inside the car until I enter. The beige leather passenger seat has a few tears, but is in otherwise good condition.

"Did you have a good day at school?" The parent behind the wheel is, inexplicably, my father.

I quickly write on the piece of paper. "Yes, Dad." I lean

over and kiss him on the cheek and he smiles.

"I really missed you, my *solnyshko*."

After watching some TV, I text Spencer, a guy I've partied with over the last year or two. He's generous with his substances and too fucked up most of the time to expect anything in return. Usually, I'd want Adderall, or LSD if I'm really desperate, but today is different. I ask him if I can come over and he replies with the tongue emoji.

Like most of the girls I went to Windemere with, Spencer was given access to an insane amount of money at a young age. Instead of investing it or accumulating real estate, he decided to fashion himself as a modern-day Hugh Hefner, only wearing robes and pajamas around his bohemian drug den, on the border of Hollywood and Little Armenia, surrounded by a rotating cast of aspiring models and actresses who are paid one way or another to be there. Like so many of his kind, he's short on charm or kindness and has a new crew of hangers-on each time I run into him. Carla once warned me that he gets off on pitting girls against one another, but I never stayed long enough to notice.

"I didn't know the lady made house calls in the daylight." His wavy hair is longer than I remember, almost Jesus-like, and he's wearing an amulet around his bare chest, which has stubble from shaving, and a pair of harem-style pants that make him look like a reject from the *Aladdin* musical at Disneyland.

"Is that to protect you from trouble?" I finger the green ornament and pull him closer toward me.

"I guess it didn't work because trouble just found me." He wears a goofy grin. "God, I forgot how much fun you are."

" 'Flirting is a woman's trade, one must keep in practice,' " I say in my best British accent. I sit down on his midcentury sofa, hands between my knees, and revert to my regular voice. "I need something from you."

"And what would that be?" He looks down at his groin.

"Not that. I want H."

"You don't want that." He sits next to me and puts the palm of his hand under my shirt and over my heart. "You need to heal whatever's going on in here."

"I didn't come here for an inspirational quote you found on Instagram."

"Fine. Just don't say I didn't warn you." He goes upstairs for a few minutes and returns with a small Baggie and straw. "It will take about ten minutes if you snort it." I throw down a roll of cash on the table and put the bag in my pocket. I feel better already just knowing I have it.

"Aren't you going to stay awhile? Marissa's not going to be back for a few hours." His rakish smile implies too much.

"I hate to buy and run. Maybe I'll come back tonight. You know I'm a creature of the night."

"You better. I have plans for you." I give him a lingering hug, enough to placate him so I can get out of here without incident. "Be careful with that. Start with a bump, not even a line, and wait."

"It's not my first time," I lie.

It's hard to believe that Spencer, someone who means nothing to me, is the last person I will ever speak to. I look at my phone for a few minutes and read a few texts. My Contacts list is a mess of first names and identifying information. There's Aleisha Stylist, Cat Makeup Artist, George Photographer, Jason Bowling Alley, Martin Band Guy From Spaceland, and Yao Writer. It's like going back in time. I don't remember half of these people and most of my real friends are long gone in their marriages and parenthood and marathon running. When I really want to torture myself, I go on Facebook so I can see everyone's smiling faces and vacations and dogs and babies, knowing that I'll never have a part of that. I've been left behind, incapable of normalcy or anything resembling it.

I just want to go to sleep and I begin the process of doing what I need to do. My landlord is coming by in the morning to personally evict me since I refused to answer his letters, so I have a bit of a deadline. I start with a line and wait twenty minutes. The initial feeling is pure euphoria, but then I suddenly throw up. I knew to expect this so I just sit back down and allow myself to sink into a deep relaxation. If I thought I could keep this going, I could just become a heroin addict, but seeing as I have no job, no apartment, and no savings, I'm pretty sure it wouldn't be long before I was on the street. Feeling confident and somewhat invincible, I decide to do more, and that's the last thing I remember.

Chapter Twenty

Caryn

"How are you handling everything?" Susan is the therapist I've been seeing regularly for the last few years, and twice a week since finding out about Sasha.

"I'm still in shock, but it's clear to me now that Sasha had problems way before the Copeland case. Perhaps he exacerbated them, or maybe it was a combination of the self-medicating and anxiety and the media attention and then being outed. I feel certain she knew her name was released, even if it wasn't on the evening news, and couldn't handle that." I don't know what I'm saying right now, I just feel like I should say something since Susan charges $175 an hour.

"She's not my patient and I've never met her, but from what you've told me so far, it sounds like she may have suffered from mental illness." I always find Susan's throaty voice to be soothing. "Mixing medications with alcohol and drugs is never a good idea. She was likely not thinking straight."

"She sounded crystal clear in the letter." I play with an errant thread on the hem of my dress. "That's what haunts me."

"I just mean that when someone is suffering from something like depression or bipolar disorder, they need to be under a doctor's care. From what you mentioned last time, there were various prescribed medications found at her apartment. She was obviously suffering from something and perhaps devising her own concoctions based on how she was feeling each day or week."

"Whatever it was, she decided she had suffered enough." I stare out the window at the ever-present traffic on Mid-Wilshire.

"And have you come to terms with that?"

"I don't have a choice, do I?"

"I guess I should rephrase that." Susan crosses her legs. "Do you feel like you understand her suffering and what led to such an unfortunate outcome?"

"I do."

"What I'm trying to get at here, Caryn, is that I want to make sure you aren't blaming yourself for her death."

"I think that's inevitable, and I hope it will pass over time, but maybe it won't. I keep thinking about what would have happened if I never wrote the article, if there was never an investigation, or a call for victims to come forward. Would she be happy and alive?"

"And what do you think?"

"I don't know. I don't know if she was ever happy."

"What she did, her twisted idea of revenge, was not something that a mentally healthy person would do. Even the victims who have suffered the worst abuse don't retaliate like that. Copeland's son is just a kid." She shakes her head from side to side in judgment.

"I understand the point you're making, but I also realize that she was pushed to her limits. She felt revictimized by the case, and knowing he would probably be out in six months due to good behavior was too much for her to bear. The DA told us she was furious about the plea deal, which I didn't know at the time. The counts he pled to were much more mild and sanitized than what happened between them for so many months. That's why she didn't come to court. She was irate at the DA, at Windemere, and at herself. It wasn't because she was scared to face Copeland. She didn't feel that pleading to reduced counts and charges meant justice was served. She wanted a trial and I'm sure she wanted an apology."

"From who?"

"From Windemere. From Copeland. From her mother. Her own mother didn't stand by her when her stepfather was molesting her. What does that do to a kid's psyche?"

"You've mentioned before that she had other demons."

"She did not have an easy life. She was erratic the few times I was around her, but she showed up when it mattered. She cooperated with Windemere and the police. She met with the DA on several occasions and wrote an incredible victim impact statement that was read aloud in court. She wasn't incoherent. One of us would have done something if we thought she was suicidal."

"Perhaps try thinking about it this way: If you had never written your article, then Dr. Copeland would still be teaching at Windemere and possibly abusing further victims."

"I know, but Sasha would at least be alive."

"That's a false equivalency, Caryn."

I want to roll my eyes but I don't. I'm exhausted from talking about Sasha every waking moment for the last few days. I feel like I could nod off right here on Susan's plush sofa while she goes about her day, seeing patients and making calls.

"If you didn't come forward, another victim would have, eventually. Would that have triggered a similar response? What about a similar crime at a different school? We just don't know."

I know this is possible, but it's not what actually happened. Whatever we continue to learn about Sasha and her mental state, I think Jane, Eva, and I will always feel that we contributed to this devastation. For as long as I can remember the sound of her voice and things she said, I will be analyzing each and every word for a clue or warning. That's the thing about suicide. It only offers more questions and gives no answers.

I tell Susan the one thing I know for sure: "Sometimes getting the thing you want most feels different than you thought."

She nods politely and then says our time is up.

I woke up early this morning because the sun was bright and streaming into my room through a sliver that was left uncovered by the plantation-style shades my mother convinced me to install. I can't go to the charity luncheon she begged me to attend because there's a memorial for Sasha today. I have the ultimate excuse and everyone understands. "I'm so sorry for your loss," people say, or if they want to be extracreative, they say things like, "She's in a better place now" and "She's no longer in pain."

Jane has Ben to comfort her, and I'm glad. She always acts like she's made of steel, but I know she feels things intensely. That's why she's such a great reporter. She can put herself in anyone's shoes and empathize with their situation. Eva, who is probably praying for Sasha's soul at this very minute, has Jesse and her girls and her faith. She has the luxury of believing that angels took Sasha because God and heaven have other plans. The grief counselor Susan referred me to said that religious people often fare better when it comes to mourning, but I don't have a religion. I'm not feeling sorry for myself; these are the facts.

Grace insisted on coming with me today because I've been distracted and prone to embarrassing breakdowns in strange places such as the fruit aisle of the grocery store and inside the locker room at my Pilates studio. I've never been to a memorial service and have no idea what to expect. And while I knew personal things about Sasha because of the case, I can't pretend I really knew her. I'm going because I'm desperate to understand what happened.

We both wear black dresses since it's the right thing to do, and I grab the biggest pair of sunglasses I can find. Grace drives us and opens her purse to show me the extra tissues she packed for me. Even though we're the same age, she's more of a mother to me than my own. I hope no one asks me how I knew Sasha or what my favorite memory of her was.

We run into Jane and Ben in the parking lot of the seaside church. The sky is clear and the ocean breeze feels nice. I introduce Grace to them, finally. Ben gives me a big hug even though I've never met him in person and asks me how I'm doing. I tell him I feel guilty. Jane turns to me. "If Sasha blamed you for anything, then why would she send the letter to you and not me or Eva or anyone else?" She says some version of this every time we speak. I keep telling myself the same thing, but my brain won't accept the message.

Jane tries a different approach: "I know this is going to sound harsh, especially as today is such an awful day, but consider that this has nothing to do with you and everything to do with her family, her upbringing, her abusers, her brain chemistry, her drug use, her drinking, her relationships."

"I know, you're right. You're always right." I'm acting like a child, but no one prepares you for things like this. Not your parents. Not your schools. Not your friends. You can meditate or do yoga or watch a million TED talks, but your mind has other plans.

"It's not about being right, Caryn. I'm not going to have you blame yourself for the rest of your life. You did the right thing." She steps closer to me. "*We* did the right thing." I know she's referring to writing about Copeland and cooperating with the investigation, but I can't help but think she might also be referring to Sasha's letter. We never offered it up as evidence and certainly never brought it to her family's attention. We never even told Eva about it because we didn't think she could handle its contents. As we walk toward the church, Ben and Grace begin talking about USC and Jane hangs back with me for a moment.

"This is between us, okay?" Jane says.

"What is?"

"What I'm going to tell you." My stomach flutters in anticipation. "I would never do this, but I'm doing it because I hope it will make you feel better. Not today, but maybe one day."

"What is it?"

"When I interviewed Sasha for the story, we spoke for over an hour. I used a few quotes from her because that was all that was needed at the time, but there was a lot more that she said."

"About Copeland, you mean?"

"I hate to betray her confidence, but she did tell me this for a newspaper interview."

"Just tell me, Jane."

"She had attempted suicide twice before. Before ever hearing your name or mine. It runs in her family, too. Her favorite aunt died the same way. I didn't use it because I was afraid Windemere would try to discredit her."

"I'm sorry, but how does suicide run in a family? I've never heard such a thing."

"Because no one wants to talk about it and yet it's a leading cause of death for someone in her age group."

"That can't be right."

"You can look it up. My point is that suicides can be traced to heritable factors like depression. It doesn't mean that you're destined to kill yourself just because it's in your family, but the other factors in her life certainly didn't help her live a long and healthy one. I'm sorry to drop this on you right here, but I wanted to tell you. I don't want you to shoulder this on you own. You have to accept that Sasha was not well."

My bottom lip begins to tremble and I realize I can't stifle my emotion with a witty retort today. I remove my sunglasses so I can wipe away the tears forming at an alarming pace. Upon seeing this, Jane instantly pulls me toward her and holds on tight. "I wish she had more time to find the right help," I blubber, wetting the entire left side of Jane's black silk blouse. This is the first time we have ever hugged.

"I know. I do too." She rubs my back, comforting me the way I imagine nice white mothers do with their kids.

I part from the embrace first, surprised to see that Jane's eyes are also watery and red. "Do you know that before my internship I once waited in line to meet you?"

"You're kidding." She pulls a napkin from her bag and hands it to me.

"It was the L.A. Times Festival of Books. It was a hot, crowded day, but you were up there, cool as could be." Jane blushes the same way she does when she tells me something nice about Ben. "If you told me back then that we'd be here now, I wouldn't have believed it."

"If you told me that *you* would ever call me 'cool,' I wouldn't have believed it." She uses her thumb to wipe the last of the moisture from under my left eye. "You know, emotion is a good thing. It can help you with your reporting. The ability to put yourself in someone's place, to feel their pain or excitement or concerns, is the key to it all."

"I'll keep that in mind." I squeeze her hand. "Thanks, Jane."

She puts her arm around me. "We better get inside."

The four of us sit together inside the simple church, a strange location since I'm positive Sasha didn't go to a house of worship and would probably find the choice to be an outrageous one for someone who had the phrase "Love is Hell" tattooed in small script just above her heart. It crushes me that there are so few people here. I don't know if it's because she had alienated herself from so many or if it's because she didn't die of cancer or in a car accident or something else that people feel more comfortable openly mourning.

A few moments before the service starts, Eva walks in with her husband. She looks frail and stricken with grief, and I know in this moment that no matter what, we will never tell her about Jack.

I can barely follow the service, led by a random man who

clearly never knew Sasha, because a photo of her has been blown up to poster size and is sitting on an easel near what I assume are her ashes. Every time I look up, I see her green eyes staring back at me. Those eyes. How could someone so lively now be housed in a small urn? Grace puts her arm around me and I think about what Sasha's life would have been like if she had known kindness. Her dazed mother is sitting in the front row with a few family members. Some random friends are scattered throughout the pews, and then there's us.

I'm scared to talk to her family members since I don't think they know about the case and I don't want to have to lie to them about anything. As soon as the service is over, Jane says they have to go because she's speaking at a journalism conference later today, but Grace and I stay with Eva and Jesse for a bit. He gets us waters and sodas and I ask Eva how she's holding up.

"I didn't know her well, but the loss feels like a family member or something. It's devastating."

"I know."

"I wish I tried harder to get to know her."

"We tried. I thought I knew about putting walls up, but Sasha was expert level. There's a lot that she went through even before Copeland that made her that way."

"I know, but it doesn't make it any easier to accept."

"Of course not."

"When I think about what she dealt with all these years, you know, to get to that place, I just get so mad. Not just at her, but at everyone who failed her and took advantage of her throughout her life." Eva becomes emotional again and Jesse suggests she visit the ladies' room to clean up.

We do some awkward mingling with a few of the other friends who are here. Laila says she's Sasha's best friend from childhood, but that the two hadn't spoken in many years. "Her mom asked me to be here. It's just awful. I always knew she struggled in life, but I never thought anything like this could happen."

A funky hairdresser named Carla tells us a story about Sasha go-go dancing at a local nightclub in her twenties, when she somehow lost balance and fell off the stage, accidentally knocking a patron out on the way down. "I'll never forget that image of her, slapping this guy's face awake while she downed his drink. We had plenty of adventures like that in those days."

As Grace makes polite chitchat with the others, I steer Carla a few feet away from the group. I have so many questions, and if I can get the answers to even two of them, I'll be pleased.

"So, is that how you guys met? Dancing?" I ask.

"Yeah, we were just babies." Carla smiles like she's playing a highlight reel in her mind. "It was a club in Hollywood that's long gone. I used to see her all the time, but the last few years she was more withdrawn. She said everyone was getting married and having kids, and I think she felt left out."

"She had a recent ex-boyfriend, right?" I turn to make sure no one is listening to us. "I remember her mentioning someone."

"Yeah, but it wasn't serious, although I'm sure to her it was. He just needed a place to stay and a warm body to lie next to."

I ask Carla if Sasha was ever in love. "Always." Her brown eyes light up. "All she ever wanted was to be in love and get married." I'm surprised to hear that Sasha desired anything conventional.

Carla tells me about the hair salon she owns, and the last time she saw Sasha. She reminisces about the time they got roped into an expensive cult-like self-help seminar by another friend. "I was buying it all hook, line, and sinker," she laughs, "but Sasha, who had out-read everyone there, would quote from ancient philosophy and question all of the group's tenets. She's the only person I know who ever got herself kicked out of a pyramid scheme." I giggle, which feels wrong at a funeral, but I can't help it.

I don't want to leave Grace on her own much longer so I get to the heart of the matter. I lower my voice since we're standing about fifty feet away from her family members. "Do you know her mother?"

"Yeah, I've met that witch a few times over the years," she says. "They weren't always estranged, but things were always bad between them ever since Sasha's dad died."

"Do you know how he died?" I stir my drink in an attempt to act nonchalant when all I want to do is ask Carla to spend the next hour with me trying to make sense of Sasha's life.

"I believe he had an undiagnosed heart condition, but I don't know the details. She never liked to talk about personal stuff like that." I nod along. "Remind me, how did you know her?"

"We both went to Windemere" is all I'm ready to say.

"Oh, right. God, can you think of someone less Windemere than Sasha?" Carla nudges me with her shoulder like we're old friends. "But I can see why she wanted to go there. She was brilliant. Too brilliant for this world I guess."

"I know she had a tough time with her stepdad," I say.

"He was pretty evil," she says. "Once her dad died, there wasn't much money left, so her mom married the first man who promised to take care of them. Her mother was a Russian immigrant with little education and no career. I think she was dependent on men for everything, then and now."

My own parents are far from perfect, but at least they kept us safe. "I didn't know her all that well," I admit, "but I liked her a lot. I'd never met anyone like her."

"And you never will."

I ask Carla if we can exchange numbers because I'd like to at least try to stay in touch with someone who was close to her.

Before we go, Eva approaches me. "I already talked to Jesse about this, but I wanted to tell you too." She removes her sunglasses to reveal swollen, tired eyes. "It's looking like a settlement offer from Windemere is coming soon, and I think it's what's best given everything that has gone on. I'm not sure I can handle a civil trial right now. I doubt the school would want one either, especially given the latest circumstances."

"Of course, I completely understand."

"Whatever money we get, part of it will go to an annual college scholarship for girls in Sasha's name. Her cousin told me that she always wanted to be a writer or musician, so I thought maybe an arts scholarship. We haven't worked the details out, and have to figure out how to go about it, but I can let you know."

I feel an enormous lump in my throat and tears form in the corners of my eyes. "I think she would really love that."

We say our goodbyes and Eva holds my hand for a moment. "We have to stay in touch."

"Of course we will. The *Daily* offered me a job, so I'll be there with Jane. You won't be getting rid of us anytime soon."

"That's incredible, Caryn, I'm so happy for you."

"Grace and I will be moving downtown next month, so I can be closer to work and out from under my father's thumb. Even though the salary's crap, I think I'll be happier being on my own." Grace beams with pride and I feel a surge of affection for her.

Eva gives me a final hug and whispers, "It's freeing when you realize you don't have to live the life your parents did."

After we get back home, I'm not sure what to do next. My emotions are thoroughly depleted; there are no tears left for me to cry. I feel like I could eat something, but am not in the mood to be surrounded by people who are enjoying life. If Sasha didn't get to enjoy life, then why should they? I don't need Susan to tell me that I'm angry; I know I am. It's going to take time. This is my first real heartbreak. Almost intuitively, Grace begins chopping vegetables and announces she's going to make us a late lunch since we felt weird munching on cheese and crackers at the service. "It'll be ready in about twenty minutes."

"Amazing Grace."

She laughs. "For chopping vegetables?"

"For everything."

I go into my room to lie on the bed. I could read for a bit or watch part of a terrible reality show. I could call my mom back. She's been leaving me hysterical messages since she found out about Sasha. I can be moody and keep to myself, so I'm sure she's convinced I could be next, as if suicide is something you can catch in an afternoon. I wonder if she's sorry for all the times she told me I brought shame to the family because I got an A minus instead of an A, or because I chose to be a writer instead of a doctor. I'm too tired to talk right now—to her, to Jane, to anyone.

After a few minutes of staring at the ceiling, I take Sasha's letter out of my desk drawer and read it one last time. I place it back in the envelope and address it to Dr. Gregory Copeland, Inmate Number 4519243 at the Metropolitan Detention Center. After sealing the envelope shut, I rifle through a few drawers looking for postage. I come upon a sheet of stamps left over from the holidays. There are four different designs and types of the same motif: flowers. I remove the rose sticker and affix it to the envelope.

The house smells good, like some combination of garlic and butter and magic, and I'm practically salivating. I always tell Grace she could be a chef if she ever changes her mind about becoming a biologist.

"I'll be back in two minutes." I grab my sunglasses and keys off the table by the door and head outside. I walk to the end of the block, which is lined with enormous magnolia trees that have been here long before I ever was, and drop the letter in the big blue mailbox on the corner. I make it just in time for the two o'clock pickup.

When I return, Grace is plating our meal, so I get the water glasses and set the table.

"How are you doing?" she asks. "All things considered."

"I'm feeling a little bit better already."

ACKNOWLEDGMENTS

To my husband, Tim, thank you for never questioning why I choose to spend most weekends writing instead of socializing with others like a normal person. Writing a novel is hard, but being with you is the easiest and best part of my life. Thank you, Mom and Dad, Chelsea and Brian, Roger and Marsha, and Dianne and Johnny, for always supporting me in everything I do.

Many thanks to my earliest readers who provided valuable feedback: Nancy McNamara, Andrew Grant Jackson, Emily LePlastrier Civita, Claire Veroda, and Evette Fisher. Thank you, Kim Askew, for your mighty heart and constant enthusiasm for my endeavors.

I'm appreciative of Margaret Sutherland Brown, who always has answers to my questions, and Kimberly Brooks, for the many lessons on life and art. A special thank you to the team at Griffith Moon for creating such a beautiful book, and to Susannah Noel, editor extraordinaire, for making this novel so much better.

Michael Chwe, Pamela Jaye Shime, Dana Danesi, Ayesha and Robin Mahapatra, Alexandra Rowe, Jan Schultz, and Josh Stephens provided me with helpful assistance during the research process, for which I am most grateful.

A special thank you to the current students and alumnae who I interviewed for this book but preferred not to be named here. You know who you are.

ABOUT THE AUTHOR

Victoria Namkung's journalism and essays have appeared in *The Washington Post*, *Los Angeles Times*, *NBC News*, and *VICE*, among other publications. She is the author of the romantic thriller, *The Things We Tell Ourselves*, and a contributor to the award-winning anthology, *Asian American Youth: Culture, Identity, and Ethnicity*. Victoria has previously taught courses at UCLA, UCSB, and 826LA, and resides in Los Angeles.

VictoriaNamkung.com
Facebook.com/VictoriaNamkung
@VictoriaNamkung

CPSIA information can be obtained
at www.ICGtesting.com
Printed in the USA
LVOW12*2306290318
571736LV00003B/28/P